Published novels:

Historical
Kitty McKenzie
Kitty McKenzie's Land
Southern Sons
To Gain What's Lost
Isabelle's Choice
Nicola's Virtue
Aurora's Pride
Grace's Courage
Eden's Conflict
Catrina's Return
Where Rainbow's End
Broken Hero
The Promise of Tomorrow
The Slum Angel
Beneath A Stormy Sky

Marsh Saga Series
Millie
Christmas at the Chateau (novella)

Contemporary
Long Distance Love
Hooked on You
Where Dragonflies Hover (Dual Timeline)

Short Stories
A New Dawn
Art of Desire
What He Taught Her

Dedication

To my beautiful daughter,
Eleanor Grace.

Book 2
Marsh Saga Series

AnneMarie Brear

Chapter One

London, May 1921.

Prue Marsh sauntered through the elegant shop belonging to Mrs Eve Yolland, dressmaker. The walls of dark mahogany shelving held bolts of material; linen, cotton, silk, damask, crepe georgette, velveteen and wool. The colours were arranged in shades from light to dark from white to black and every shade in between. Excellent light came from the large front windows facing the street, illuminating the tasteful, and discreet arrangement of accessories any woman should have the need to purchase. Assortments of beaded bags, satin purses, lawn handkerchiefs, kidskin gloves, jewelled headdresses, fans and shimmering shawls drew Prue's attention. But today, her hands merely drifted over the displayed finery, her mind wandering.

Restless.

She was always restless. Her mama said she needed a husband and a house to organise, but such mundane options failed to inspire her. And that was the problem. She wasn't inspired by anything at the moment.

Summer was fast approaching, and invitations were arriving at Elm House, her home in York, thick and fast for all sorts of entertainment like garden parties, social dances, private dinners, musical soirees, house parties and picnics, but she'd meet the same people again, the people she'd known all her life and it wasn't enough.

So, she'd left Mama and her younger sister Cece and escaped to London to stay with her grandmama and hope the London scene would be more entertaining.

'Prue!' Grandmama's raised eyebrows and sharp look snapped her back to the present.

'Sorry. What did you say?'

Her grandmama, Adeline Fordham, was not one to ignore, even if it was unintentional. Grandmama led the way to the shop's entrance. 'I asked if you needed more time or are you happy to move on?'

'I'm finished.' She nodded her goodbyes to Eve Yolland and her assistants, before leaving the building and stepping into the brand new motor car waiting at the curb side. The dark green Sunbeam, Grandmama's latest acquisition, shone like a new penny in the sunshine.

Once Higgins, the chauffeur, closed the door and climbed behind the wheel, Prue settled back against the leather seat.

'Right. Enough.' Grandmama peered at her. 'I refuse to spend another moment with you in this mood. What is the matter? For weeks you've been walking around London as though some great misfortune has befallen you. I insist on knowing the cause of it, or you can go back to your mama in Yorkshire.'

'I'm fine. Tell Higgins where we need to go, Grandmama.'

'Home, Higgins, if you please.'

'Home?' Prue frowned. 'Don't we have another appointment?'

'We do or did. But this is more important. So, you can either talk on the way home, or if it is of a delicate nature,' she directed at look at the back of Higgin's head, 'we shall wait until we are behind closed doors.'

'There is nothing to talk about.' Prue stared at the passing people walking along the streets of Westminster.

'I beg to differ.' The superior expression on Grandmama's face was familiar. 'You are depressing me, girl, and if I wanted to be depressed, I'd visit my neighbour, Felix Truman, and listen to him talk about his collection of snails! Why a man in his eighties wishes to have a collection of snails is beyond me. You can't pass him in the street without receiving a lecture on his latest procurements. So, out with it.'

Sighing heavily, Prue knew she'd not easily divert her when she had the bit between her teeth. 'Honestly, Grandmama, nothing has happened.' She shrugged one shoulder, a sense of hopelessness descending again.

It shocked her more than anyone that she felt like this. Never in her life had she been so uninterested in anything. Frankly, it worried her. She was always the one in the family to start a party, or a game. She considered that laughing and having fun was the only way to be. She left being serious to Cece, who'd made it into an art form and bored everyone with her

4

stuffiness, and Millie, her older sister, had the homely attributes for being a wife and mother that suited her perfectly. Yet, Prue wasn't ready for any of that.

'Ah, of course.' Grandmama patted Prue's knee, nodding her head wisely. 'I understand now. Silly of me not to see it before.'

'See what?' She turned to look out of the window at the passing rows of houses as they entered Mayfair, where Grandmama's townhouse was situated.

It took a moment for Grandmama to turn back to her, and when she did a small smile played about her lips. 'I forgot how much like me you are. Millie has my strength, but in a quiet, efficient way, and Cece has my kindness and sweet nature, but you, you have my restive character, my spirit of adventure. I should have done something about it earlier.'

Prue grinned at Grandmama declaring her sweet nature. There was nothing sweet about Grandmama. Adeline Fordham was known for speaking her mind and didn't suffer fools gladly. Prue glanced back out of the window as clouds skidded over the sun. 'Whatever do you mean? Done something about it?'

'The war interrupted things, but everything is settling down once again now. It's time.'

Higgins slowed the automobile in front of the white-painted terraced house and Kilburn, the butler, rushed out to open the motorcar's door.

Alighting, Prue waited for Grandmama to accompany her up the three short steps to the shiny black front door. 'You're talking in riddles. Time for what?'

'Why, to take you abroad, properly, not just to Millie's chateau in France.'

'Abroad?' Following her into the parlour, Prue slipped off her gloves, wondering if she'd heard correctly. No one travelled abroad now, or hadn't done for years, not since the war started in '14 and then afterwards the Spanish Flu epidemic had decimated hundreds of thousands of people and Europe had plunged into greyness. There was no incentive to travel to countries fighting bankruptcy and restrictions.

'It's high time we sampled the delectable delights of travelling to other places, my dear. High time indeed. And *you* especially.' She sat down at her rosewood desk in the corner and selected several sheets of writing paper. 'You, my dear, need to explore the world as I did before I married. There's nothing better than experiencing foreign cities and people. It broadens one's mind.'

A bud of excitement grew in the pit of Prue's stomach. Abroad. Travelling. Yes. Absolutely, yes. 'When can we go, Grandmama?'

'As soon as I can arrange it, which will take some time. I've a busy couple of months ahead of me. I'll send word to your mama today of our intentions.' She bent over busily writing. 'And do not blame me if you have a fabulous time, Prue, and never want to come home. Your mama will find fault with me, of course, and it's quite possible that you'll meet the man you will marry while we're at it.'

'I'm not looking for a husband.'

'Why ever not? Don't be ridiculous. Marriage is what you need, eventually.'

Prue thought of the happy marriage her eldest sister, Millie, had achieved with Jeremy, and their new baby. 'I meant I don't want a foreign husband.'

'What is wrong with that, pray? Some foreign men are rather charming.' Grandmama chuckled, the lines crinkling around her blue eyes that she had passed onto her daughter and three granddaughters. 'It's a matter of selecting the right one, and with your handsome features, you will be in high demand, trust me. But remember, don't always aim high. Some of the nobility around the world, like here in England, are penniless now. The inheritance from your late papa isn't large enough to restore some ancient Italian title back to its former glory. Some of those European titles and estates will need generations to claw back their former wealth.'

'Grandmama, I'm not looking for a title.'

'There isn't anything wrong with a title, just be selective, that's all I ask.'

'I want to marry for love.'

'Quite rightly, too. However, fall in love with a young man who has vaults full of money. The new rich are a good start, don't worry about backgrounds. The richest families in England have a trade somewhere in their lineage. Keep an open mind.'

'Does it have to be so regimental?'

Grandmama raised her eyebrows innocently. 'It's the truth. Because of the war whole fortunes have crumbled along with the lives of family heirs. You only have to remember our friend, Monty Pattison, to see that. So be careful. The last thing you want is to marry an impoverished foreigner.'

'I have every intention of being choosy. I won't settle for anyone, even if there is a shortage of men now.'

Grandmama adjusted her glasses. 'I'll start sending out letters of enquiry today, for we need a good ship to take us. However, I doubt we'll be able to leave before July. I've too many functions to attend before I'm free to go.'

'What about Cece? Should she not come with us?'

'I don't consider this trip is right for your sister. She is devoted to your mama at the moment and well ...'

'Perhaps I should stay with Mama, too.' Guilt filled her. She'd thought only about the fun of such a journey and not about leaving her mother and sister behind in York, especially as Papa died a little more than a year ago.

'I don't imagine your mama needs you as much as she relies on Cece, those two are cut from the same cloth, aren't they?' Grandmama continued jotting down plans.

'No, Cece is different from me in many ways and enjoys the more homelier comforts. She has never mentioned her wish to travel.'

'Cece will stay home. I'll make it up to her in another way, buy her a cottage somewhere. You and I will go. One granddaughter is enough to put up with, never mind two. Besides, you and Cece fight like cats and dogs and I'll not have you two ruining what is probably going to be my last trip.'

'Where shall we go? America?' Prue clapped her hands unable to hide her excitement. 'New York!'

'Lord no, not America. With prohibition there I'd find it tiresome trying to enjoy a meal without a good glass of wine.'

'There's always ways and means of getting alcohol, I'm sure.'

'I'm not spending my time consorting with blackmarketeers just to obtain a case of wine and run the risk of being arrested.'

'I would have imagined you'd enjoy the contest of obtaining secret alcohol and not getting caught.' Prue raised her eyebrows in challenge.

'Perhaps, a few years ago I'd have risen to the test of beating the authorities, but not now, I'm getting old. No. I'd rather we started with India first.'

'India? Gosh.' Prue's eyes widened in astonishment.

'You have an aversion to India?' Grandmama peered over her glasses at her.

'No, not at all.' In truth she'd rather go to America, but anywhere was better than staying home in Yorkshire. 'I never even considered going to India.'

'Your Uncle Hugo and Aunt Daphne will put us up at their house in Bombay. Though we'll have to put up with them in return.' Grandmama grunted. 'I love my son, but his choice of wife leaves a lot to be desired. However, the food there is simply divine. Also, if Hugo doesn't come home to England then this may be my last chance to see him. I'll not be making the trip again.'

'India sounds so exotic…' Prue gazed out of the window, not really seeing the green garden square set in the middle of the townhouses for the inhabitants to use as their own personal garden. Instead she thought of what she knew about India and that was very little.

Grandmama finished one letter and folded it. 'After India, we'll go to Italy. It is one of my favourite places. I have friends in Palermo who are forever asking me to visit. I would like to see them again. George Johnston, especially, was a good friend of your grandpapa and he's getting rather ancient and not terribly robust any more. It would be good to see him.'

'Italy. I can hardly believe it.' Prue's imagination ran wild. 'Two beautiful countries to explore.'

'Perhaps after Italy we'll go to Switzerland. We'll decide that later.'

'What about the effects of the war? Mama says—'

'Your mama says too much, always has done since she was taught to speak. Foolish notion it is to wish for a child to say their first words, for we are forever regretting it, wishing they'd just be quiet.' She turned in her chair, her pen poised. 'Prue look at what the war has done, what it has destroyed. Those of us that are left must put the world to rights again. It's our duty to those who died for us. To do this, we need to live, for them, for ourselves. Your mama is all doom and gloom, preaching that the world has changed and all that nonsense. Well, yes, it has changed. But that doesn't mean we can't enjoy what is left. And enjoy it we shall!' She paused. 'Unless you wish to remain in England and forgo exploring different countries?'

'No! Thank you, Grandmama, but you are right. I need to travel, to discover, to ...'

'To *live*, my girl. It's as simple as that. By your age I had ridden across parts of Africa by camel.'

Knowing the story well, knowing all her grandmother's travel adventures, Prue hurried to kiss her cheek. 'Tell me your stories tonight, at dinner, will you?'

'I will, my dearest one, but soon, you will have your own to tell, or at least some of them. You will find that some stories are better left locked away in here.' Grandmama tapped her head and winked.
'Sometimes, the greatest stories are never told.'

Chapter Two

A pianist played quietly in the corner of the steamer's dining room as background music to the clinking of glasses and cutlery, the chatting and laughing of the first-class passengers.

Dessert - raspberry tart and cream or a gooseberry fool - was being served to the tables and Prue was doing her best to pay attention to the older man, Mr Richardson, on her right, but instead her gaze drifted to the women in the room as she studied their evening wear. Her silk and crepe georgette dress of silver and grey fitted in perfectly, but she noticed that those who shared the captain's table wore extra jewellery. She made a mental note of that, for tomorrow it was their table's turn to dine with the captain.

Grandmama was a little cross that it had taken eight days to be invited to dine at the captain's table, but there were many first-class guests all vying for the opportunity, and despite her wealth and breeding, Grandmama was down the list behind a couple of governors of Indian provinces, several British Crown high officials and the odd minor European royals.

11

'More champagne, Miss Marsh?' Mr Richardson asked, lifting the bottle from its stand.

'No, thank you, Mr Richardson. I deem I've had enough for tonight.'

'Ladies?' he asked Grandmama and his wife, who both shook their heads. Mr Richardson's agreeable wife sat next to Grandmama and they were deep in conversation, but across from her, Prue was rather taken with the Richardson's son.

Laurence Richardson constantly wore a bored expression, he picked at his food, barely spoke and yet there was something about him that Prue was drawn to. She had no idea what it was. Laurence wasn't necessarily the best-looking man on board, and in the week since they sailed from Tilbury Docks in London, she'd danced with most of the men in first class, so she knew who stood out. Despite that, Laurence Richardson had been attentive to her when they stopped for six hours at Marseilles, the Richardsons had joined her and Grandmama for a short shopping trip and coffee in a café before they all returned to the boat. Prue had taken some photographs with her new Kodak Brownie camera while in Marseille and Laurence also had a similar camera, it had given them something to talk about, especially as onboard there was a dark room for photographers to produce their films. Prue hadn't developed hers yet and asked Laurence for guidance.

From the week's dinner table conversations, she understood the Richardsons were departing the steamer in Egypt. Mr Richardson had an import business in Port Said and they were spending their annual six months there to oversee their interests. Mrs Richardson had no love of Egypt but refused to stay in England by herself while her husband was away and so with good grace, she accompanied him every year.

Prue finished her gooseberry fool and dabbed a napkin at her mouth, she'd not followed a word Mr Richardson had said about market shares, and having drunk too much champagne, she needed fresh air.

With a slight smile she excused herself and rose from her chair. 'I'll take a walk around the deck, Grandmama. Please excuse me,' she said to the table.

'I'll be in the games room if you need me. Mrs Richardson and I are going to play cards against the Elwin sisters,' Grandmama told her, nodding to another table where two women were talking animatedly with the captain. 'They beat us last night and we'll not let that happen again, will we, Mrs Richardson?'

'No, we shan't. It's terribly upsetting letting the side down. I do apologise again, Mrs Fordham.'

Grandmama gave her new friend a quelling look. 'No need to apologise *again*, Mrs Richardson, just be more attentive in the next game. I am not used to losing. It gives me indigestion and a bad night's sleep.'

'Do you wish for company on your stroll, Miss Marsh?' Laurence Richardson asked, rising as well.

Surprised, Prue nodded. 'That would be nice, yes.'

Together they left the dining room and Prue paused to collect her white sable wrap from the holding closet. Fortified against the evening chill, they headed for the stairs to take them up to the upper first-class deck.

Here, during the day, Prue played shuttlecock, quoits and deck tennis, card games and charades with other like-minded passengers, or she'd sit on a deck-lounger and read. So far, they'd had good weather the entire voyage.

At night however, the stars glittered in a black sky and she often took a stroll with Grandmama after they'd spent the evening watching a theatre show or listening to the band. It seemed strange now to walk the dimly lit deck with Laurence. It gave the occasion a sense of intimacy, or was she reading too much into it?

'I've the dark room booked for a few hours tomorrow afternoon,' Laurence said as they strolled. 'Would you like to develop your film, too?'

'I would indeed, thank you, but you'll have to show me how to do it. I impulsively bought the camera before we sailed, and I've not learned how to develop the photographs myself yet. I have no idea what to do.'

'It's easy enough if you are careful. I can show you.'

'Thank you.'

'You must be excited about visiting India?' he asked as they passed another couple.

Prue breathed in the salty sea air. The soft slapping of the waves hitting the hull was rhythmic and soothing. 'Very much. I've never been to India, and I haven't seen my uncle and aunt for years. Have you ever been?'

'No. I should like to go though one day if I can escape my desk. My father is keen on teaching me everything there is to know about the family business, whether I want to participate or not.'

'You wish to do something else?'

'I want to go and live in America!' he said passionately. He stopped and gripped the railing. 'It is all I want.'

'Then why don't you go?'

'And disappoint him and mother? No. I am not that cruel. There are other ways in which I am not the ideal son. I can't keep adding to the pile.'

'I also wish to visit America. I want to go shopping in New York.' She joined him by the rail, turning her back to the cool breeze so she could see him properly in the golden light spilling over the deck cast by a wall light. She wondered if he'd try to kiss her. He had appeal and she felt the need to be kissed on such a night.

'New York, what a place it must be. I imagine it to be quite spectacular.'

Prue watched the emotions flit across his face. 'What would you do in America?'

He stared down at the churning black sea beneath them. 'You will assume I am strange.'

She lightly touched his arm. 'I will not. I am very modern.'

He took a deep breath and let it out. 'I would like to become an actor in the movie films.'

'An actor?' Shocked, Prue smiled at him, liking him even more. 'I adore watching films. I go whenever I can, which is often. You would be perfect for it. With your brooding looks and manner, I could see you on the screen, truly I could.'

'You think so?' He brightened at this.

'Absolutely. You could be the next Charlie Chaplin.'

'I very much doubt it, Miss Marsh.' He chuckled. 'I want to be me. I did very well at it in my university theatre group. I received rave reviews, but Father will not hear of it. He reasons it to be a passing fancy.'

'Why not go to America and try your luck and prove him wrong?'

'My parents would be scandalised. It is not the done thing, you know? I am to take over from my father in the business and be happy with that. I am an only child, you see. I wish I wasn't.'

She was sorry for him. 'Only you aren't happy to manage your father's business.'

'Not in the slightest. Imports and exports bore me to tears.' He straightened and held out his arm for Prue to take. 'Enough of me. Tell me of your plans, Miss Marsh.'

'I don't really have any. I simply want to travel, have fun, enjoy every day.'

'I've never met anyone like you before. Someone who laughs a lot and wrings out the amusement in everything you do. I see you during the day, having the best time on deck with lots of gentlemen giving you their attention, begging you to partner them at one thing or another.'

'I am having a wonderful time onboard. It is nothing like I expected. But you should have seen me a few months ago. I was miserable, not knowing what to do with myself. I couldn't find any pleasure in my days at all. That's why my grandmama decided we should go on this trip, to give me an adventure and cheer me up.'

'It has worked then it seems?'

She grinned as they strolled. 'Heavens, yes. Now I wake up every morning eager to see what the day will bring.'

'Lucky you.'

She squeezed his arm. 'Don't be downhearted, Mr Richardson. You've met me and that can only be a good thing!'

He laughed gently. 'Is that so?'

'Of course!' She stopped as they heard the music coming from the ballroom. 'In two days, you shall be leaving us. Why don't we dance until the sun comes up, what do you say?' she challenged.

'I'm not a very good dancer.'

She laughed and playfully hit his shoulder. 'Call yourself an actor! Shame on you. You must learn how to dance well for the movie business. I'll teach you.'

'I'm not sure, Miss Marsh.'

'Don't be frightened. It's only dancing, everyone does it. Come on!' She took his hand and opened the door leading into the ballroom. 'I dare you to have a good time.'

He shrugged his elegantly suited shoulders. 'Very well.'

~ ~ ~ ~

Port Said was a hive of industry and noise as the passengers disembarked. Prue kept a hand on Grandmama's arm as they negotiated the dock and inched through the crowded passenger control and out onto the teeming streets. The heat was incredible, and Prue's white linen dress soon lost its crispness.

Behind them, the Richardsons were organising their luggage and searching for their motor car and driver amongst the seething traffic congestion of the narrow streets of the docks.

'Good luck in everything you do, Miss Marsh.' Laurence shook Prue's hand as Grandmama said goodbye to his parents.

'Thank you, and I wish the very best to you, Mr Richardson. I'm so pleased I met you. I really enjoyed your company. We had a fabulous time, didn't we?'

'We did.' He laughed in the soft way he had. 'You are indeed an excellent lady who I am delighted to call my friend. Would you care to write to me?'

'I would, indeed.' From her bag she gave him her card and he gave her one of his. 'Do remember though that I'll not be at that York address for a year or so. I'll write to you first from India and then you'll have my address.'

'Excellent. Embrace every moment on your travels.' He took a step back. 'Goodbye then.'

'And thank you for all your help with my photographs.' She leaned closer to whisper to him. 'Go to America.'

He saluted to her as he walked away.

'Well, that's that then,' Grandmama said coming back to her. 'Shall we find our driver?'

In the bustle of finding the hired car they had booked with the onboard chief purser, Prue took stock of her first experience of Egypt and Egyptians. She glanced at several things at once. The docks were crushed with people: hawkers wearing baggy trousers and bright fez hats who cried out their wares, while senior porters whistled for lackeys to carry luggage. Children begged, women with blank faces sat on the roadside selling vegetables, baskets, strings of beads, woven shoes and all manner of goods. In contrast wealthy locals rode in carriages and motor cars, clogging up the narrow roads.

'There, number eighty-six.' Grandmama pointed to a man holding up a sign. 'Give him your bag, Prue.'

Prue dutifully gave the driver their over-night bag and climbed into the motor car beside Grandmama.

'Shepheard's Hotel is the best in Cairo,' Grandmama said, passing a note to the driver, which were the instructions for him about the next two days and all written in French by the purser, who assured them that French was the main language in the port. Grandmama spoke to the driver in French and he smiled and bowed, happy to do as they wished.

Grandmama settled into the seat and took her fan out of her handbag. 'It's infernally hot here. I last stayed at the Shepheard's Hotel with your grandpapa about twenty years ago. It'll be pleasing to be off the boat for a night and stay in the decent hotel while the boat travels along the Suez Canal, for the canal isn't terribly exciting, and it's most revoltingly hot at night to sleep. Still, that won't change when we return and board at Port Suez. But this little side trip is an opportunity to show you Cairo, if only very briefly.'

'I'm eager to see the pyramids. How long will it take to arrive in Cairo?'

'A few hours, depending on the state of the roads and the ability of this driver.'

They wove through the streets and Prue gazed up at the large ornate British colonial buildings standing side by side to the local structures, which were square-shaped and built from pale sandstone blocks or simply timber. Beautifully designed mosques with their tall minarets dominated the area as they sped out of the port and into the countryside.

'That Laurence Richardson,' Grandmama said, waving her fan, 'he's not for you.'

Prue arched her eyebrows. 'Really?'

'Definitely not.'

'Why?' Prue played along although she had no romantic interest in Laurence at all. He was a good, kind person who she hoped to be friends with for a long time, but he wasn't for her. He was too serious, and a little troubled she felt.

'You are the wrong sex.'

Prue blinked rapidly. 'The wrong sex?'

'You are not stupid, girl. You understand what I mean. Laurence is a lovely young man, and most eligible, if you ignored the fact he only has eyes for men.'

'That's not true,' Prue protested.

'Why are you so defensive? Has he promised you anything?'

'No, not at all. We have a friendship that isn't romantic in the slightest.'

Grandmama nodded. 'I rest my case.'

'You're wrong. We have only known him for ten days or so. How can you make such a judgement?' Prue wasn't totally convinced herself. Only that she'd never met a man who liked other men and not women and wasn't sure if she could pick them out or not.

'I am right, my dear. When every other man on board that boat wanted to partner you in games or on the dance floor, or would smile at you as they passed, or dipped their hat to you, when did Laurence ever do that to any woman? Having sat beside you each meal time did he never once flirt with you?'

'That means nothing. I'm obviously not his type of woman.'

'Nonsense. You're every man's dream. Tall and blonde, energetic and funny. You have pedigree and wealth. Those blue eyes of yours could bend any man to your whim.' Grandmama looked out at the desert they travelled through. 'His mother told me he hasn't once shown any interest in the young debutants thrust before him. She greatly hoped you might be the one since he took an interest in you.'

'We enjoyed each other's company. We shared an interest with our cameras and photography. He taught me how to develop my film in the dark room.'

'I feel sorry for the poor boy. He'll have to live a lie for all his life.'

'He wants to go to America and be a film star.'

'Then he should go and do that. Americans who work in that industry are far more tolerant to that type of thing, if handled discreetly, from what I've been told, anyway. He'll be able to hide it better there than in England.'

'Are you terribly sure about this, Grandmama?' Poor Laurence.

'Trust me, dear. I have seen it before. I had a very good friend when I was younger who was male orientated, and of course it is illegal to be so. His life was one of hiding unless he was with people he trusted. He killed himself in the end.'

'How tragic.'

Grandmama stared into the distance. 'When you write to Laurence always be kind. He'll not have a very good life hiding who he really is. Be his friend, always.'

'Naturally, I'll be kind.' Prue spotted her first camel, but the shine of the day was gone.

She was quickly learning that life was not all fun and games. She suspected for the first time, she was seeing the world as an adult, someone who was no longer playing at being a grown-up. Her parents had cosseted her and her sisters all their lives, and rightly so, but it didn't really prepare them for the real world. Papa had forbidden Millie to become a nurse in the war to protect her from seeing sights that would upset her, yet she had married a man with shell shock. Jeremy's condition nearly destroyed their marriage. If Millie had been a nurse tending to injured soldiers perhaps she could have handled the situation better? But like all the Marsh sisters they waltzed through life sheltered by doting parents and knowing only the teachings of their strict governess. None of which equipped them for the world outside of their home.

Chapter Three

In the blazing August sun, her eyes shielded against the glare, Prue gazed at the Sphinx. Around her several dozen tourists did the same. People from all walks of life, all colours and religions stood as she did and took in the wonder of the statue. They'd left splendid Shepheard's Hotel at dawn and travelled by hired motor car straight to see the pyramids before the heat of the day became too intense, but Prue felt the heat was at boiling point the clock round. There seemed to be no relief from it.

'I expected it all to be bigger,' she muttered to Grandmama as she took a photograph with her Kodak Brownie.

Grandmama wiped the sweat from her forehead with a white handkerchief. 'Funny that, I did too when I first visited.'

'I'd built up an image in my mind that it would be enormous, rising into the sky.' She took a few more photographs, including one of Grandmama's profile as she stared at the pyramids in the distance.

'Unfortunately, when we do that, the real thing will always disappoint us.'

Hawkers threaded through the crowds plying their wares of trinkets and knick-knacks. Prue bought a wooden carving of the Sphinx and popped it into her bag.

'Why do you buy such rubbish?' Grandmama shook her head.

'To remember this day by.'

'That's what that expensive camera is for.'

'Yes, but I also want to fill a house one day with all my photographs and souvenirs from around the world.'

'Then purchase something more suitable.' Grandmama took Prue's arm as they pushed through tourists from all parts of the world. 'Let us find our driver and head back into Cairo. I'd like to buy a few silk shawls, and maybe a rug to send home to London. I need to replace the one under the dining table. We've time before we are driven back to Port Suez and board the steamer.'

After once more crossing the River Nile, which yesterday Prue had hoped would be something beautiful and majestic, but in truth was just another river flowing through an overcrowded city, their driver edged the motor car into the bustle of teeming thoroughfares.

The streets of Cairo were streaming with all varieties of vehicles and pedestrians, mainly men. Prue had shopped in London and Paris many times, but nothing prepared her for the chaotic Cairo streets.

In a large souk on the outskirts of the city, they stopped to shop as the call to prayer sounded. Grandmama led the way, using her walking cane to swipe at unsuspecting individuals who dared to get in her way. Prue held her arm tightly so as not to be swept away from her as the crush of hot sour-smelling bodies pushed her this way and that.

Not being able to speak the Egyptian language they took their guide along with them and between him and Grandmama bargains were fought over in French and finally money exchanged. Grandmama bought two bright red ornamental rugs, a hanging lamp in shades of blue, and while she bartered for the best price on a pair of silk slippers, Prue sauntered to the next stall and bought pastel-coloured soaps and scarves in pink and green tones.

'Tell me you didn't pay full price, girl?' Grandmama asked as they returned to the motor car, which was surrounded by beggars and trinket sellers that the driver was shooing away.

'I'm afraid I did. Unlike you, I have no wish to stand there arguing like a fishwife,' Prue replied as the motor car sped off with its horn blaring and the driver waving his hands angrily at people and slow-moving traffic.

Grandmama laughed. 'Why that's the fun of it. You must try it for it gives one such a sense of wellbeing when you win!'

The warm wind on her face made Prue tired after their early start to the day, and as they sped along at a fast pace that she found invigorating but which Grandmama announced was suicidal, she looked out at the changing landscape. The city fell away behind them and gone were the buildings and palm trees and instead, stretched out for as far as she could see, was nothing but sand and dust. The odd squat square buildings they passed were the same colour as the surrounding pale scenery, even the mosques were drab and uninteresting. This part of Egypt was poor and sparse, and Prue was happy to return to the ship. She hoped India wouldn't be as disappointing.

'Your thoughts?' Grandmama asked.

'I don't quite know what to make of it, really.'

'Don't be too harsh in your opinion. You've only seen a small part of a beautiful country.'

'Yes, that's true but where is the beauty? It's not in Cairo.'

'There are parts of Egypt that are lush and green, not like this desert. Along the length of the Nile the countryside is very different to here. Perhaps one day you will see another part of Egypt and change your mind.'

'Perhaps.' But Prue wasn't convinced.

'You said you wanted to have an adventure and to travel and that means seeing the ugly and the beautiful.' Grandmama frowned. 'Are you regretting your words?'

'No, no, not at all.' Prue sat up straighter. 'Egypt might not have been what I expected but I'm still very glad I came. I already have stories to tell my children one day. I can tell them I sailed across the Mediterranean and stayed in a lovely hotel in Cairo and now I've seen the pyramids and Sphinx.'

'And we still have much more to explore. After sailing down the Red Sea, stopping at Port Aden and then navigating across the Arabian Sea, we'll be in Bombay. India is a special place, and one I think you'll fall in love with as I did.'

~ ~ ~ ~

Prue leaned over the ship's rail and gazed in wonder at the sight before her.

Bombay.

India.

The aromas of spices, of the salty sea splashing against the ship and the docks, the stench of rotting vegetables, the cries of hundreds, no thousands of people working on the wharves all carried across the water to envelop her. The sky was heavy and low with cloud masking the hills beyond the bay and making the air thick. Boats and water crafts of many sizes crisscrossed the bay. Below the steamer's deck, Indians in canoe-shaped vessels paddled up to the side of the hull waving their goods in the air, hoping a naïve passenger would send over some money and in return receive some sort of garment. No one paid them any attention. The purser and crew had already warned them of such activities and to not trust the water vendors.

A few drops of rain hit her and reluctantly Prue left the rail when she noticed passengers returning inside to get out of the weather and ready themselves to leave the ship.

Hurrying down the narrow corridors, she quietly entered the cabin and sat at the desk. Outside the window rain fell in a sheet, washing the deck, and giving the ship's crew a difficult job of docking and bringing up the luggage in such slippery conditions.

With Grandmama taking a nap in the opposite bedroom, Prue gently took out her leather writing folder which held sheets of paper, envelopes, a fountain pen and ink cartridges.

1st September 1921

Dear Millie,

Prue

I do hope you have received my last letter which I posted from Port Aden, it was our next stop after leaving Port Suez and Egypt. In that letter I wrote about our overnight stay in Shepheard's Hotel and the splendour of the service we received. It was divine! If you didn't get the letter, let me know and I'll describe it again in another.

What a dreary place Port Aden is! Gosh, I was glad to return to the ship after half an hour there. It was full of men who stared openly at me and some gave me looks that made me shiver. I had heard that it was a unique place to visit and there would be lovely walks along the shore we could take to stretch our legs, but the atmosphere made it impossible for us passengers to relax so we didn't venture far from the dock. I saw no beauty there and was greatly disappointed.

We left Port Aden and thankfully the uncomfortable and draining heat of the Red Sea didn't continue as we travelled across the Arabian Sea. I have never experienced such heat as I did as we travelled the Red Sea. I took the opportunity many times to sleep on deck with other like-minded passengers. Men were kept down one end of the deck and we women at the other end with a divider placed in between us, all very proper.

Grandmama warned me the Arabian Sea could be choppy, and much cooler and she was correct. Some passengers were very seasick, especially after the calmness of the Suez Canal and the Red Sea. It was a bit of a shock to us all at how rough the last leg of our journey would be.

Anyway, we are now finally here in Bombay and waiting to depart from the ship. We sailed into a wide bay an hour ago, but there is much confusion as to where we need to be docked and our luggage is waiting to be brought up and so on. Therefore, I thought I'd write you a quick letter to say we are safely in India. We shall be collected by Uncle Hugo from the quay. Grandmama sent him a telegram from Port Aden informing him of our arrival information.

I can't put into words how thrilled I am that we are here. I'm hoping India is exciting. I'm sure it shall be simply because we are staying at Uncle Hugo's house and will have the comforts of a home and with us staying months, we can form friendships and have many options of entertainment.

That said, I shall miss this boat and the other passengers. Grandmama and I have had such a good time on board, really. There was always something to do and people to talk to. Lots of games were played and even a theatre night was held by the passengers where everyone put on a performance. I sang a song with a piano accompaniment, though the man playing it wasn't very good. Still, I received a round of applause.

We've met some grand people – a good deal of them British returning to India. You'd be surprised how many single women are on this ship with the main intention of getting themselves a husband once in India. Apparently, there is an enormous amount of single British men wanting wives. Grandmama had to chaperone a few of these desperate young girls as they would flirt with the ship's crew and male passengers in a most alarming way (and that's saying something coming from me!) We've had two engagements on the voyage and these people were complete strangers on embarkation in London! I was asked myself by a gentle older man who has a tea plantation in Ceylon, but I declined him, he then

*asked for Grandmama to become his wife. You should
have seen her face. It was a picture, and she sent him
off with a flea in his ear, but I suspect she was
secretly flattered. It was very sweet.*

*Right, a series of whistles have been blown and I
must go and pack my last things.*

*I'll write again very soon. Give my love to Jeremy
and Jonathan!*

*Your sister,
Prue.*

As Prue sealed the envelope and wrote the address
on it, Grandmama came out of the bedroom.

'Are we all ready?'

'Just a few things to finish off and I'm done.' Prue
hurriedly packed, the pit of her stomach tight with
anticipation.

'Well then, let us find a porter and get off this ship.
It'll be mayhem trying to get through customs and
finding Hugo.'

As though fate was listening to Grandmama, they
spent the next hour disembarking and queuing up in
the British built customs' building on the dockside.

The heat and the humidity took Prue's breath away
as the crush of passengers fighting to find their
luggage and have their paperwork stamped grew into
the predicted mayhem.

'Why we must be treated like cattle is disgusting,'
Grandmama snapped, her grey hair limp from
perspiration. 'All this standing about! Look at that
official over there. If he goes any slower at reading
those passports, we'll need camp beds to sleep the
night!'

Prue flicked a glance at the calm and methodical British official seated behind the nearest desk to them. 'I'm sure he's doing his best. There are a lot of people to sort through.'

'Doing his best? A sloth would work faster!'

With their papers finally accepted, Grandmama led the way out of the customs' building and to the luggage area. She dabbed at the sweat on her face and neck with a handkerchief. 'We should have waited to come later in the year. Arriving in monsoon time is not ideal.'

'But you said you didn't want to wait,' Prue reminded her as they finally found their luggage.

'That's because at my age waiting can be fatal.' Grandmama folded her fan and tapped it against her other hand. 'Let us see if my son has the good sense to bring a large enough motor car.'

Prue, being taller than Grandmama spotted Uncle Hugo first and waved to him happily and at that same moment, the clouds suddenly sent down another deluge of rain so fast and heavy that Prue gasped.

'Hurry, Mama!' Hugo had no time to welcome them properly but ushered them into a stylish white motor car with the hood up. A porter quickly tied the trunks to the rack at the back of the motor car with the help of Hugo's driver. The rain lashed down in a torrent as Hugo threw the smaller bags onto the front seat and then climbed into the back with Prue and Grandmama.

Outside the steamy windows, the colours and smells of India changed into a watershed of puddles and blurry faces rushing past.

'Thank goodness you were there, Hugo.' Grandmama wiped the drops of rain off the front of her apple green dress.

31

'Why you came in monsoon season, I don't understand,' he replied, brushing the water off his hat.

'Well! That's a greeting if ever there was one,' Grandmama scoffed.

'Forgive me, Mama.' Hugo dutifully leaned over and kissed her cheek. 'I am that pleased to see you, naturally, and you, Prue.' He kissed Prue as well and sat back with a happy grin. 'It's been forever since I've seen you and look how well you've turned out. All grown up now, I see. Jolly good!'

'Thank you, Uncle.' Prue smiled.

'You'll have all the men at the Club seeking you out. We'll have to keep an eye on you for there are some dashing cads about, you see. However, I'm friends with many a good chap and we'll have you partnered at every dance, you see if we don't!' He braced himself as the driver halted for a running pedestrian, and then again for a Brahma cow, which slowly made its way through the assortment of people and vehicles.

'Is your home far, Uncle?' Prue asked, staring at the bullocks pulling carts, the swarm of people carrying goods on their heads, the stray dogs, the horse and carriages, which also fought for space with the horn-tooting automobiles. It was all so crazy.

'No, indeed. We live on the edge of Malabar Hill, one of the best districts in Bombay. Although this weather will hinder our progress. The rains turn the streets into rivers. However, our house is well situated on a slight rise and on the outskirts of the main hub of the city, but not too far away that it's inconvenient to attend my work, the Club or several of our friends' houses. Daphne prefers this house to the last one we had which was closer to town, but the smells we had to endure there from the sewers was rather intolerable.'

'And how is Aunt Daphne?'

'Eager to see you both.' Hugo gave another wide smile. 'Her cousin's daughter, Gertie, is here staying with us. I'm sure you'll like her.'

'Is she part of the latest Fishing Fleet to arrive?' Grandmama asked with a smirk.

Hugo flushed slightly. 'That is a very unflattering term, Mama, but yes, she came out from England to find a husband, but hasn't been successful yet.' He turned to Prue. 'What about you, niece? Are you a member of the Fishing Fleet, too?'

Laughing, Prue shook her head. 'No, I'm not fishing for a husband, Uncle.'

'Then that is a loss to all single British chaps in India.'

Prue sighed happily, remembering that her uncle was a nice man, easy to get along with. It would be no hardship to live with him for several months.

The crowded city fell behind them and they travelled through a more open and leafier area with glimpses of the bay between tree-lined bungalows and substantial villas.

Eventually, the driver pulled to a stop at a large set of iron gates that were opened by an elderly servant. The rain stopped as suddenly as it had started, and they swept up a drive lined by hibiscus bushes and frangipani trees. The house itself was a large bungalow with a wide veranda wrapped around all sides.

As they alighted from the car, the sun shone, and Aunt Daphne and another taller, thin woman came out to stand at the top of the steps.

'We're home,' Uncle Hugo announced, helping his mama up the stairs.

'Mother, so wonderful to see you,' Daphne said in her high, excited voice that Prue remembered so well. 'And Prue, delighted to have you with us. This is my cousin's daughter, Gertie Fuller. I'm sure you'll be great companions to one another as two single women.'

'I'm thrilled to be here, Aunt.' Prue kissed her aunt's round cheek and remembered her scent of lavender. Aunt Daphne had put on a lot of weight since she last saw her, but her kind smile was still the same.

Prue shook Gertie's hand. 'I'm pleased to meet you, Miss Fuller. I hope you and I can get up to all sorts of mischief.'

The faint smile Miss Fuller wore fell and startled she looked at Daphne before her eyes narrowed at Prue. 'Mischief? I do not think so, Miss Marsh.'

Prue's heart sank a little. Miss Fuller stood with her back ramrod straight, she was in fact on an even height with Prue, but there the similarities ended. Miss Fuller wore a prim high-necked white blouse and long black skirt with her uninspiring brown hair pulled tight into a knot behind her head. She looked like a school governess.

Daphne fluttered around them and then led the way inside. 'Gertie will show you to your room, Prue, so you can freshen up. Mother let me show you where you'll sleep. Hugo, are you staying or returning to the office?'

'Alas I must return to work, but I'll be home for six and over dinner I'll catch up with you both then.' With a cheerio he turned and jogged back down the steps to the motor car.

Prue gazed around the large living room, noting a table fan whirling the humid air about the room. Comfortable wicker chairs were placed around a low cane table and French doors were open to the veranda allowing the scent of the recent rain to drift in.

'My uncle has electricity?' Prue asked Gertie, gesturing to the fan.

'Barely. Electricity is extremely unreliable. We are lucky to have it for an hour a day. India is very primitive. Daphne crows to her friends about having electricity connected yet when she has a dinner party she insists on candles, it saves her embarrassment when the electricity stops working. Do not rely on it. Always use your paraffin lamp by your bedside instead of the ceiling light as you'll suddenly be plunged into darkness and crash into things.'

Along a corridor, Miss Fuller led Prue to an end room. 'The bathroom is the second door on the right back there,' she announced before opening the bedroom door.

Inside was a large four-poster bed with netting hung and tied to each post. Again, French windows opened out onto the veranda. A large wardrobe stood against one wall and next to it was a set of drawers, which had a porcelain wash basin and jug.

A young Indian woman stood by the bed and, placing her hands together in front of her, bowed.

'That is Ganika. She'll see to all your needs,' Gertie said, wiping the drawers with a fingertip and scowling even though her finger was clean.

'It's very nice.' Prue placed her small bag on the bed and bowed her head to Ganika.

'Always check your shoes for scorpions,' Miss Fuller warned.

'Thank you for the tip.' Prue pulled off her gloves.

'You'll soon learn to hate India,' Miss Fuller sneered. 'It's a hot filthy place full of disease and stink. Everything turns to rot after a while.'

'You don't like it here then?' Prue said, with a cheeky lift of her lips.

'What is there to like?'

'I'm sure, but there must be some wonderful attributes to the country.'

'I've yet to find them. I wouldn't trust any Indian.' Miss Fuller turned her back on Ganika. 'So, if you have expensive jewellery give it to Hugo to put in his safe. I'll leave you to freshen up.' Miss Fuller left without further comment as two male Indian servants came in carrying Prue's trunk.

Prue nodded and smiled at the young men, who wore white tunics and yellow turbans. They didn't speak or even raise their eyes to her and hurried out.

While Ganika unpacked, Prue unpinned her hat. She washed her face in the basin and sponged the back of her neck. Her dress had quickly dried in the heat and would have to do until the rest of her clothes were unpacked and the creases dropped out.

Dying for a drink, she made her way back onto the veranda where the others were sitting on cane furniture.

Aunt Daphne was pouring out cups of tea. Behind her chair, a tall servant stood with his hands behind his back watching her every move. Aunt Daphne waved towards him. 'That is Rama, our khansama, butler if you like. If you need anything at all, speak with him. His English is excellent. Sit down, my dear.' Aunt Daphne waved her to a chair. 'You must be so tired. I was just saying to Mother that we, Hugo and I, decided not to entertain tonight or accept any invitations for this date to give you both time to rest after your voyage.' Aunt Daphne passed around plates of sticky sweet pastries.

'That is good of you, Aunt,' Prue said, pouring herself a glass of cold water.

'That water is safe to drink, as we get it brought in specially but do not trust water anywhere else. Also ask for tea wherever you go, so it'll have been boiled.' Daphne turned to Grandmama. 'I've already had your cards made up and dropped off at certain friend's houses, as is custom. I deemed it prudent to do that to save you the time and worry of sorting it out yourself.'

Grandmama bristled. 'I brought my own cards, Daphne. I did write and tell Hugo that.'

'Well goodness! He forgot to pass that information on to me. Never mind, it would have held up the visiting, as least this way the courtesy of dropping a card has been done. You have replies already.' Daphne clicked her fingers and Rama left the veranda to instantly return with a silver platter holding slim square cards. 'We have a great many friends, Mother.' Daphne passed the cards to Grandmama.

'And you imagine I am without contacts as well?' Grandmama quirked an eyebrow. 'I was in India before you were even born, girl. My diary is bursting with names I can assure you.'

Daphne looked uncertain. 'Er... well, I simply thought you would enjoy meeting many more.'

'I appreciate your concern, Daughter-in-law, but please understand that I am quite capable of seeing to my own friends. However, I am sure Prue could do with some of your introductions as mine are of my age.'

'That is true. I know no one out here.' Prue sipped her tea, wanting her aunt to feel needed. 'I would be happy to meet your friend's daughters, Aunt.'

Daphne clapped her hands. 'How splendid! Yes, that is excellent. Society is returning from the mountains in the north now that summer is over. Bombay will soon swell with all sorts of entertainments. We'll have you dancing every night if you care for it and by day the amusements never stop. We'll have you married by Christmas!'

Prue jerked. 'I have no wish to be married, Aunt.'

Miss Fuller glared at her as though she'd said something despicable. 'No wish to marry, Miss Marsh? Why ever not?'

Prue chuckled. 'Because I don't wish to be tied down to a man before I've even lived.'

Grandmama laughed. 'Good girl!'

Miss Fuller blinked blankly at her. 'I fail to understand your meaning. Surely acquiring a husband is the best thing a woman can do? How could you consider yourself complete without a husband or children? That is the role God gave us to fulfil.'

'Those things are noble indeed, and in time I'd like to achieve all that but for now, while I am young, I intend to travel and explore and have fun.'

'Fun? How utterly tiresome.' Miss Fuller frowned and turned away, disappointment filling her eyes.

Prue sipped some more tea and ignored the other woman. In that instant she knew they'd not be friends.

Chapter Four

A huge cheer roared up from the crowd and Prue whipped around to see what the cause was.

'Oh, I say, good shot!' Hugo clapped soundly at the charging polo players out on the field.

Using her hand to shield her eyes from the sun, Prue scanned the horsemen. She'd been introduced to many of them before the start of the game, and one fine handsome officer by the name of Captain Lewis had kissed her hand like a gallant knight and said he'd ride for her today and if they won, he'd declare the victory to her.

In the four days since her arrival, Prue had found India to be a hive of wild extremes. Within the British class system, one could pretend they were still in England, yet the moment one left the confines of a British house or the Club then the reality of the true India would swarm up and choke you. Crazily, she loved both worlds.

'There you both are!' Aunt Daphne puffed as she joined them.

'Sorry, my dear.' Hugo took her arm. 'Prue and I were getting a closer look at the field.' He paused as two horsemen came thundering so close that the ground vibrated under Prue's feet.

'I couldn't find you, Hugo.' Daphne fluttered a fan before her flushed face. 'I've left Mother in the stands by the refreshments bar talking to some lady who knew a friend of your father's.'

'Really? Shall we return to them?'

'I'll stay here, Uncle. I like being close to the action.' Prue waved them away, glad to have some alone time.

Since arriving she'd not had a minute to herself unless she was in her bedroom. Aunt Daphne had them out morning and evening, and well into the night. Mornings were for shopping and running errands and the occasional visit to one of her friends, then they'd return home in the middle of the day to eat, rest and nap as the heat built. Afterwards, refreshed, if there was such a word in the energy-sapping warmth of India, they'd receive visitors and make more calls themselves, before eating again, bathing and dressing for a late dinner and whatever night entertainments were arranged, dinners, theatre, cards at the Club, dancing and movie film nights.

Prue enjoyed the constant activity of the mornings and nights, but during the middle of the day she grew bored and restless. Having naps at noon was alien to her. Miss Fuller would stay in her room for hours on end and Grandmama and Daphne too would sleep, but Prue found herself laying down for ten minutes before needing to get up again and wander restlessly around the quiet darkened house.

As the horses galloped past, she spotted Captain Lewis sitting on his fine animal. He gave her a salute and she waved back. As he rode away, she strolled the perimeter of the polo boundary. She wore a khaki *topi*, the hat that was recommended to wear in this climate. Her linen green dress was sleeveless, and her lacy parasol was no match for the burning sun.

Suddenly she was knocked from the side. A small Indian child mumbled something to her and then ran off. She instantly grabbed her purse tighter.

'You did the right thing, holding that purse tightly,' a man said, coming to her side. 'Are you all right?'

'Yes, thank you. No harm done.'

'You can never tell which of them are thieves or not.' He bowed slightly and held out his hand. 'Ajay Khan.'

'Prue Marsh.' She shook his hand, liking his smile and the kindness in his dark eyes.

'Can I escort you back to your party, or to one of the refreshment bars?'

'Thank you. Yes, I'd like a drink,' she said impulsively.

They fell into step and from the corner of her eye, Prue took in the man walking beside her. He wore a white linen suit, which contrasted against his light brown skin. A white trilby hat sat low and jauntily on his sleek-backed black hair. He was handsome and lean and something in her chest tightened when he turned to politely guide her up the steps to the wooden building.

'I have not seen you about here before.' He ordered two lime and sodas without even asking her preference.

'No, I've only been in India for less than a week. This is my first polo match in this country.'

'Ah, fresh off the boat. How are you liking the exotics so far?'

'Very much.' She nodded her thanks as the Indian bar attendant gave her the drink.

'Cheers.' Mr Khan clinked his glass to hers.

'Cheers,' Prue replied. 'You are the first person I've spoken to without first being left a card.'

'Cards are overrated, wouldn't you agree?' He drank deeply from his glass, his intelligent eyes not leaving her face.

'It's the polite way of meeting people.'

'Yes, and the British are very *polite*.'

She bristled. 'And what is wrong with that?'

'Nothing, nothing at all.' His gaze roamed the crowded room.

The light chatter and laughter filled the air with the background noise of the people clapping the polo. Two young Indian boys stood on either wall and pulled ropes to flap the long fans up in the ceiling – a fruitless task for the air was heavy and thick.

'Do you have family here?' Mr Khan asked.

'Yes, my uncle and aunt Fordham.'

'Your uncle is in the army?'

'No, The Indian Civil Service.'

'As I am.'

'Really? You might know of him, Hugo Fordham?'

'Alas, I do not. There are a great number of us, and I am not British enough to mix in the correct circles.'

'Not British enough?' she quizzed. Although he spoke excellent English, and his skin colour was light, he wasn't British.

'I'm Anglo-Indian, my father was British, my mother Indian. Something which is no longer favoured unlike a hundred years ago when no one cared.' His curt tone couldn't be hidden.

'Oh, I see.' Prue was embarrassed she'd asked, but it answered why he spoke with a perfect English

42

accent. She put her drink down, only half-finished. 'Thank you, but I must go. My grandmama will be worried about where I've got to.'

'I have made you uncomfortable.'

'No… well, a little.'

'Forgive me. That wasn't my intention. Sometimes I'm a little too quick to assert my parentage, just in case people come to the wrong conclusion.'

'Which would be?'

'That I'm an Indian trying to be British. I'm not. I'm proud of my Indian heritage.' Yet still he spoke of it as though in a challenge to her.

'And so you should be,' Prue answered lightly.

'I suppose that after spending my entire life in England trying to fit in, and not doing so because of the colour of my skin, I'm a trifle defensive about it.'

'That's understandable.' Prue finished her drink. 'I really must go.'

'Let me walk you back to them.' He swept his arm wide, indicating for her to leave first. 'You never know, another child might bump into you and take your purse this time.'

'I am stronger than I look.'

He gave her a slow appraisal that sent shivers down her spine. 'I agree, Miss Marsh. I don't suppose much would bother you at all.'

Pleased that he had seen that in her, she held her head high as she headed towards the stands at the bottom of the field. 'And what do you do in the I. C. S., Mr Khan?'

'I'm a lawyer.'

'And are you married?'

'Are you proposing, Miss Marsh? I've heard that some British women are extremely forward, but I must warn you I am selective in the women I conduct myself with.' He laughed.

She blushed. He was outrageous and no gentleman. 'I am not proposing, Mr Khan.'

He shrugged. 'Shame.'

Prue walked on. Were all Anglo-Indian men so forward? She sneaked another glance at him, wishing he wasn't so handsome.

'Will you come to dinner with me, Miss Marsh?'

Her stomach clenched. She wanted to say yes.

'Miss Marsh!' The strident and disapproving tones of Miss Fuller cut through the murmuring crowd surrounding them.

Prue sighed but pasted a smile on her face as Miss Fuller pushed her way through a group of Indian men and stopped before her.

'Goodness me! We've been so worried.' Miss Fuller put a hand on her heaving flat chest. 'I've walked miles, I'm sure of it, looking for you!'

'I'm sorry.' Prue glanced behind Miss Fuller as Uncle Hugo made towards them as well. 'I haven't been gone too long, have I?' In all honesty she assumed it had only been ten minutes since Uncle Hugo left her.

'Hugo has been back with us for half an hour.' Miss Fuller's vociferous tone made Prue wince.

'The fault is mine, miss.' Mr Khan bowed.

Miss Fuller barely glanced in his direction. 'You may go, sir.'

Prue stiffened at her rudeness but was saved from commenting as Uncle Hugo reached them.

'There you are, my dear. No harm has come to you, has it?'

'No, Uncle. I merely was walking, and a child bumped into me, and Mr Khan here,' she indicated the man beside her, 'gave me assistance.'

'Indeed? Golly, I'm much obliged, kind sir.' Hugo shook Khan's hand vigorously. 'Much obliged.'

'The pleasure was mine.' Khan's smile seemed a little too smug for Prue's liking.

'Shall we go?' Miss Fuller didn't wait and turned on her heel.

Prue held out her hand to Mr Khan. 'Thank you again.'

As he took her hand, she felt the edge of a card pressed against her palm.

'Good day to you, Miss Marsh.' He left them and was soon absorbed into the crowds.

'We should go, my dear.' Uncle Hugo took her arm. 'Your aunt is eager to return home and rest before the party tonight.'

'Uncle?'

'Hmm?'

'Could we invite Mr Khan for dinner one night?' Prue asked as they left the noise of the crowds and walked through the rows of motor cars to her uncle's vehicle.

'Khan? To dinner? Heavens, no. We thanked him for his help, that is more than enough.'

'But we started talking, and he seems intelligent and kind.'

'I'm sure he is. However, he isn't British, my dear.' Uncle Hugo's mouth became a thin line and his grey eyes softened in apology. 'It's not the done thing, my dear.'

'What do you mean?' Though she knew of course exactly what he meant.

'The chap is not one of us.'

'He's half British and what does that even matter? We are in India, not England. Surely socialising with Indians is accepted?'

'It's not enough for him to be only half British.' He stopped a few yards from the motor car where Daphne and Grandmama had been joined by Miss Fuller. 'Society won't accept him.'

'I'm not asking for society to accept him. I'm asking if he can come to dinner. He's a lawyer, not a street sweeper. You deal with Indians every day at your office.'

'But I don't dine with them. My dear, you need to understand there are rules here. Living in India is hard enough without giving offence to people. If we dined with individuals outside of our class, we would soon find ourselves without friends.' He held up his hands as though in surrender. 'They are not my rules, but our people are steeped in tradition here. The class divides are stronger out here than in England.'

'That is incredible. He works for the I.C.S. as you do.'

'Yes, and he is probably a very decent chap, who I would likely deal with in my position at the office, but outside of that, our paths do not cross.'

'That is ridiculous!'

'Sadly, it is the way of the world, my dear. It is no different to being back home, really. You wouldn't invite someone to dinner who was outside of your circle, now would you?'

'True,' she agreed reluctantly. 'However, if he is from a good family, he could join our circle, couldn't he? I don't see why the colour of his skin should matter. The Viceroy and his officials dine with Indian princes and maharajahs.'

'That is different, and you know it. There is a divide.' He helped her into the motor car.

Grandmama took her hand. 'Is everything all right?'

'Yes, Grandmama. I suppose it is,' she answered with a sigh. In truth she was becoming aware that there was a very different aspect to living in India. Since leaving London she was continually being educated.

'We must have a wonderful rest when we arrive home,' Aunt Daphne chatted. 'Tonight's party is going to be fabulous. Lord Reading, the Viceroy of India, is attending, did I tell you?'

'A dozen times,' murmured Grandmama.

'It's such a pleasure to have him in Bombay.'

At the front of the automobile, Hugo turned in his seat as the driver sped them away from the polo field. 'He may not yet attend, my dear. For there has been an uprising in the south. Tensions are running high.'

'Silly uprisings!' Aunt Daphne waved away his concerns. 'There are always uprisings somewhere in this blighted country. We shall not let rebels ruin our night. There will be many important people there. We must look our utter best, of course. I am so pleased you will witness such a grand evening, Mother, for I'm sure these gatherings are far different from what you remember in your time.'

'My time?' Grandmama looked affronted. 'Girl you make me sound ancient. Remember, I was travelling the world when Hugo was born, and he is the same age as you. So, do not make me sound decrepit and not consider your own age.' She leaned in closer to Daphne. 'And am I still not travelling at what you call my *great age*?'

'I do not mean to give offence, Mother.'

'And do you suppose I never attended to a fancy function?' Grandmama snorted in contempt.

'Well, yes, I'm certain you did but never with a Viceroy attending, I'm sure.'

'Good God! Let me tell you, I've dined with Princes and Maharajas, Sheiks and more members of the nobility than you've had hot dinners.'

'Yes, of course. I do forget your history, Mother. Hugo doesn't speak of it much.'

'Yes, because he was decently brought up. We do not flout our contacts in public, Daphne, it's bad taste.'

'Yes, Mother. Forgive me. Now, we are to arrive at eight and it would be wise for us all not to wear the same colours, or varying shades of the same. Gertie is wearing apricot and I'm wearing olive...'

Prue let Daphne's ramblings roll over her head and tuned out. Her thoughts were of Ajay Khan, and twisting a little in her seat, she held the card down by her thigh where no one could see it and traced a finger over his gold embossed name.

~ ~ ~ ~

In the Grand Ballroom of the Taj Mahal Hotel, Prue waved her fan before her hot face. She'd been dancing for nearly an hour and unlike England, the heat of the room and pressed bodies were stifling in the humid air of monsoon season. Outside, rain hammered the road in front of the hotel and the gardens at the back, and no one was leaving the ballroom to venture out in it. This meant of course that the dance floor and refreshment rooms were heaving with bodies in the dank tropical air.

'Here, Miss Marsh, a drink.' Captain Lewis in full dress uniform handed her a gin and tonic he'd gone to fetch after their dance.

'Thank you.' She sipped eagerly, her throat dry. She glanced around the lavish room looking for her grandmama and spotted her talking to Lord Reading, the Viceroy. Prue smiled as behind Grandmama Daphne was fidgeting trying to not be overwhelmed by the exalted company.

'Do you ride, Miss Marsh?' Captain Lewis suddenly asked, smoothing back his oiled black hair. The handsome officer was a foot taller than Prue and had a well-trimmed moustache that gave him a dignified air.

'I do, Captain, but not as well as I would like. I outgrew my childhood pony and never replaced her. I much prefer to drive motor cars. My two sisters and I all can drive.' She liked the captain, he was enjoyable company and during their dance he'd asked her subtle questions about her family, but not in such a way that Prue felt he was testing her worth.

He tilted his head. 'Really? You drive? How fascinating. However, I was going to ask whether you would care to go for an early morning ride with me?'

'Early morning?'

'Yes, many riders take advantage of the cool dawn air to exercise their horses. It's far too hot later in the day.'

'I'd like that, yes,' her answer was spontaneous.

He smiled warmly. 'Excellent. I'll arrange a day.'

'Can I borrow someone's horse or hire one? My uncle doesn't keep a stable.'

'Indeed. There are horses to hire at the stables close to the barracks. I'll take care of everything.'

'Thank you. I look forward to it.'

'Prue!' Aunt Daphne's excited voice pierced the air.

Turning, Prue waved in her direction and with some shoving and excusing herself Aunt Daphne made it through the crowd to her side.

'Oh, I declare, the stuffiness in this room is unbearable. We came down from the hills far too soon. Simla is much more preferable than Bombay at this time of year.' Daphne dabbed her sweating face with a handkerchief.

'I doubt there is any society left in Simla, Mrs Fordham, they've all returned south. You'd be bored within a day being up there without friends.' Captain Lewis grinned.

'How true you are, Captain, but still such humidity cannot be borne.'

'Did you want me, Aunt?' Prue reminded her.

'Oh, well, not truly. However, I did want to tell you some delicious news. Your grandmama has managed to receive an invitation to Government House next week and we are all invited as well. Isn't that delightful news?' Daphne near jumped for joy.

'Happy news indeed, Aunt.'

'She has also invited a great many people to our home for dinner next month. I'm all in a dither as to how we'll manage. Our dining room isn't so large...' A flicker of doubt crossed Aunt Daphne's eyes.

'I'm sure with more staff we will manage just splendidly.'

'You think so? There is so much planning to be done.'

'Perhaps a dance with me, Mrs Fordham will sooth your mind?' Captain Lewis asked gallantly.

Daphne blushed and patted her hair. 'Goodness, Captain, that would be charming, truly it would.'

Once the captain had whisked her aunt into the middle of the dance floor, Prue sauntered to the open doors and enjoyed the coolness of the fresh breeze coming off the bay. The rain had stopped, and the insects once more sent up their night-time serenade.

She smiled a welcome as Grandmama came to stand with her.

'That captain saved your ears I imagine, by whisking Daphne away?'

Prue nodded. 'She was very excited by your exploits tonight. You've performed miracles I believe by obtaining an invitation to Government House, not to mention the dinner we'll be hosting next month.'

Grandmama waved her hand as if it was no big deal. 'To be honest, I had forgotten a relative of Lord Reading's is an acquaintance of mine and once we started talking, we got along famously. The man and his wife are very easy to converse with, thankfully. Sometimes, these men and their wives are like talking to sheep, all dead behind the eyes, bleating nonsense no one wants to hear. Thankfully, Reading seems a sensible man. He also spoke of my dear Edward.'

'He knew Grandpapa?'

'Amazing, isn't it?' Grandmama's expression fell a little. 'Edward would have enjoyed tonight.'

Prue broke the sudden silence. 'I fear you will be praised and blamed in equal measure over the next few weeks. Aunt Daphne is all a flutter over the idea of hosting an important dinner.'

Grandmama smoothed down a lace ruffle on her dress. 'She'll make it more than it is. A few interesting people having a simple meal. That's all it's meant to be. No fanfare. A quiet night that's all I intended it to be, but she'll make it a performance, you watch. Anyway, it'll keep her occupied and out

of our hair.' Grandmama raised her head and scanned
the crowd. 'With subtle comments about the
requirements of the dinner party, I can keep Daphne
from accompanying us on various excursions for
days.'

This time Prue laughed. 'Grandmama!'

'Well, let's face it, having her and miserable Gertie
with us every day is extremely tiresome. We have to
go to Daphne's dull shops, her dull friends' houses,
her dull parks and so on. The woman doesn't stop
talking from the moment she opens her eyes until she
closes them at night. We need to escape the torture
from time to time.'

'She must be lonely most times. Before Gertie
arrived, and us, she must have spent long days alone
for Uncle is always at the office or away on business.'

'Do you blame him? It's a wonder he's not deaf
from all her talking. No, I'll not feel sorry for her,'
Grandmama grumbled. 'The woman wants for
nothing. She has a servant for every conceivable task.
She doesn't even wash herself in the bath she has
someone to do that!'

Prue's eyes widened. 'Gosh!'

'I tell the truth. Daphne prides herself on not having
washed her own body in years. Such idleness. The
woman doesn't walk anywhere. Have you noticed? Is
it any wonder she's fat?'

'Grandmama!'

'Well, she is. Why hide the fact? She does nothing
but sit around and eat and drink all day. I'm certain
I've gained a pound in a week just by watching her.'

Prue hid a grin behind her fan.

Suddenly, Gertie was standing in front of them as if
by magic. 'Hugo is ready to return home, Mrs

Fordham. He says he has a headache, and an early start in the morning.'

'It isn't even late.' Grandmama frowned.

Captain Lewis brought back Daphne who was blushing like a girl and perspiring like she'd been manning the bellows at a blacksmith's.

Miss Fuller swept her gaze over the captain as though he was nothing but a beggar. 'Daphne, Hugo is ready to leave.'

'What? Now?' Daphne protested, patting a handkerchief at the perspiration pooling on her neck.

'He has a headache and an early start in the morning,' Miss Fuller spoke as though she carried all authority.

'We are not ready to depart quite yet,' Grandmama broke into the conversation, her gaze narrowed at Miss Fuller. 'Tell Hugo to go home. We'll find our own way later.'

'I should go,' Daphne's eyes were downcast.

'No.' Prue put her hand on her arm. 'Stay and enjoy yourself. You've been eager for this night all week.'

'I will accompany Hugo back home. I'm not in the mood for this, anyway.' Miss Fuller sighed as though everything was a trial.

'I'm sure Hugo can manage to go home alone,' Grandmama snapped. 'He's a grown man not a child.'

'I wish to go, Mrs Fordham. Goodnight all.' Miss Fuller left them.

'Perhaps I should go with them?' Daphne queried hesitantly.

Captain Lewis offered his arm. 'Come, Mrs Fordham, let me find another dance partner for you, and perhaps Mrs Fordham senior will join me in a dance too?'

Grandmama waved him away. 'Those dances aren't slow enough for me, Captain, but take Prue and Daphne while I mingle for a while. There's a Prince over there that I believe I once accompanied on a tiger shoot.' She left them to enter a circle of elite Indian men, many of them princes.

Prue watched her in awe. Her grandmama was one in a million.

Chapter Five

'I really don't think she should go alone,' Aunt Daphne was saying as Prue entered the veranda for breakfast.

'She's a grown woman and certainly capable of venturing out of this house alone,' Grandmama countered back, sipping her tea.

'Are you talking about me?' Prue asked, pouring herself a glass of orange juice.

'Dearest, you must reconsider about going out on your own.' Daphne spread a thick layer of marmalade on her toast. 'I really don't approve. What would your mama say?'

'I'll be fine, Aunt. I've been in India for three weeks now and not been out by myself in all that time. At home in York, or even in London, I come and go as I please.'

'Bombay isn't sleepy York or civilised London. Can you not wait until Gertie is feeling better then go with her? Perhaps I should go with you instead?'

'How is Gertie this morning?' Prue tried to deflect the subject.

'In bed still. She doesn't wish for a doctor though, and say's it's probably something she ate at the Club dinner yesterday. Are you ill at all?'

'No, I'm perfectly fine,' Prue replied. 'I'm rarely ill.'

'Yes, me too, and we all ate there. It is a worry.' Daphne forked some eggs into her mouth. 'I'd take you into town, of course, but I've a dress fitting this morning, then Mrs Hemmings is calling at eleven, oh and the new dining room furniture is to arrive today, though naturally one never knows a time with these people. I've ordered crates of new china service for our dinner party and they have to be inspected. So, I simply don't have time to spare for you today, dear niece. Perhaps if you were to go tomorrow? I could take you then, or Gertie could—'

'Daphne, enough!' Grandmama barked. 'Prue wants to go shopping this morning and she can. Hugo's motor car is here waiting to drop her off anywhere she pleases.'

'But the city is so crammed with people, Mother. It's not seemly for a young single woman to be gallivanting about by herself. Indian men find British women very appealing. They are all sex mad here, if you pardon my language. I really am worried that Prue might be abducted and never seen again!'

'I wish you were abducted,' Grandmama whispered under her breath but Prue heard her and bit her lip to stop from smiling.

'And not only that,' Daphne continued, 'there is such unrest in the country. The Indians are crying about injustices at every turn thanks to Gandhi. Hugo was only saying last night that two British owned warehouses were set fire to down by the harbour. I must insist that Prue stays home today.'

'Prue is going to shop in the heart of the city and not be anywhere close to rebels burning down warehouses. She wants to take some more photographs as well. She *goes*.' Grandmama picked up the newspaper and shut everyone out.

'Then take Ganika with you, for a servant accompanying you is better than being alone.'

'I'll be fine, Aunt. I am looking forward to having a day by myself.'

'If you wait, I'm sure I have a friend who is free this afternoon…'

'No need. See you later!' Prue quickly kissed Grandmama's cheek and hurried down the steps to the waiting motor car.

She asked the driver, Jal, to take her to the Fort district and sat back as the gates closed behind them.

Excited to be by herself for the first time, Prue opened her handbag and checked that she had Ajay Khan's card inside. From the information on the card she knew his office was located in the Fort district, an area where many lawyers and bankers had offices, and near the harbour, but she ignored that. She'd be nowhere near any trouble.

She was keen to see Khan, if that was even possible and she hoped it would be. She'd not made contact with him since meeting him at the polo match. Yet, he'd been on her mind a lot since then. None of the British men she'd met at the Club or social events had attracted her attention as much as Mr Khan had done. She was eager to find out more about the man.

In the crush of Monday morning traffic, Prue sat impatiently as the driver tried to traverse the hectic conditions. In narrow roads, horses and carriages, bullocks pulling carts, rickshaws and other vehicles all vied for the same space on the crowded streets.

Men and women, nearly all carrying pots or baskets of produce on their heads, also tried to make their way through the swarming thoroughfares. Shops had their goods on the side of the street, taking up the room people needed to walk, which in turn forced them to walk into the road, slowing down the traffic even further.

After ten minutes of sitting in the motor car and only crawling a few yards, Prue refused to wait any longer. 'Stop here. I'll get out.'

'Here, memsahib?' Jal shook his head. 'Not close to Fort, memsahib.'

'I'll walk. It's not far is it? Straight down towards the harbour, yes?'

'Yes, memsahib.'

'Go back to the house. My grandmama wishes you to take her to the Yacht Club.'

'Very good, memsahib.'

Prue alighted from the car and hurried down the street. The smell of rotting vegetables and garlic filled the air. She turned a corner and kept going, hoping she was heading the right way. The stench of open sewers made her gasp. She received curious glances from Indian men busily toiling on a building site as she passed. A mangy dog gave her a sniff, but she hurried on. The heat was already dropping the curls she'd put in her hair last night, but there was nothing she could do about that now.

Heading closer to the harbour the sounds of ships' horns carried. There was a sense of freedom in her that she'd not experienced before. Despite having been out alone in York or London, they were home to her, whereas here, in a foreign country hardly knowing a soul or the languages, she was giddy with the excitement of it.

The traffic was fierce and to cross any road took wits and courage. She skirted the busy roads circling the Flora Fountain, a lovely monument of a Roman female statue atop of a large fountain. She stopped to take a photograph of it.

Prue headed for a small park edged between two large buildings. She sat on a low stone wall for a moment to catch her breath as the heat built. Around her women in colourful saris stood talking, their small children playing in the water spouting from a broke water pipe. She took some more photos, smiling as the children played.

When she'd drawn enough stares, Prue put her camera away and moved on to search for the street that Khan's office building was situated. To her left the large imposing Crawford's Market created traffic jams as thousands of people came and went from the market. The crush of bodies combined with the heat and tangy smells of the stalls made Prue a little light-headed. She wished she'd eaten breakfast before setting out.

From a side street a man on a bicycle nearly collided with her and she jumped back in shock. He spoke in his native language but swore at her in English.

'You should look where you are going!' she shouted back.

A group of ragged children swarmed her from out of nowhere. Prue clenched her fists, glaring angrily at the children who yelled in her face. Their brown skinny arms reached to touch her, little hands pulled at her dress, her bag, her camera, their begging and pleading voices whirled into a chaotic noise. She pushed through them to get clear, but they followed, their demands growing louder.

'Miss Marsh?'

She looked up into a shadowy doorway of a large white building and as if by magic Ajay Khan jogged down the two steps into the sunshine. 'Mr Khan!'

'This is a surprise.' He turned swiftly to speak harshly to the begging children and as a group they darted away down back alleys. He took a step closer to Prue. 'Are you hurt? Did they rough you up?'

'No, I'm fine. Hot, that's all.' She felt flustered by his closeness. She was hot and sweaty and yet he seemed cool in a white shirt and pale cream linen trousers. She was dismayed that she looked a fright.

'Have you become separated from your family?' He looked around as though expecting a member of her family to suddenly appear.

'No, no. I'm quite alone today.' He seemed as handsome as ever and she was aware of his hand on her arm, sending tingles along her skin.

'Shall we go for some tea perhaps, to settle you?'

'Thank you, that would be nice.' She pushed a damp curl off her hot forehead. She needed to get her hair cut short and forget about trying to curl it, it was the only way to have it in this climate.

'Wait here, I'll fetch my hat.' He disappeared inside the building for a moment before returning with his hat sitting jauntily on his head as it had at the polo match.

'Come, let me take your arm and we'll dodge the madness of the traffic and go to Crawford's Market.' With his hand on her elbow she hurried beside him as they ran across the street and into the burgeoning market place.

The crush of people made it difficult for them to talk, as often Prue had to fall behind Mr Khan in single file to slip between stalls. After several minutes of doing this, Khan stopped and ushered her inside a rundown looking stall.

'Don't let appearances fool you.' He indicated for her to sit at a shaky wooden table. 'This place does the best food, I promise you.'

She sat stiffly on the edge of the chair as he stepped to the serving counter. Around her Indian men sat drinking and smoking, chatting away and staring at her openly.

Khan brought back a tray of small plates filled with delicacies and two cups of milky tea. 'I bought a variety as I sensed you might like a little of each.'

'Thank you.' She turned to sit facing away from the group of men, but out of the corner of her eye she saw an older man sat on the floor, he was chewing something browny-red and was swaying as though in a daze.

Khan glanced around him and grinned at Prue. 'That old man is high on betel nut. You chew it and it takes all your cares away.'

'Like laudanum or opium?'

He raised his eyes in surprise. 'Yes, but I suppose in a gentler way. It stains your mouth though, very unpleasant.'

'Mama had a friend who was addicted to laudanum. They used to find little bottles of it all over her house.'

'What happened to her?'

'She was put in a mental asylum in the end.'

Khan frowned. 'Shall we discuss something nicer, like this food. Have you tried any of these before?'

Prue looked at the assortment before her. 'No. The cooks at my uncle's house serve us British food or curries. My aunt imports from England crates of sweet foods like biscuits and chocolates. She's not one for trying new things.'

'Will you try one?'

'Of course.' She was always eager for a challenge and she didn't want him to think she was a timid British woman.

'Try this.' He indicated one of the dishes.

She tore a piece of what she imagined was a crepe and dipped it in the dish of mango yoghurt. It was tasty and refreshing. She liked it.

'You have a camera,' he stated.

'Yes, I enjoy taking photographs. I'm building a good collection. I want to document my travels.'

'You must take one of me.'

'Very well.' Prue took out the camera and got it ready as Ajay leaned back in the chair, relaxed and sure of himself. Prue captured two photos then put the camera back in its case.

'So, Miss Marsh,' Khan said as he scooped up with his fingers some flaky fish seeped in coconut milk. 'Is it fate that we meet again, or design?'

'Why did you give me your card?' she countered, not wanting to look as though she'd gone purposely to find him.

'I didn't contemplate that you would give me your card that day, not a good British woman like you.'

'How do you know I'm a good British woman?'

His lazy gaze raked sensually over her body. 'I know your type.'

'My type?' That irritated her. She didn't want to be defined by a type. 'I think not.'

He chuckled. 'Whether you like it or not, Miss Marsh, you are who you are. There is no shame in that. Take it from me, for I have gone through years of hell trying to find out just what type *I* am!'

'Should I feel sorry for you?'

He grinned and tilted his head. 'Not in the least.'

'Then I won't.' She raised her eyebrows at him. 'Yet you must have thought I would be willing to accept your card? I mustn't be that *good* then?'

'I took a chance, yes. I found you extremely alluring. I wanted to see you again. How else could I do that when we've not been introduced in polite society?'

Her stomach twisted at his mention of finding her alluring. 'I could have thrown your card in the bin.'

'But you didn't.'

Prue blushed and lowered her lashes, pretending to concentrate on the food.

'You were standing outside my office building for a reason.'

She shrugged and had no cause to play games with him. She was not a silly young girl of eighteen having her first crush. She was twenty-three and had her fair share of flirtations and, if she included the disastrous involvement with Wyn last year, she could easily say she was a woman who knew what she wanted.

She ate some fish, the sweet coconut sauce delicious. 'I'll admit that I wanted to see you again. You seemed interesting. There's no harm in meeting you again, is there? Unless you aren't a gentleman, or you lied and you are married?'

'Do you want me to be a gentleman, or married?' Khan sat back in his chair, studying her and Prue's heart clenched at the intensity of it. Despite the swarm of people, the heat, the smell and noise around them, it all dimmed into the background when he looked at her.

Her heart thumped in her chest. 'I don't imagine I do.'

63

'Many people, no, a *great deal* of people will not like it. British and Anglo-Indians do not mix – ever.' Khan sipped at his cup, looking at her over its rim. 'But you are restless. I see it in you. A kindred spirit, I suppose.'

She stiffened slightly that he could read her so easily. 'I'm travelling to have some adventure.'

'What kind of adventure do you want?' his voice was silky smooth.

'Any that comes my way.' She picked up a pale caramel square. 'This looks like fudge.'

'It is. It's almond fudge.'

She bit into the sweet sugary treat. 'Lovely.' When she looked at him, his gaze was on her mouth. She swallowed and licked her lips.

'I must get back to the office.' He stood abruptly. 'I shall take you back to the main road.'

She stood also but shook her head. 'Thank you, but no. I shall walk around the market.'

'Is that wise? You may get lost and there is unrest in the city, especially towards the British.'

'Are you trying to frighten me?'

'I'm trying to be sensible, Miss Marsh. I would not want harm to come to you and I am the last person you were seen with.' His gaze flicked around the throng of people surrounding the eatery. 'Your safety is paramount.'

The coldness of his tone irritated her. 'I'll be fine. Thank you for the tea and food.'

He stood very close to her. He smelt of sandalwood. 'Your card.'

She hesitated only for a moment before opening her bag and giving him one of her cards.

'Until next time.' He grinned and tipped his hat to her before walking briskly away.

For several minutes she stood in the food stall. The whole meeting couldn't have taken more than half an hour and she was left unsatisfied and yet thoroughly intrigued by the encounter.

~ ~ ~ ~

Bombay, September 30th, 1921

Dearest Millie

Sorry I'm late in writing this letter! It's been very hectic here. Each day there is always something to do. Well, I have made sure I have something to do! Most British women I've met spend a great deal of time doing nothing but visiting each other and complaining how dull India is. I am out every day, which means I receive censure from Aunt Daphne and her friends but sitting around the house or sleeping most of the afternoon certainly isn't for me. I take myself off to the theatre and watch the latest movie film, at the moment they are having a re-run of Charlie Chaplin's movies. Yesterday, I watched The Vagabond.

Oh, before I forget, the dinner we hosted last night was a tremendous success. Grandmama was the attraction, of course. She has such a way with her. Our guests were some of the most important men in India, yet Grandmama treated them like family and they enjoyed that very much. We had no pomp or ceremony. Grandmama even asked Lord Reading to pour her a drink! I truly thought Aunt Daphne would faint at the cheek of it, but he happily got up and made her a whisky and soda. Our guests stayed very late as they all sat on the veranda talking. It was a brilliant success thanks to Grandmama.

You asked me to tell you more about my days, so I'll try.

After breakfast, I go out each day to visit the markets and do a little shopping. Sometimes, I go to the Club with Grandmama and meet her friends, also I take walks in the parks, some of which are extremely pretty. You know me, I must keep busy or I'd simply die of boredom, and by going out I don't have to partake of Aunt Daphne's boring tea parties with her narrow-minded friends. Even Grandmama takes herself off to the Club every day, even if it's to sit and read, otherwise I think she'd say something to those women and cause offence. She is a card, isn't she?

I have been riding early most mornings with Captain Lewis. He sends a motor car for me at dawn and when I arrive at the stables, he is ready and waiting on his horse and has my mount ready to go. We ride for an hour along the harbour foreshore or sometimes through the parks. India is beautiful at that early time of the day. The sky is pink, and the heat has yet to fry us. It's an hour when everything is peaceful and tranquil – just us and the birds. After our ride we go to the Yacht Club for breakfast and then I return home for a bath and start the day of social visits or sightseeing.

You have asked about Captain Lewis, but I cannot tell you more than I already have. He is a gentleman, an officer in his regiment, a respectable dancer and conversationalist and an interesting riding partner. Everyone has a good opinion of him. However, he doesn't make my heart thump in excitement, and he should if he was to be considered as a potential husband, don't you agree?

The family believes he's a good catch, and Aunt Daphne talks of him as though he is some sort of demi-god! He pays her a lot of attention and she laps it up. She feels I should snap him up as quickly as possible. Poor Aunt Daphne, she is full of fancies. I, however, do not wish for a husband, and certainly not one who would remain in India for years. I would be trapped.

The truth is India is a hotbed of extremes and the British go about with their heads in the sand as to how the Indians regard them. There is trouble all around the country. We have been spared a lot of it, thankfully. Only strikes remain ongoing and causes a great disruption.

Hand on heart I cannot blame the Indians for striking, they are treated poorly. Of course, I do not understand all the political issues and won't bore you with it all, but Grandmama was mentioning that perhaps we'd soon travel on to another country before it all gets out of hand.

Millie, I cannot tell you how I struggle here. Me, the one who never cared about social conscience in my life! But I see the poor children in the streets, the lepers, the maimed, all living like abandoned dogs and I can't stand to witness it, especially when I am surrounded by comfort.

Here, Prue paused. Voices came from outside her bedroom. Uncle Hugo's soft murmurs and Gertie's more forceful tones before footsteps sounded of them walking away.

Sighing, Prue tried to gather her thoughts to continue writing, but a glance at the clock on the chest of drawers showed she should be getting ready for the party. She quickly reread over what she'd written. She desperately wanted to mention Ajay Khan but what could she say? That she'd met a dashing Anglo-Indian man who she gave her card to but hadn't heard of since they shared a meal in a market? She'd sound foolish. She hated that Ajay Khan was on her mind so much.

Aunt Daphne's birthday dinner is being held at the Club this afternoon and Gertie has been a nightmare for days with her plans for it to go well. The woman barely has a kind word for anyone and with her organising the party, she's become a dragon and has poor Uncle running around obeying her every whim. I try to like her, but she is unlikeable. Gertie treats people as though everyone is beneath her and she isn't even high born! Grandmama is struggling to keep her temper with her at times. What with Gertie's sourness and Aunt Daphne's excitable ways it is difficult to not speak sharply to them.

I sense that is why Grandmama is keen to move on. She received a note from a friend in Italy inviting us to visit and Grandmama is tempted to leave before Christmas, which upsets Uncle Hugo greatly for he wants us to stay here a year or more, but that is too long for either of us.

I will send this letter in the morning. I've to write to Mama and Cece as well, plus my new friend Laurence, whom I mentioned to you in previous letters.

Mama said in her last letter that she was planning another visit to you, that must make you happy. Cece I rarely hear from. Does she write to you? Is she upset with me for going on this trip with Grandmama and she wasn't invited? I'll send her some gifts.

Give my love to Jonathan. I long to see him! You must send a photograph of him soon, and I'll send you some photographs I've taken as well. Uncle Hugo has had one of the outbuildings in the garden converted into a dark room for me. It was very good of him and now I can develop my photos myself.

Tell Jeremy we could do with a crate of Chateau Dumont champagne sending to us. The stuff Aunt Daphne buys is not as nice as yours. Uncle Hugo says he'll put an order in but never does. So, please send us champagne!

Much love,
Your sister, Prue.

With a speed she was proud of, Prue quickly changed into a satin and chiffon dress of dusky rose that had printed roses on the flimsy light skirt that drifted around her knees like tissue paper. Her hair had been washed the night before and curled by Ganika and she added a comb to one side of her head which held small dainty white roses. Her make-up was done subtly and quickly, her lipstick a blush pink to match her outfit.

A knock on the door heralded Grandmama as she was slipping on her shoes.

'Oh good, you're ready.' Grandmama wore a pale blue outfit and a wide hat. 'No hat, girl? You'll boil alive in the heat. It's a garden party, remember?'

'I've my parasol. I didn't want to wear a hat again, it squashes my curls.' Prue pulled on her white lace gloves.

'Better to have squashed curls than boiled brains!'

'I'll take the risk.' Prue collected her handbag and parasol and lastly her camera. 'We are ready?'

'Listen,' Grandmama pulled her back before she could leave the room. 'I've accepted my friend's invitation to stay with them in Palermo, but that we wouldn't be there until the end of November. That gives us another two months here. I've not posted the letter yet if you want to stay longer? Or are you happy for me to go ahead?'

'Yes, I am happy to leave at the end of November, but Uncle Hugo will be disappointed we aren't staying for Christmas.'

Grandmama's expression became sad. 'I know, but he's not a child. I would like him to return to England to live but he says he won't for years yet. Evidently he's not considering me in my old age so why should I think of him?'

'He might change his mind about England once we've been gone a while and he misses you.'

'We'll see.' Grandmama looked doubtful. 'Right let us go and spend an afternoon listening to Daphne and her tedious friends wish her a happy birthday every five minutes. I wouldn't mind if the food and drink was suitable, but Gertie's organised the menu and it's as bland and boring as she is!'

'In my letter to Millie I asked her to tell Jeremy to send us a crate of his champagne.'

'Just a crate?' Grandmama scoffed. 'Living with this lot we need ship full!'

Chapter Six

Prue edged her way through the stalls of Crawford's crowded market. To her left and right were industrious men plying their trades. She glanced at the turbaned man sharpening knives, the barber with his queue of waiting men and boys, the grain sellers, the shoemakers, the goldsmiths and the tinsmiths.

She dodged around large pots and urns, a vegetable stall and a wide area spread with colourful rugs and carpets. Some stallholders, all smiles and hand gestures, begged her to come to their stall and buy something, telling her their goods were the best on offer. She declined politely, skipping around harassed mothers and babies and walking fast past the next seller who had the same intention to inform her of his excellent goods and prices.

The humidity seemed so heavy today, tempers flared between stallholders and a group of particular men were arguing aggressively.

Prue slipped down between two stalls into another row and wondered if she should make for home. After all, she'd not bought a single item and her enthusiasm to go shopping for gifts for Cece and Mama was waning with every moment.

As she stepped out into the busy street and walked along the swarming roadside, the first drops of rain landed. Prue groaned and looked for the nearest door back into the covered market building, but as everyone had the same idea, she was soon crushed between hot sweaty bodies. The drops turned to a sudden heavy downpour of monsoon.

Getting soaked by the second, she used her elbows to barge through the people no longer caring if she annoyed those she pushed past. The stench of body odour and stale spices mingled with trodden on fruit made her gasp.

Once inside, she stood and wiped the rain from her face, her hair dripping and her dress sodden.

'When the air is too heavy to breathe, it is time to get inside before the rain starts,' the soft voice whispered in her ear.

Turning, Prue looked into the dark eyes of Ajay Khan. 'Oh, it's you.'

'It's me.' He nodded. 'I saw you about ten minutes ago.'

'Ten minutes ago?'

'I followed you, watched you.' He stood very close to her.

Prue swallowed, her eyes not leaving his face. 'Why?'

'Because I like the look of you. You are beautiful, graceful, even more so when you don't sense anyone is watching you.'

She swiped at her wet hair, knowing she must look a dreadful sight, but he took her hand and lowered it.

'You are beautiful. In any state.' Still holding her hand, he started threading through the crowd and she followed him, not caring where he led.

Eventually, after traversing to the other side of the market, he guided her back out into the downpour and laughed at her shocked face as they splashed through puddles crossing a road and down an alley.

'Where are we going?' she called out as he pulled her along.

'What does it matter?' he laughed back at her, rain running down his face.

She grinned, feeling alive and excited. She no longer cared that she was soaking.

Suddenly, he opened an iron gate and pulled her into a small square courtyard. Khan pushed her gently against the wall and kissed her deeply.

Surprised, Prue stood still as he plundered her mouth, then in an instant she was kissing him back, holding his shoulders tightly, demanding as much as he was.

His hands roamed her body, outlining her contours through the wet dress, which moulded to her body like a second skin. She shivered at the erotic sensation, eager for more. Her stomach clenched as he pressed against her.

Moments later he took a step back and at the same time the rain stopped as easily as if a tap had been turned off.

'You kiss very well.' His statement made her smile.

'Thank you.' She looked around at the white painted walls, the tiled floor of the courtyard. 'Where are we?'

'This is my home.' He watched her closely. 'Will you share my bed?'

Her eyes widened at his abrupt question. 'Gosh...
um ...'

'I want you and I believe you want me too.'

'I don't even know you!'

He shrugged one shoulder. 'Why should that
matter? What difference would it make if we'd
known each other three minutes, three hours or three
years?'

'It's not so simple.' She was lost for words, but her
body ached for his touch. 'People simply don't go
around getting into bed with strangers!'

'They should. The world would be a happier place
instead of having all these rules and regulations. Why
not go along with what your body tells you it wants?'

'Because it leads to trouble.' Now the heat of the
moment had passed, she felt uncomfortable in her wet
clothes. Her shoes squelched with water.

'Come inside and I will fetch you a towel.' He
walked under a dripping roof gutter to a green painted
door.

'No, I think not.'

He turned back to her, a grin playing on his lips.
'You are frightened?'

'No!'

'You are. You want me, admit it.'

'None of this makes any sense.'

'Why? Because I am not British? Can you only
want a white man with impeccable credentials and
pedigree?'

'No, I didn't mean that.'

'I judged you to be different, Miss Marsh, but
underneath you are just the same as all the other
memsahibs.'

'Don't call me that!' she snapped.

'But that is what Indians must call white women, they are superior to us.'

'Stop it!'

He took three long strides and was nose to nose with her, pressing her against the wall again. 'I'm not good enough for you, am I?'

'I… You…' She hated that her words wouldn't come. Her mind was a jumbled mess. Her body screamed in silent want. She'd never experienced such a need in her life, even with the men she'd flirted with in the past.

'Go home, Prue Marsh.' He stepped away and after a long look, stepped inside and shut the door.

Prue stumbled out into the narrow street. To her right was the noise from the ships and boats in the harbour, so she knew to go left and head back up towards the city streets.

She'd walked many roads before she found her way back to an area she recognised. She needed to get home, to change her clothes, but her legs stopped moving and she leaned against a wall. How had all that happened so quickly? Ajay Khan was like a drug. Her was her opium. A taste of him and she wanted more. She had to get a grip of herself. This wasn't meant to happen. She must be in control, not him.

'Are you unwell?' A tall elegant Indian woman in a deep purple and gold sari stood beside her.

Prue stared at the woman, mesmerised by her stunning exquisiteness. 'Oh, I…'

'Let me help you.' The woman clicked her fingers to her servant that stood a few paces behind. She spoke to him in her language and he disappeared in a flash.

'We shall get you home, yes?' The woman's gold bangles jingled as she placed her hands together in front of her. 'You are safe now.'

'Thank you.'

'You live with Hugo Fordham, yes?' Her smile was lovely and kind. The gold in her ears shone as the sun broke between the clouds.

'I do. How did you know?'

'I live a few streets away from you. I've seen you walking many times in the Hanging Gardens.' She bowed her head shyly.

'You have?' Prue wondered if there would be any more shocks for her today.

'I, too, walk there most evenings. I am Nina Patel.' She spoke excellent English, her movements supple and serene.

'I'm Prue Marsh, but do you know that as well?' Prue smiled to take any sting out of her words.

'No, I did not know your name. Now I do.' Nina bowed her head in acknowledgement.

Before Prue could respond, a sleek white automobile pulled up beside them and the servant sent off before, jumped out of the front passenger side and opened the door for Nina.

'Come,' she said to Prue. 'I shall take you home.'

~ ~ ~ ~

'You are invited to tea at the Patel's residence?' Aunt Daphne needed to sit down as she heard Prue's statement.

'Yes, Aunt.' Prue, after bathing and changing, now sat on the veranda enjoying scones and tea. The episode with Ajay Khan had been pushed to the back of her mind for now, as she discussed how she'd been brought home by Nina Patel.

'You understand who they are, don't you?'

'How could I possibly, Aunt?'

Grandmama sipped her tea. 'I'm sure you'll delight in telling us, Daphne, so you might as well get on with it.'

'Well,' Aunt Daphne sat straighter in her chair, and even put down her second scone. 'The Patel family are very wealthy, I mean extremely. They are in shipping, I believe. But they aren't just ordinary Indians, no they are Parsi.'

Prue looked blankly at her aunt. 'I've no idea what that is.'

Grandmama spoke before Daphne could. 'They are descendants from Persia, my dear. They came to India centuries ago to escape religious persecution from the Muslims.'

'Not only that,' Daphne butted in as though that information didn't matter, 'the Patel family are descendants from Persian royalty I was told. Very elite. They don't mix with anyone. That's why when you say you are invited there, I find it incredible! Are you sure you aren't mistaken?'

'Don't talk nonsense, Daphne,' Grandmama snapped. 'Prue might have been soaked through, but she didn't have water in her ears. If this Nina Patel invited her for tea, then I don't think Prue could have mistaken that for something else!'

'Truly, Aunt,' Prue said more gently, 'Nina invited me for tea tomorrow afternoon. She's sending her motor car for me even though they live only a few streets away and I told her Uncle Hugo had a motor car.'

'That's a sign of a decent family.' Grandmama
nodded wisely. 'Sending their own car to collect you
is dignified.'

Aunt Daphne stuffed her mouth with scone, shaking
her head in amazement at the same time. 'What news
to tell Hugo!'

'You'll have to wear your best day dress, my dear,'
Grandmama frowned, 'for there can be no chance of
error if you become a friend of a Parsi. Excellence is
what they strive for in everything.'

'Yes, I can imagine. Nina is incredibly beautiful.
She wore so much gold. I would guess she even had
gold thread in her sari.'

'It would be, yes.' Grandmama poured more tea.
'They have exquisite taste.'

'You must study everything, Prue,' Aunt Daphne
gushed. 'Then you can tell us it all when you return
home.'

'I'll do my best, Aunt.' Prue smiled.

'Oh, you'll miss my friend, Mrs Baker's, afternoon
tea party. That is a shame indeed.' Aunt Daphne
quickly brightened. 'However, being in a Parsi home
would be far more exciting for you, I'm sure. I heard
they eat off gold plates, you know.'

Grandmama rolled her eyes. 'I bet they have
elephants in the gardens, too.'

'Do you think so, Mother?' Aunt Daphne gasped.
'No.'

Aunt Daphne's eyebrows rose as Gertie joined
them. 'Oh, there you are. I thought you'd sleep all
afternoon.'

'Forgive me. I wasn't feeling well again.' Gertie
took two steps towards the table and suddenly fainted.

Aunt Daphne screamed making Grandmama jump.

Prue hurriedly knelt beside Gertie.

'Shut up, Daphne!' Grandmama demanded as Daphne continued to wail.

Grandmama issued quick instructions to Rama who had been standing at attention near the table.

'Gertie.' Prue tapped the other woman's pale cheeks.

'Is she dead?' Daphne hollered.

'No, of course she'd not dead, you stupid woman!' Grandmama snapped.

Gertie's eyes flickered, and she lifted her head.

'There, see, she's coming back to us,' Prue crooned. 'Let us sit you up slowly.'

'I do apologise,' Gertie murmured, as Prue helped her into a sitting position. 'Forgive me.'

'Water!' Daphne poured iced water from a jug but managed to spill more on the tablecloth than what went into the glass. 'Good Lord, Gertie. To faint and you've only just left your bed! You must be dreadfully ill. This is so upsetting! Shall we take her to the hospital?' Daphne cried harder, her hands shaking.

'Seriously, calm down or I'll slap you!' Grandmama snatched the glass out of Daphne's hand and passed it to Gertie.

After Gertie had sipped at the water, Prue helped her up into a chair.

'I am most sorry,' Gertie said again.

Grandmama poured her a cup of tea. 'I've sent for the doctor. You've been unwell for many weeks and it's time you needed a professional's opinion.'

'Oh, no, Mrs Fordham, I'm sure I don't need a doctor.'

Aunt Daphne wiped her eyes with a napkin, then spread more cream and jam onto another scone. 'No, Gertie. I agree with Mother. You are my family and how could I look your parents in the face again if anything happened to you? A doctor is required. No arguments.'

Gertie glanced away into the garden. 'I'm sure I'll be fine,' she whispered.

~ ~ ~ ~

As the sun rose in a coral-hued sky, Prue sat on the borrowed horse called Ginger, and looked out over the bay. Ships and boats of all sizes rode at anchor while further out to sea, a few vessels were steaming on to other ports.

'Did you enjoy the dance, last night, Miss Marsh?' Captain Lewis asked.

'I did, Captain. I'm sorry you weren't there. Some of your fellow officers said you were on duty.'

'A last-minute clash of schedules, unfortunately. I was deeply annoyed that I missed another chance to dance with you.'

'I can confess that my feet ache this morning. We arrived home at three o'clock this morning and I only had an hour's sleep before your motor car came to collect me. So, forgive me, if I am not at my best.' Prue laughed. 'I danced all night.'

'Yes, I heard. My fellow officers had nothing but praise for your stamina and beauty.'

'They were lovely men, truly. Very attentive.'

Captain Lewis laughed. 'Naturally, every British bachelor in Bombay wants to meet the enchanting Miss Prue Marsh. You've set tongues wagging and many hearts fluttering.'

Prue chuckled, delighted to be so popular. 'I'll soon be replaced when the next boat from England arrives with another group of London debutantes.'

'None will be as lovely as you.'

Slightly embarrassed by his constant compliments, Prue walked her horse on a bit.

'See that steamer there?' Captain Lewis pointed to the left where a large steamer was pulling into the docks. 'That's arrived from England.'

'It has?' Excitement filled Prue. 'That means we'll have mail. I might have letters from my sisters and Mama.' For a moment Prue had a sudden longing to see them, to hear her mama's gentle laugh, to see Cece's quiet censure in her eyes even though she'd grin at something stupid Prue had said or done, and she missed Millie's tight embraces which told her just how much she cared.

'It's also the steamer I'll be travelling to Ceylon.'

Prue turned in the saddle to stare at him. 'Oh, you're leaving?'

'For a few months, that is all. My regiment has been sent to Ceylon, a routine operation.' He let his horse nibble at the grass. 'Damned bad luck, actually. I was hoping to spend more time with you.'

'I see.' She stared back out to the steamer again, half-heartedly wishing she too could go on the steamer and sail to somewhere new. India was interesting and exotic, but she was keen to keep exploring. The days with her fussing aunt and solemn Gertie were beginning to wear her down, and she'd heard nothing from Ajay Khan since the kiss in the courtyard.

'I will miss our morning rides, Miss Marsh.'

Prue flashed a smile at him. 'I will too, Captain. They have been a pleasurable part of my day.'

'I'm glad. May I write to you while I'm gone?'

'If you wish.' Her attention was caught by movement further along the road that edged the park they were in. She thought she saw Uncle Hugo's car go past. How odd.

Captain Lewis turned to stare as she did. 'Is something wrong?'

'No, at least I don't think so. I imagined I saw my uncle's motor car go by, but surely it is too early, it's not even six o'clock. He said he was going to stay home today.'

'We can return to the stables if you wish?'

'Would you mind?' Prue gathered the reins and brought Ginger about. 'It's just that Gertie, Miss Fuller, has been ill recently. The doctor came last week and didn't seem concerned and said it was likely a fever of some sort but since then Gertie hasn't left her room. We are all a little worried. My aunt has been terribly upset.'

'Sickness can strike very quickly out here. I imagine your aunt must be going out of her mind with worry.' Captain Lewis grimaced, knowing Daphne as well as Prue did.

'Yes, it's been... difficult indeed. Uncle Hugo can't seem to settle to anything either at the moment. The house is a trifle disturbed to say the least.'

They negotiated the path back along the foreshore and headed for the stables.

'Have you seen your new friend in recent days?' Captain Lewis asked.

Prue knew he meant Nina Patel for they talked about most things on their morning rides. 'Yes, I've had tea once more at her house since my first visit last week.'

'And that went as well as the first visit?'

'It did. I met her mother and father and also her two brothers and younger sister. They are all extremely nice. Nina and I walked in the Hanging Gardens and I took some photographs for my collection.' Prue thought of the Patel family, with their engaging smiles and warm welcome. She'd stayed longer than she had expected to for they were all keen to ask her questions about her life and family. Nina's father had lived and worked for many years in London and had business interests there. He spoke excellent English as did all the family.

'Will you be going there again?' Captain Lewis asked.

'Yes, they invited me back next Thursday.'

Crossing a small grassed area, Prue jerked in the saddle as she saw Uncle Hugo's motor car parked outside a square building. She knew it to be his car for Jal, his driver, was behind the steering wheel.

'Miss Marsh?' Captain Lewis halted his horse beside Ginger.

'What building is that, do you know?'

'It's a hospital from what I can read on the sign above the door. My Hindi reading isn't great. I can speak it better than I can read it.'

'A hospital?' Prue's heart squeezed. The sign above the door was not in English, which was unusual. 'What kind of hospital can you tell?'

Captain Lewis peered to read it. 'A private hospital from what I can gather. It will be for the wealthy Indians to attend. Why?'

'That is my uncle's motor car parked out the front.'

'Right, well.' Captain Lewis seemed uncertain as to what to do next. 'Could he be fetching the doctor for Miss Fuller?'

'Perhaps. Why would he be going there though? We have a doctor, an English doctor, only on the next corner from the house.'

'I don't know, Miss Marsh. Why don't I take your horse back to the stables and you go and find your uncle? Unless you want me to wait with you?'

'No, no, thank you.' Prue quickly dismounted and handed him the reins. 'Thank you, Captain, that is most kind of you.'

'I hope to see you before I sail?'

'Hopefully, Captain!' She ran from him across the road and after a glance at Jal sitting in the driver's seat, she entered the foyer.

A small Indian man stood behind the desk sorting through papers.

Prue brought her hands together and bowed. 'Namaste. May I ask as to whether my uncle, Mr Hugo Fordham, has come in here?'

'Certainly, memsahib.' He bowed. 'Sahib Fordham is with Doctor Wadia. Upstairs, third door on the left.' He bowed.

'Thank you.' Worried, Prue hurried along the corridor and up the staircase. She strode along the silent corridor but only counted two doors on the left. She stopped and turned about. There were three doors on the right. At the door she thought to be the correct one she hesitated to knock. This was private business of her uncle's. What gave her the right to intrude?

She waited a few moments, pacing the floor, then rushed back down the corridor and outside only to find her uncle's motor car gone.

Stunned, she stood on the street. Had she imagined it all? It had definitely been Jal in the motor car, and the porter said her uncle was with a doctor. How had she missed him?

Feeling ridiculous in her jodhpurs yet not riding a horse, she began walking home as the call to prayer filled the air. The streets were growing busy as the city woke to a new day, yet Prue felt disconcerted.

First, Gertie was ill and now perhaps her uncle? Was he very sick? So sick he didn't want anyone to know or worry and that's why he saw an Indian doctor at the crack of dawn before anyone was awake? It had to be or why all the secrecy?

Anxious, she hailed a passing rickshaw, who took her the rest of the way home. At the gates, she bade him to wait until she could send a servant down to pay him. Prue noticed her uncle's motor car was in the drive and Jal was wiping it over with a cloth. He didn't look at her.

Walking up the steps, the sound of weeping greeted her. In the corner of the veranda where the rising sun didn't reach, Prue could make out Gertie, hunched over in the dimness.

'Gertie!' Prue hurried to her side. 'Are you sick again?'

Gertie leaned back, her pale face streaked with tears, her eyes red. 'I'm not sick, only of heart.'

'Whatever is the matter?'

'Nothing, nothing at all.'

'I beg to differ. Nothing at all wouldn't make you cry like this.' It was the first time Prue had seen the other woman with her defences down.

Standing, gathering her dressing gown about her, Gertie moved away. 'I said, it is *nothing*!' She stormed inside.

Prue stood on the veranda trying to decide if she should follow Gertie or not. The woman had not given her any reason to foster a friendship between them. In fact, Gertie went out of her way to not be in Prue's presence, and barely spoke to her when she was.

When Uncle Hugo came out and smiled at her she
stared at him, not knowing whether to mention that
she had seen his motor car at the hospital or not.

'Did you enjoy your ride, my dear?' he asked,
sitting at the table as a male servant came around the
side of the house from the kitchens with a tray of
coffee.

'I did, yes.' She watched the servant place the tray
on the table then Rama stepped out of the doorway
and poured the coffee for her uncle.

'Memsahib?' Rama asked, lifting the coffee pot.

'No, thank you, Rama.' She watched her uncle, who
seemed totally at ease, if not a little pale. 'You are up
early, Uncle?'

'Couldn't sleep. I decided I'd do some more of your
aunt's jigsaw puzzle while everyone slept. It always
surprises her to wake and find more pieces put into
place.'

'You should have come for a ride with me and the
captain.' She watched his face closely, knowing he
was lying.

'Perhaps another time, my dear.'

'Captain Lewis is leaving for Ceylon shortly. I'll not
be riding much myself unless you wish to accompany
me? We go on such nice rides around the city and
down by the beach. Not many people are around so
early. You could fit it in before leaving for the office.'

'I've not really got the time, dearest.' He didn't
meet her eyes. 'Besides, I'm not a great one for
riding, sorry.'

'I'll have to go alone then.'

'Yes, sorry.' He stood and picked up his coffee cup.
'I'd best wake your aunt, she's looking forward to
today. She likes watching the ladies' gymkhanas. You
should have entered one of the events.'

'I'm not a good enough rider to go over jumps as they do.' She smiled woodenly. 'I'm also happy to watch. Will Gertie be coming, too?'

He froze. 'I don't think so.'

Prue chewed the inside of her mouth. Something was not right.

Chapter Seven

Prue laid in the hammock strung between two trees in the front garden and opened the envelope. Above her, birds twittered casually not at all perturbed by her presence. The house was quiet, only Gertie was at home and she was reading on the veranda. Prue had happily forgone shopping with Aunt Daphne, and Grandmama was spending the afternoon with Uncle Hugo visiting an old friend of Grandpapa's.

Prue needed today to recover from another party last night, where she had drunk too much and danced with eager men too long but enjoyed every moment of it.

Opening the letter, Prue smiled seeing Millie's familiar handwriting.

Dearest Prue,

How you must be enjoying India. The sights and sounds you write about fill me with jealousy! Dances with the Viceroy in attendance, garden parties, Club dinners, polo matches and so much shopping. It sounds such fun and also quite exhausting! I'm so

*pleased you are having the best time of it. And who is
this Captain Lewis you ride with each morning? Is
something developing between you both?*

Prue snorted. 'Not likely, sister,' she murmured. Her
thoughts strayed to Ajay Khan, but she couldn't write
of him. Millie wouldn't understand the forbidden
allure of Ajay. Prue didn't understand it herself.
When she was with him, he turned her into a pool of
longing. Yet, weirdly, she barely thought of him
when she was busy doing other things. It was all very
confusing.

She continued reading.

*No matter if this Captain is not for you, I trust you
are having the time of your life. I can live the
adventures through you while being in France and
learning the champagne trade. Being a wife, mother
and the mistress of Chateau Dumont is more than
enough for me at the moment.*

*Jeremy is very busy expanding our distribution and
is working so hard I barely see him, but he's happy
and content. His 'episodes' have lessened greatly this
year. Naturally his nightmares are not completely
gone, but they are not as frequent as before. When he
isn't focused on the estate, he spends time with local
soldiers who fought in the war. They have created a
little club for themselves in Épernay and once a week
Jeremy goes and spends a few hours chatting with
them.*

*Jeremy has only just returned from a trip to London.
Monty is running the office there and doing very well
with it. Next time I shall go with him, but I didn't
want to leave Jonathan as he's being very disturbed
of late due to him cutting some more teeth and he's*

been grumpy with it. I didn't want to leave him when he was so miserable.

Jonathan is growing so fast. I doubt you would recognise him now. You wouldn't believe it but he's nearly crawling. Apparently, he's not as advanced as other babies his age are, but the doctor assures me that is because he was born so early and is a little delayed. I'm sure he'll catch up very soon.

Mama arrives soon for a visit and Jacques will be coming from Paris. Jacque's wife died suddenly two weeks ago from a heart attack. Very shocking. Jacques is much saddened by it, of course, but I also assume he is somewhat relieved to be free of the burden of being in a loveless marriage and he no longer has to endure the unpleasantness of a divorce.

How Mama feels now I do not know. Has she spoken to you about Jacques and their future? Time will tell obviously.

And to answer your question in your last letter, no I haven't heard much from Cece.

Mama wrote to me last week and said Cece was spending a great deal of time with Cousin Agatha, who has been unwell. I still believe Cece would have wanted to go travelling with you and in my opinion it was mean of Grandmama not to include her. I hope Grandmama makes it up to her in some way. I asked Cece if she wanted to come and spend the summer with us here, but she declined. Whether she comes at Christmas, I do not know but I'd like to think she will as I know Mama wants to. I do feel sorry for Cece as she seems to have no sense of purpose in her life. What do you think?

Prue paused in reading and thought of her younger sister. Cece was a difficult character, not as easy going as her or Millie. However, perhaps she should try harder with Cece. Suddenly she had an idea and smiled to herself. She'd invite Cece to join her and Grandmama in Italy!

She lifted her head at the sound of the gates being opened by the old Indian servant who lived in a small hut tucked behind bushes near the end of the drive. Her uncle's motor car drove through the gates and Prue climbed off the hammock to go meet it.

Jal stopped the car and another servant ran out from the garage to open the door for Grandmama. Prue waved and was about to speak when she noticed the thunderous look on Grandmama's face.

'Grandmama?' Alarmed, Prue hurried to her side.

'Please, Prue, don't talk!' Grandmama brushed past her and mumbling under her breath stomped up the steps and inside.

'Uncle?' Prue quizzed him as he slowly walked past. 'What has upset Grandmama?'

He wiped a hand over his face. 'Me, Prue, me.'

Left alone on the drive, still holding Millie's letter, Prue was at a loss.

A sound hissed behind her and for a dreadful moment Prue froze. Had a snake had slithered into the garden?

'Prue!'

She turned and stared in amazement at Ajay Khan standing on the other side of the gates.

She hurried down to him. 'What are you doing here?'

He grinned cockily. A bicycle was leant against the fence. 'To see you of course! Can I come in?'

'No!'

A stony expression replaced the grin. 'No?'

'Forgive me. I'm being rude, but now isn't a good time.' She glanced back at the house, but no one was on the veranda and the only person about was one of the gardeners weeding the flower beds beside the house.

'Will there ever be a *right* time, Miss Marsh?'

She riled at the accusation. 'Don't have that tone with me! Not after the last time we met when you—'

'When I kissed you? A kiss that you wanted just as much as I did?' he taunted.

'Stop it,' she snapped, but her weak body tingled at the mention of that kiss. So far it had been the best kiss of her life and she wanted to repeat it.

'Meet me.'

Her heart thumped. 'When and where?'

'Tonight. In the Hanging Gardens. Ten o'clock.' He sauntered back to his bicycle. 'Will you be there, Prue Marsh?'

She raised her chin at the challenge. 'You'll have to wait and see, won't you?'

He hopped on the bicycle, his eyes boring into hers, but from behind him she noticed a motor car coming down the road and realised it was Aunt Daphne being dropped off by one of her friends.

Prue quickly ran across the gardens before her aunt could spot her and sidled around the side of the house. Here, small huts filled the space, and it was where the servants cooked and slept. Prue bowed her head at one of the female servants called Adi, who sometimes sang softly as she cleaned the house. Prue passed the kitchen and the tantalising aromas of curries and spices tickled her nose and she was abruptly very hungry.

Going the back way into the house, Prue stopped at Grandmama's bedroom and knocked on the door.

'I'm indisposed!' was the reply.

'Are you really, Grandmama?' Prue spoke through the timber.

'Prue? Get in here.'

Disturbed by the brusque tone, Prue opened the door and stood in the doorway.

'Get in here and shut the door!' Grandmama snapped.

Prue quickly did as she was told. Grandmama never spoke to her like that ever. Had she found out about Ajay Khan? She edged further into the room.

Grandmama sat on the chair by the French doors that were open to let in the slight breeze. 'We have a problem.'

'We do?' Prue swallowed, anxious. In truth she'd not really done anything bad with Ajay. It was a few secret meetings and a passionate kiss.

'I was hoping we could travel to Italy earlier than we planned for I am weary of Daphne and her tedious friends. I went to book the tickets this morning.'

'And?' Prue relaxed, this had nothing to do with her.

'And I was happily chatting away to Hugo about it as we drove to the ticket office. I jokingly said that he would miss me no doubt and he said he would, but there was something in his tone, something like relief.'

'Relief?'

'Indeed. I expected arguments that we hadn't stayed long enough and so on, but he said none of that. I got the impression he wanted to get rid of me.'

Prue frowned. 'Are you sure? I very much doubt Uncle would want you to go before Christmas.'

'Let me finish.' Grandmama put up a weary hand. 'He is my son and I know when he's keeping something from me, I always have known. He could never lie to me.' She took a deep breath. 'Anyway, I judged that he was hiding something and started questioning him. Why did he want me gone? Had I said something to annoy him, perhaps? Though I couldn't imagine what it could be for I have been on my best behaviour and kept my mouth closed as much as possible.'

Grandmama pushed herself up from the chair and walked to the French door. 'I eventually wheedled it out of him and what he said has shocked me to the core. I am actually lost for words. I don't think that has ever happened to me before.'

'What did he say?' Prue thought of the hospital visit and suddenly sat on the bed. 'I saw him, Grandmama.'

'Saw him? What do you mean?'

'I saw him visit a private Indian hospital the other morning. I was out riding with Captain Lewis and noticed the motor car parked out the front. Jal was driving, so I wasn't mistaken. Goodness, is Uncle Hugo very sick?'

'Sick?'

'Will he recover?'

'What are you talking about? A hospital?' Then Grandmama's expression changed to one of clarity. 'Now I see. Hugo must have been there to book an appointment or gain some advice. In secret. The last thing he needs is for all of this to become public knowledge, which is why he visited an Indian doctor. He wouldn't run into someone he knows there.'

'What is wrong with him?' Prue hoped it wasn't anything fatal.

'He's going to be a father.'

Prue blinked, confused. 'A father? I thought he was ill?'

'He's not ill in the slightest, except possibly in the head!'

'I don't understand.'

'It's easy to understand, girl. Your uncle is going to be a father.'

Surprised, Prue stared at Grandmama. 'You mean Aunt Daphne is having a baby? At her age? She must be at least fifty? Is that why he was at the hospital for her to see someone?'

Grandmama's lips thinned. 'No, it's not Daphne. She, *his wife*, isn't pregnant.'

'Oh ...' Prue gasped as the knowledge sank in. 'Oh, dear. He has got someone else pregnant,' she stated the obvious.

'Yes, and I'm guessing my son went to that hospital to see what he can do about it! Possibly through them he can arrange to send the baby to an orphanage, or a private family adoption.'

'An orphanage?' It seemed terribly real now. 'Who is the woman? Is she Indian or British? Is she an acquaintance?'

'Indeed. That is why I am so shocked.' Anger flushed Grandmama's cheeks. 'It's the one you'd least expect. The one who is all buttoned up like a nun in an abbey. Who is severe and condescending, cold and calculating, and whose looks cut through you as though you are beneath her.'

'Not Gertie,' Prue whispered, going cold.

'Yes, the little trollop. His wife's cousin's daughter. The single woman living under his very roof! Can you consider such a thing? I certainly cannot. He must have been off his head.' Grandmama slapped her hand against the wall in disgust.

95

'I am so shocked.' Prue couldn't believe it of her uncle.

'That is an understatement.' Grandmama paced the room. In an instant she'd marched out of the bedroom and down the hall and without knocking, she barged into Gertie's bedroom.

Prue scrambled to follow her.

'You! You little slut, get up and go into the sitting room,' Grandmama snarled before storming out.

Prue stood in the doorway and stared at Gertie, who was lying on the bed, looking decidedly ill.

'I'll not!' Gertie whimpered.

'It's best that you do,' Prue answered sadly.

Prue walked into the sitting room and sat down on the edge of the cane sofa. With his back to them, Uncle Hugo stood by the drink's cabinet pouring himself a large whisky while Grandmama gripped the back of a cane chair. Rama stood regally beside the door leading into the dining room, silent and unobtrusive as always.

Outside the birds called in the trees and one of the gardeners was humming. Prue could hear Aunt Daphne calling goodbye to her friend and wished her aunt didn't need to come inside.

They all turned as Daphne came up the veranda steps and through the open door. 'What a lovely visit I had with Mildred. She is such a sweetie for dropping me back home. We've just organised a picnic for Saturday. We did it in the motor car a moment ago, aren't we impulsive? No checking our diaries or anything! A simple snap decision. A picnic on Saturday. Isn't it wonderful to be so impetuous? I must do it more often,' Daphne said as she placed her bag on a side table and unpinned her hat.

Daphne flopped onto one of the cushioned cane chairs. 'Do you know Mildred's brother is selling his tea plantation up in the Darjeeling area? He's decided to return to England. He misses his children who never came back to India after being sent away to boarding school many years ago, and now his dear wife has died he feels he should be with them and finally see his grandchildren who he's not even met yet. Mildred will miss him, of course, but then she only saw him during the summer when she travelled up to his plantation to escape the heat here. Now she'll have to come with the rest of us to Simla for the summer.'

Daphne stopped talking and glanced around as Gertie joined them hesitantly. 'Ahh, Gertie. Nice to see you out of your room. Are you better? Perhaps you'll come with us to the Club tonight. There's a comedy show on. I am so excited to see it. I do enjoy a good laugh.'

'We aren't going to the Club tonight,' Grandmama's voice cut through the air. Everyone stilled.

'We aren't? But why?' Daphne pouted, wiping the perspiration from her face with a handkerchief. 'I simply must have a bath. Has the show been cancelled? Such a shame. We'll go to the Club and have dinner and then see a movie film, shall we? Rudolph Valentino is playing. Prue likes him, don't you, dear?'

Feeling uncomfortable, Prue nodded to her aunt.

'We aren't going to the Club or to watch a film, either,' Grandmama grounded out. 'We are staying home.'

Daphne's shoulders sank. 'Why? Is someone coming?'

'Because there is something that needs to be discussed.' Grandmama glared at her son. 'Tell her.'

'Mama,' Hugo pleaded. 'Now isn't the time.'

'You are joking, aren't you?' Grandmama's blue eyes widened. 'When exactly is the right time? When she,' Grandmama flung a pointing finger at Gertie, 'has a stomach the size of a watermelon?'

'Mama!' Hugo groaned.

Gertie started crying and Daphne glanced wildly from one to the other.

Prue shrunk back on the sofa, wishing she was invisible, or that she could discreetly leave the room, but she knew Grandmama would bark at her to sit. So, she remained silent and watched members of her family fall apart.

Hugo threw back the rest of his whisky. 'Daphne, let us go into the bedroom.'

'Which one?' Grandmama asked. 'Yours or Gertie's?'

'Mama! You aren't helping!' Hugo lashed out. 'This is between my wife and me.'

'Really? If you'd kept other things between just you and your wife we wouldn't be in this mess, would we?'

'Mama, you've made your feelings absolutely clear, but this is none of your concern and it is between my wife and I.'

'I would have thought *that one* over there needs to be involved as well.'

'Mama, please!'

'What did your papa always tell you as a young man? You do not pollute your own drinking well,' Grandmama cried. 'Why didn't you listen to him!'

'Because I'm not as saintly as Papa was.'

Grandmama's gaze narrowed. 'Do not dare speak of your papa in such a way. He was no saint, but he treated his family with love and respect!'

'And I could never match up to Papa's high standards,' Hugo spat. 'India was my chance to get away from the family yoke. I didn't meet your high standards as a son, did I? I couldn't be trusted to be responsible for the family money when Papa died. Papa gave you sole control in his will, but as his son and heir I should have been in control of everything.'

'You didn't show us that you had the self-control to be responsible for such a task. That's on you, my boy,' Grandmama scoffed. 'You spend money like water. You've no knowledge of how to make more, which is why you still work for I.C.S. and you've not made a wealth of your own. Your inheritance won't last forever.'

Uncle Hugo threw back the last of the whisky. 'My inheritance? Don't make me laugh. You pull the purse strings on that for both me and Violet.'

'Absolutely I do. Until you can show me otherwise, I'll continue to control the family money until I die. And going by your current situation, I've made the right decision. So, do not stand there and try to push the blame of your own inadequacies on me! You are responsible for your actions, Hugo. Now stand up and be a man and accept it.'

'I do accept my responsibilities! I told you that I'll fix this. I don't need your interference.'

'Enough!' Daphne shouted, pushing her bulk up and out of the chair. 'There is to be no more shouting.'

'Daphne,' Hugo took a step towards her, 'we need to talk, rather urgently.'

'No. Stay where you are, Hugo. I do not want you near me right now.' Two large tears slipped from

Daphne's eyes. She turned an accusing look towards Gertie. 'I know your dirty little secret.'

Gertie jerked, her hands trembling where she clasped them in front of her. 'You do?'

'I was listening outside the door when the doctor was examining you. I heard him say you are very likely to be pregnant. I know you denied it, too, but it's true, isn't it? And looking closely at you your stomach is round. I'm not imagining it.'

Gertie's mouth opened and shut a couple of times. 'Daphne…'

'Quiet.' Daphne turned to her husband. 'And Jal has told me he has taken you and Daphne to the private Indian hospital to talk with Doctor Wadia about this predicament. You forget, Hugo, that Jal was a loyal servant of my father's long before he became your driver. He will never lie to me.'

'How did you guess it was me though?' Hugo asked in surprise.

'Because you assume I don't know you after thirty years of marriage.' Aunt Daphne's tears continued to fall but Prue was in awe of her aunt's hidden strength as she faced them. 'Do you not think that I've always known your desire for children? Children we never had? I was expecting something like this to happen years ago, perhaps with some anonymous Indian woman, but never with my very own relative.' Her chin wobbled. 'I saw the secret looks you both shared, the times when I was away from the house and Gertie had a sudden headache to stay behind and you returned from the office unexpectedly. I might look senseless, Hugo, and perhaps I am, really, but I do understand some things.'

'Daphne…' Hugo held out his hand to her. 'I'm incredibly sorry. I never meant for it to happen.'

'Which part, the affair or the child, you weak conceited man?' A dead look came into Aunt Daphne's eyes.

'Both.' Hugo's face fell, and he no longer looked the dashing handsome uncle Prue loved, but instead he was an ordinary man who'd been found out.

'Now we have to find a solution to this problem,' Grandmama said quietly.

Aunt Daphne grimaced and took a deep breath. 'I've already thought of that.'

Uncle Hugo's face revealed his shock. 'What do you mean?'

'We keep the child,' Aunt Daphne's voice trembled. She straightened, her head held high. 'We take the child and raise it as our own.'

'No one will understand.' He rubbed his hands over his face. 'How do we explain we abruptly have a child at our age?'

'Once the child is born, we are moving away. We shall return to England, or at least move to another part of India. You will put in for a transfer elsewhere. I really don't care where we go, but we do not stay in Bombay.'

Uncle Hugo nodded, his face grey. 'If that is what you want.'

'I don't *want* any of this!' Aunt Daphne screamed. 'But it is what I *have* to do!' Then she paled. 'Unless you are leaving me for her?'

'Gosh, no!' His eyes widened. 'Definitely not.'

Gertie whimpered.

'Good, because if you were, I'd ruin you both. The lies and scandal would destroy you, I'd make certain of it.' Daphne wiped her face with the back of her hand and took a deep breath. 'Gertie will return to her parents and the child will be raised by us.' Aunt

Daphne turned an icy stare on her cousin. 'You will not leave this house until it is born, no one is to see you! Then you are to be gone, and you will never contact any of us again.' With that Daphne rushed from the room, her sobbing echoing down the hallway.

Not saying a word, Gertie slunk away.

Uncle Hugo stormed out of the front door calling for Jal to take him to the Club.

Silence descended on the house and the whole time Rama didn't move a muscle.

'Well. That discussion finished far quicker than I expected.' Grandmama blinked rapidly.

'It was awful,' Prue murmured.

'Agreed. I didn't realise Hugo held such condemnation towards me and Edward.'

'It's all due to money.'

'The root of all evil as they say.' Grandmama nodded and sat down, looking old suddenly. 'Hugo never showed Edward that he could be responsible enough to take control of the family money. He always had debts and lived a good life. When he married Daphne, we hoped he would settle down, but of course he didn't. The debts simply grew larger. Your grandpapa once again paid off the debts and acquired for Hugo the position in the I.C.S. to help him sort his life out.'

'I never knew any of this,' Prue whispered.

'Why would you? You were only a child. It's not something we wish for people to know. When your grandpapa drew up his will, we understood it would cause comments and maybe Hugo would be unhappy about our decision. But we both underestimated how deep his wounds were.'

'It's a day for revelations, it seems. I cannot help but feel truly sorry for poor Aunt Daphne.'

Grandmama sighed. 'I must say for the first time in her life, Daphne has stood up for herself and made sense. I never thought I'd see the day, or that she had it in her. Remarkable.'

'You agree to her plans?' Prue walked to the drink's cabinet and made them both a gin and tonic.

'Make that a double, and yes, I do agree. They make a decent argument. Does Gertie want to be lumbered with a bastard and a ruined reputation? Keeping the child will give her no chance of being happy. Who would accept her? Besides, Hugo is the child's father, he should raise it. He has the opportunity to give it the best in life, Gertie doesn't. No, Daphne has obviously been contemplating long and hard about it all.'

Prue gave the gin to Grandmama and sat down again. 'But why not say anything before now? How did she manage to keep it to herself? She must have been so hurt and angry, yet she's behaved normally.'

'Has she?' Grandmama twitched her lips. 'No, if I think back, there have been signs, but we missed them. She's been more talkative than normal. There's never a moment's peace when she's about as though silence would allow her to ponder about things she didn't want to acknowledge, and she's been drinking a lot. Nothing too much that causes comment, but she has been putting it away. I did notice that.'

'Aunt Daphne might have been hoping it was all not real. Perhaps she thought if she pretended it wasn't happening it would go away? Who knows?' Prue swirled the ice in her glass. 'But you had no inkling of what was going on with Uncle Hugo and Gertie?'

Grandmama sipped her gin. 'No, not until today.'

103

'How will they live under the same roof for months until the baby is born?' Prue didn't think she could do it if she was in Daphne's shoes.

'That remains to be seen, but Gertie is further along than you'd imagine. It's why she's kept hidden in her room and has worn flouncy clothes recently.'

Prue shook her head in wonder. 'I missed all the signs.'

'You had no reason to look for them. You were busy enjoying yourself. Why would you consider your uncle was having an affair under his very own roof?'

'True. I never thought that of him.'

'He's a man, they are all capable no matter what age they are. Never grow up, men.'

'When is the baby due?'

'November, they believe.'

'November! Next month!'

'Yes, Gertie's not very big at all, which is a concern, but she's not eating and what she does eat doesn't stay down for long.' Grandmama sighed heavily again. 'It's changed our plans, my dear. We will have to stay around here for a little longer, at least until the baby is born. Unless you want to return to England by yourself? I wouldn't blame you if you did. It'll not be a barrel of laughs around here now.'

Prue shook her head. 'No, I won't leave you.'

'Thank you, dear. I must confess I'm pleased you're here. You are the only one around here who isn't stupid.'

Chapter Eight

Later that night, Grandmama's words echoed in her head as Prue made her way in the dark to the Hanging Gardens some streets away from the bungalow. At that moment she felt a little stupid to be out alone at night walking the streets for the sole purpose of meeting a man she didn't know that well. It was indeed, very stupid!

Still she kept going. A tingle of anxiety shivered down her skin, but it was equally matched by a throb of excitement at doing something wicked. Once before she'd behaved just as wicked. Last year she'd met a man, Wyn, and for a few crazy weeks she thought herself to be in love with him, but when they met in Calais, when she was on her way to visit Millie in France, she'd realised her mistake. It hadn't been love only lust. That doomed love affair had been short and sweet. Lots of promises were made, but in the end, she'd not gone any further with Wyn than kisses and embraces. Despite being in a hotel room overnight, she'd refrained from sharing his bed.

Wyn hadn't been the man for her, but she'd come away from that experience wishing she'd known more about the act of sex. What would it have hurt for her to sleep with Wyn? No one would have found out, and she wouldn't be so curious any more about what making love was like. She had friends who'd done it. Why shouldn't she?

A cat ran out from behind some crates. Prue jumped, her throat closing in fear for a moment, then she breathed and continued on. The city sounds came to her on the warm breeze. From another street she heard the clopping of a horse's hoofs on the cobbled road, the creak of a cart. A dog barked from behind a fence and as she passed a house a baby was crying.

Once into the park itself, she hesitated, not knowing which path to take. The shadows thrown by the moon and eerie night calls of unseen animals made her quiver. She should turn back. She was putting herself in danger.

A hand touched her waist from behind and she screamed.

Ajay Khan laughed. 'I couldn't resist.' He swept her into his arms and kissed her hard.

Prue stiffened for a moment then softened into his embrace. His kiss was demanding, taking not asking, and she liked that to begin with, then she leaned back and gazed at him in the dim light.

'What is wrong?' Ajay frowned, tightening his hold on her ready for another kiss.

'Wait, let me catch my breath.'

'Let us go under the trees over there. I want to explore your body,' he murmured, nuzzling her neck.

His words and touch melted her resistance as he led her by the hand into the darker pockets of the garden.

Some inner devil controlled her as she lay on the grass and reached for him. Ajay's hands slipped under her dress and satin chemise, her skin tingled. His mouth was hot and demanding as he kissed her neck, his hands on her breasts.

'You are beautiful…' His whispers caressed her as well as his hands.

She ran her fingers through his hair, pleased it wasn't oiled, and instead smelt newly washed.

'I want you badly, Prue,' he murmured against her mouth, his knee pushing her legs apart. 'Tell me you want me, too.'

From nowhere a reasonable voice filtered through her desires. He was going too fast, his mouth all over her body, his panting loud in the silent grove around them.

'Ajay. Ajay!' He wasn't listening to her, and she suddenly sat up, pushing him away.

'What? What is it?' He glanced around as though expecting they'd been disturbed.

'You need to slow down.' She pushed her hair away from her face, heart racing. 'You're rushing me.'

'I thought it was what you wanted?'

'I do.' She pulled down her dress, covering her legs.

Standing, Ajay took a deep breath. From his pocket, he took out a packet of cigarettes and lit one.

'Are you going to offer me one?'

He shrugged. 'Women shouldn't smoke. It's not classy.'

Prue gritted her teeth. Why did he do that? He could go from being charming and sensual to cold and arrogant in a heartbeat. She got to her feet and brushed down her dress, hoping it didn't have grass stains on it.

He gave her a look over his shoulder. 'You will not have sex with me.'

As always, his abruptness shocked her. 'No. I don't think I will. Not tonight, anyway.'

'Why?'

'It doesn't feel right out here in the open.'

'And I assumed you were a modern woman.'

'I can be modern without being reckless. We could have been caught.' As she spoke, she thought of Millie and knew she'd never approve of her rash decisions.

'I'm assuming you are a virgin. Are you not curious of what it is like?'

'Of course, I am,' she defended. 'However, I've decided a quick fumble in the bushes isn't my style.' She took a few steps back towards the path. 'I'll say goodnight to you, Mr Khan.'

'I will be your first, Miss Marsh. Count on it.'

She didn't answer him as she walked quickly back across the gardens and towards her uncle's bungalow.

Would he be her first? She didn't really know if that was what she wanted. He was handsome, she couldn't deny that, and he made her want to have sex with him, and a defiant part of her believed she should just go for it and get the deed done. Yet, the sensible part of her fought for control. She wanted to be loved, really loved, by a man who would die for her. Gosh, she sounded like Cece now!

Annoyed with herself, she hurried down the street and slipped into a side gate next to the drive she'd purposely left unlocked. The bungalow was in darkness and quiet. Prue slipped off her shoes and silently padded up the veranda steps.

'Remember, my dear,' Grandmama suddenly spoke.

Prue jerked, smothering a scream with her hand.

'Remember that every action has a consequence. Now go to bed.'

Prue crept to her room. Nothing got past her grandmama, yet she hadn't censured her or asked for explanations.

As she undressed in the moonlight, she gazed at herself in the mirror, seeing her body as Khan had, the subtle curves of her hips, flat stomach, small breasts, well-shaped legs. She was proud of her body. Riding most days had given her toned muscles, and she was careful of what she ate. She leaned in closer to the mirror and pulled gently at her hair. Despite hats and parasols, the harsh Indian sun was bleaching the ends a lighter blonde than was natural. It needed cutting.

Remaining naked, for the humidity had risen sharply heralding more rain, Prue slipped between the cool bed sheets and adjusted the netting around the bed. As she stared up at the bed canopy, she ran her hands over her body as Khan had done, recalling the lust between them. Had she done the right thing by turning him away? So far, no other man had got beneath her skin as he had. There was no future for them, and she didn't love him, she knew that. It was simple desire. What harm could come from that? There was no one they could hurt with their actions as no one would ever know!

Rolling onto her stomach, she thumped the pillows into better shape. Damn it! She should have had sex with him!

~ ~ ~ ~

'Are you ready, Prue?' Grandmama called. 'Jal has come back from dropping Hugo off and we are running late.'

Prue hopped out of her room, trying to buckle her sandals on. 'Coming.'

Ganika tidied the bedroom, giggling at Prue's antics.

'Ah, Captain Lewis. This is a pleasant surprise,' Grandmama said.

Prue paused in the hallway and listened. The captain couldn't see her as he came up the veranda steps.

'Do forgive me, Mrs Fordham, for this unexpected call, but I'm away this afternoon to Ceylon and I wish to see Miss Marsh before I leave. I missed her last night at the Club and I've not had the chance to say goodbye to her.'

'She is getting ready, Captain, as we are due at a friend's house shortly. In fact, we are late, which is extremely rude of us.'

'Oh, I see. I should have sent a note but plans changed last minute.'

'Will you be gone long, Captain?'

'Six months or more,' his voice sounded dejected.

'Well, that is a decent length of time to get the job done down there, isn't it? I hear the Tamils are causing a stir for independence.'

'That is true, madam, and that is why my regiment are going there as a show of force and to tame those that may wish to rebel.'

'Excellent. All this talk of independence may lead to these countries becoming self-governed one day, but at what cost to human lives?'

'I agree, madam.'

A short silence descended, which Grandmama broke.

'I will be honest with you, Captain. I sense my granddaughter is the right woman for you.'

'Can I ask why not?'

'I don't think she is made of the right stuff to be an army wife.'

'She would never need for anything, Mrs Fordham. I can provide well for any wife I may take.'

'I don't doubt it, Captain, but that is not the point. I consider your way of life would bore her within months. Prue is not one for being at the whim of the army's decisions. Moving from place to place, seeing the same army wives day in day out. You are an officer, dear Captain, a man who is used to being guided and used to rules and regulations. My Prue is the very opposite, and I'm afraid would baulk at being told what to do, and where to live by army officials. I'm sorry, but that is my view.'

'Is it Miss Marsh's view also?'

'Dear man,' Grandmama's voice gentled. 'If she was in love with you, she'd be spending every moment with you and crying that you are going away. Instead, she's getting ready for a tea party.'

In the hallway, Prue's shoulders sagged at the truth of it.

Silence stretched out on the veranda.

'Perhaps you can write to her?' Grandmama sounded optimistic.

'Yes, I did ask her before if that would be acceptable.'

'You do know we shan't be in India for much longer? We shall be gone before Christmas.'

'I understand.'

'I will tell Prue you dropped by to say goodbye, Captain, and let you be on your way to save yourself from embarrassment.'

'Thank you, Mrs Fordham, that is kind of you.'
Captain Lewis cleared his throat. 'I wish you both
every happiness.'

'Thank you, as we wish the same to you, Captain.'

Prue felt she should go out and say goodbye face to
face but what would that achieve? She didn't want to
cause Captain Lewis further awkwardness.

Waiting a few moments, Prue stepped out on the
veranda. 'Thank you Grandmama.'

'It was nothing, dear. I'm well practised in sending
off handsome young men. Did it quite often in my
time.' Grandmama left the breakfast table. 'I was
correct though, wasn't I? You aren't in love with the
Captain?'

'No, I'm not. He's a good man, kind, but I wanted
nothing but friendship from him.'

'Just as I thought. If a man doesn't stir your blood,
he's then regarded as a friend only.'

'I'm a bit of a coward for not coming out and saying
goodbye properly.'

'And witness the man's embarrassment? No, you
did right by staying inside. You spared him his
dignity and God knows how much men take store by
their dignity. Now, let us go.' Grandmama dressed in
a soft shade of lavender, gathered her purse. 'I
deplore being late. So uncivilised.'

'Sorry.' Prue straightened her dress and adjusted her
hat, which sat at an angle over her left eye. She wore
a pretty lemon dress with short chiffon sleeves. 'I
wanted to look my best today for Nina has extended
family staying with them.'

Aunt Daphne came out onto the veranda, carrying a
pen and paper. 'You both look very nice. I'm sure the
Patel family will be most impressed by the pair of
you.'

112

'Thank you, Aunt.' Prue kissed her aunt's cheeks. 'It is a shame you aren't coming with us.'

Aunt Daphne's eyebrows puckered. 'Yes, well we all agree who to thank for that, don't we?' She lifted her head. 'Still, it won't be long until the baby is born, and I'll not have to remain here and watch over *her*. *She* will be gone, and we can move away.'

Prue had noticed that her aunt no longer mentioned Gertie by name any more. 'Has any decision been made in that regards?'

'Hugo is making inquiries.'

'Come, Prue!' Grandmama barked from the bottom of the steps. 'There isn't time for chit-chat. Goodbye, Daphne.'

Once in the car and travelling the very short journey to the Patel's splendid home, Grandmama sighed. 'Hugo believes he can get a transfer to Calcutta. He refuses to come back to England and raise the child there.'

'Why?'

'I don't know, and it hurts me that he's picked India over England. He isn't speaking to me much at the moment. There is hurt on both sides.'

'Uncle Hugo is dealing with a lot. He simply has to work it out. It doesn't mean he feels differently about you.'

'He spoke of his true feelings that day. Some things said cannot be unsaid.'

Prue grasped Grandmama's hand. 'He loves you.'

As the motor car drove through the impressive iron gates of the Patel's home, Grandmama turned to Prue. 'If he loved me, he'd come home to England. You realise that with them moving to Calcutta, this means that once we leave India, I doubt I'll ever see that child again.'

'Oh, Grandmama.' Prue squeezed her hand in sympathy. 'Uncle might change his mind.'

'Stubborn. Just as his papa was! The only good reason to have children is for the grandchildren, remember that. Grandchildren will be the love of your heart, while your own will merely give you grief!'

They climbed out of the motor car and were greeted by Nina and her father, Abi, on the white marble steps at the front of the grand house. Once inside, they were introduced to the rest of the family, many of whom had travelled from Africa.

Seated in wide cushioned chairs in a pavilion type room at the back of the house, Prue smiled at an elderly couple but couldn't converse with them as they spoke no English, however their middle-aged son, Boman, was full of beaming smiles and hand gestures and spoke excellent English.

'You are staying in India for long?' he asked Prue while Grandmama spoke with Nina and her parents.

'Not much longer, no. We hope to travel on to Italy soon.'

'Italy? How interesting.' He sat down beside Prue, his resplendent white outfit was threaded with gold in a geometric pattern. 'I have also been to Italy, more exclusively to Rome. What a place. Such history.'

'Yes, I'm excited to explore it myself.'

'I shall give you the names of some people, friends of mine, they have a restaurant near the Colosseum, most excellent. You must go there.'

'Thank you. I will try to, yes.'

'My niece tells me you are not married, Miss Marsh.' He offered her a plate of sugar-coated dates and almond fudge, which instantly reminded her of Ajay Khan and the food they ate at the market.

'That is true,' she answered, pushing Ajay from her mind. She hadn't seen him since the night in the park a week ago.

'And you have such freedom.'

'I do, yes.' She frowned, wondering why he asked such a question.

'With no husband, perhaps you would accompany me to a wedding? That is why we, my family, are here in India. A relative is getting married on Wednesday. Will you come?'

'Oh, yes you must do so!' Nina butted in, her blue sari, edged with yellow was beautiful on her slender body.

'Well, I suppose I could,' Prue answered hesitantly. 'But I do not know the couple.'

'Tosh, that does not matter at all.' Boman waved away her cares, shaking his head in the way Indians do. 'There will be hundreds of people there celebrating, you'll be one in the crowd.' Then thinking it might have sounded rude, he quickly sat forward. 'But a delightful guest in the crowd.'

'You do not have to stay long, Prue.' Nina shook her head at her uncle in rebuke. 'As long as you are comfortable, yes?'

'Have you been to an Indian wedding before?' Boman asked.

'No, I haven't.'

'Ah! That is good. You will enjoy it I promise.' Boman beamed. 'I will be personally responsible for your happiness as a welcomed guest.'

Prue couldn't help but smile at his infectious happy manner. 'That would be lovely, thank you for inviting me.'

When they moved into the marble columned dining room for luncheon, Boman sat next to Prue and that made Grandmama chuckle.

Throughout the meal he was attentive, begging her to try the numerous dishes of curries and vegetables. He asked her many questions about her home in Yorkshire, her family, her likes and dislikes, so many questions that Prue started to get a headache.

Afterwards, they sat in the garden under a large Chinese banyan tree, its shade cast a cool apron over the tables and chairs where the family and guests sat and sipped tea and nibbled on more food. A rare white peacock strutted about the lawn, while monkeys chatted in the trees, dropping nut shells on the humans below.

Nina called Boman away and took his place on the blanket at Prue's feet. 'I do apologise for my uncle's attentions. He is enamoured by you. It is not often we have British women in our home and he never witnesses it in their community in Africa.'

'He is very friendly.' Prue smiled, as a monkey screeched and swung in the branches above.

'You will come to the wedding, won't you?' Nina glanced up at the monkey's antics. 'That is Sheena, my brother's pet. She is most irritating and most bossy.'

Prue laughed at the monkey as it jumped down to the grass and ran to the others who sat by the fountain. It sat on Grandmama's lap and she didn't miss a beat as she conversed with Nina's father.

Turning back to Nina, Prue sipped her peppermint tea. 'I don't have anything to wear to a wedding. I shall have to go shopping.'

'I have the perfect thing. Come with me.' Taking her hand, Nina led Prue inside and up a wide marble staircase to her bedroom. A side door inside the bedroom opened to reveal a separate closet full of saris, choli tops, dupatta scarves and lehenga skirts.

'Oh my!' Prue stared at the array of beautiful materials of all colours.

'This is the one I was thinking of for you.' Nina pulled out a length of teal-coloured raw silk. 'Do you like it enough to wear?'

'It's beautiful.' Prue touched the sari, delighting in the way it shimmered and changed colour in the light. 'It reminds me of a peacock.'

'Yes!' Nina grinned. 'It's yours. I'll have it sent over to you. I'll take care of everything.'

'Nina, no. It is too much.'

'I want you to wear it.' She turned and pulled out a burnt orange sari. 'This is what I am wearing. We shall match together perfectly.'

'Are you sure they won't mind a British woman coming to their wedding?'

'Weddings are a celebration. It is a time of friendship, family and joy. We accept anyone as long as they are there to spread happiness.' Nina put away the saris and then grasped Prue's hands. 'You will soon be gone, and I will miss your friendship. However, we will have the memories, yes?'

Prue nodded. 'Lovely memories. My grandmama said that making memories is the best thing to do in life.'

Nina laughed. 'Your grandmama is a most amazing woman!'

'She is.'

'And so widely travelled. I would so wish to do that.' Nina fiddled with some scarfs. 'You will have the freedom I am denied. My father tells me I am to marry next spring. I am getting too old.'

117

'How old are you?'

'Twenty-five. Far too old to be unmarried my mother says. I bring shame on them.'

'Shame?'

'I reject all suitors.' Nina shrugged a bare elegant shoulder. 'I will marry next year. He is the one I've been waiting for.'

'Who?'

'The man my father says is worth the wait.' Nina giggled. 'I trust my father to pick a good man.'

'I'm twenty-three and am in no hurry to marry. Do you want to get married to a stranger?'

'Of course, I want to marry, and soon after he will no longer be a stranger,' Nina said wistfully. 'I would like someone who thinks only of me, who I can rely on, and I would like children.'

'My sister, Millie, married two years ago when she was twenty-three and I was twenty-one. Millie said something similar at the time. I didn't understand what she meant. I felt as though I knew everything back then, but I didn't, I still don't. Getting married was the right thing for Millie.'

'And it will be for you, too, when the time is right.'

'Millie has a little baby and he is adorable, but I'm not envious that she has a baby and I don't.' Prue shrugged. 'Possibly there's something wrong with me.'

'No, my friend. You merely aren't ready, as I wasn't until recently. It will happen, when fate decrees it, or when a handsome man crosses your path!'

Prue chuckled. 'Well, there have been many I liked, but I didn't want to marry any of them.' She thought of Ajay Khan. 'I met someone recently, an Anglo-Indian.'

Nina's eyes were so expressive, and she couldn't hide her shock. 'Anglo-Indian? How did you meet such a person?'

'By chance, at a polo game.'

'He is a friend of your family?'

'No.'

Nina gripped Prue's hands. 'But you mustn't do anything with him. He wouldn't be accepted.'

'That seems to be the common opinion I see.' Prue pulled away and ran her fingers along the rainbow colours of the saris. 'I don't want him for a husband, just someone to play with.'

'Play with?'

'You know, to kiss.' Prue wiggled her eyebrows suggestively, and they both giggled.

'My father would kill me!' Nina hid a laugh behind her hand.

'My papa is dead, but my mama and grandmama would not be happy with me at all.'

'Will you see him again?'

Prue nodded and grinned. 'We shall see!'

Chapter Nine

Prue stood on the other side of the gate in Ajay Khan's courtyard. She'd fended off a swarm of begging children with some harsh words, though they only finally left her when she stopped at the gate and they realised she was going inside.

Now she was here, nerves jingled in her stomach. She didn't even know if Khan was home but being Sunday afternoon, she hoped so. She'd foregone a trip to the theatre with Grandmama to come and see him and now she wondered why.

What was it that dragged her here? Khan was nothing special. He didn't try to woo her or make her feel important. There were no false promises, no love notes sent, no flowers, no romance. He'd not been in contact since the night at the Hanging Gardens. Was he using her? Did it matter? For she was certain she was only using him. But for what? Experience?

Alone at night in her bed, her body throbbed with a need, a desperate need that Ajay had woken in her. In the cold light of dawn, she understood that she wasn't wanting Ajay Khan as a husband, she wasn't even sure she liked him. She felt none of the emotions she'd read about in books. She hadn't gone off her food dreaming about him, or was inspired to write poetry about their love, or want to draw his likeness. She went for hours and hours not even thinking about him as a person. Yet she did want his body.

She took a step back. She couldn't act on this curiosity. She wasn't a whore. She had self-respect.

'Are you going to stand there all night?'

She jolted at his voice coming out of the shadows by the doorway. 'I'm not sure why I'm here.'

'You're here to see me. To finish what we started.' He walked out of the shadows and into the paling golden wash of the sunset.

'I shouldn't have come.'

'Why not? I've been waiting for you.'

'I don't believe you. You have sent no word to me.'

He laughed softly and held out his hand.

Silently she took it, and he led her inside.

The room was basic, but clean. A kitchenette to one side and a sitting room on the other. Up a short flight of steps, he guided her into his bedroom, and all she saw was stacks of books, clothes flung on a dresser and a large double bed in the middle.

She swallowed, her heart thumping. Outside the window birds chirped and twittered and the sound of children playing floated on the air. The room was bathed in an orange glow.

'I want you to stay, but if you must leave, do it now,' Ajay whispered against her ear, his hands on her hips.

'I think I should…' she whispered back as his lips hovered over hers.

'Then go…' His lips gently touched her neck, and she shivered at the delightful sensation.

Prue

As if a button had been pressed, or a trigger pulled, she brought his mouth to hers and kissed him hard. He undid the buttons of his white shirt and shrugged it off before he slipped her dress over her head.

Standing in her chemise, she gazed at his lean body, his skin the colour of light caramel. She touched his chest, liking that his dark eyes smiled at her.

There was no room for talk, or for whispered romantic words as they suddenly came together in a hard, demanding way. Prue was eager to explore his body as he was hers. Hands and mouths, lips and tongues caressed and sought, moans filled the room as the sun set casting rays across their naked sweating bodies.

When at last she could take no more, she urged Ajay to finish what he'd started, and he took delight in easing into her body and pushing her past the point of no return. She expected pain, but there was none, just a feeling of fullness and an increasing pressure that built to a satisfying ending that was over rather too quickly.

Sated and in awe of what she'd experienced, she lay beneath him until he rolled off her, panting.

As the freshness of the evening air touched her cooling body, and the sun slipped down completely. Prue lay in the dimness and stared at the ceiling, noting the thin cracks, a cobweb in the corner. The rush of blood had left her as suddenly as it arrived, and her mind cleared of its madness.

What had she done!

Scooting off the bed, she hurriedly found her clothes and dressed.

'What are you doing?' Ajay asked from the bed.

She glanced at him, pulling on her shoes. 'I must go home.'

'No. Stay. We can do it again. Slower next time.'

'No!' Fully dressed she rushed from the room and down the stairs. She dropped her sandal and quickly scooped it up again.

Ajay caught her arm as she headed for the door. 'Prue!'

'No, Ajay. I have to go.'

Still naked, he dropped her arm. 'I provided a service, didn't I?'

Unable to look at him, she bit her lip, hoping he'd let her go and not turn nasty. 'It's late.'

'Look at me.'

Slowly she lifted her head and sought his gaze.

He took a step back from her, his expression unreadable. 'Go.'

Relieved, she ran out of the house, flung open the gate and ran up the road.

The darkness deepened as she reached a main road. Rickshaws, horse and carriages and motor cars hurried past all eager to get where they were going and not concerned about a British woman leaning against a building catching her breath.

She kept walking, slower now, more in control of herself. A dog barked at her from the entrance to an alley, but she ignored it. Aromas of garlic and cumin lingered in the air as she passed the end of an empty bazaar. Come morning the place would be heaving with people and produce, the noise deafening, the air pungent. However, now all she saw was two cats and several shirtless men taking away wooden boards and sweeping the area.

Impulsively, Prue turned down another road and headed for Back Bay. The stench of open sewers filled her nose. In the shadows, rats blatantly ran in front of her and she recoiled in disgust. Outside of shops and houses, factories and slum dwellings, beggars sat with bowls in front of them, their vacant eyes lost to the world. Some slept rolled up in rags, and all the while barefoot children ran through the streets, hollering and chattering away like monkeys.

Thankful to reach the bay, she strolled along the long curving foreshore, passing families with small babies swathed against their mother's chest, old couples sitting on benches watching the water and youths in their first stages of courting shyly making conversations.

Lights glowed orange and gold as restaurants and shops lit up the night. Food carts selling an array of finger food clamoured for custom. Although Prue was hungry, she'd didn't give into temptation and buy anything. So far, she'd been saved from getting an upset stomach and didn't want to tempt fate.

The breeze off the bay was cool, reminding her that winter was not far away. Soon, she'd be experiencing an Italian winter. Would it be cold in Palermo? The urge to travel there was strong. As much as she enjoyed India, this wasn't the only country she wished to see.

A British man doffed his hat at her as he walked towards her. 'Good evening, miss.'

'Good evening.'

'You are all right?' His worried look made her smile.

'I am, yes, thank you. Simply taking a stroll.' She walked on, not feeling in any danger at all. At any time, she could hail a rickshaw, but the walk helped to clear her jumbled thoughts.

She had just slept with a man. It still felt unreal. The taboo of sex was finally known to her. She'd liked it, but the crazy rush leading up to the act alarmed her a

124

little. She'd been wild and impulsive, everything her family had accused her of, yet their comments had been spoken off-handedly, in jest. How would they feel knowing she'd acted so unwisely?

In one swift moment she had thrown away her inhibitions, her decent upbringing and her morals to lay with a man who wasn't her husband. More than that, she'd shared the bed of a man who wasn't even in her society, but an Anglo-Indian. If society found out, they'd shun her. Women in her circle didn't have sex with anyone but their husband, or perhaps a discreet lover once her marriage had produced a child or two.

She thought of Nina. Her elegant Parsi friend would never have lowered herself to have sex with a man she barely knew. Nina would remain pure for her husband.

Prue's stomach clenched. She was no longer untainted. What would her future husband say about that? A part of her wanted to go back in time and erase what she'd done. However, another part of her said to hell with it! What's done is done, and she had been adventurous and modern.

Reaching the beach at the end of the bay, Prue slipped her shoes off. Walking with the sand between her toes, she allowed her gaze to lift to Malabar Hill, to where Nina's magnificent house stood. She could never be as good and amiable as Nina, but perhaps it could be a goal to achieve?

The chilly breeze rippled the water and she shivered in her thin dress. It was time to return to her uncle's bungalow and with that decision came another – she would not sleep with Ajay Khan again, but she did want to experience sex another time.

Prue

~ ~ ~ ~

Prue laughed. Nina was speaking to her but her words were drowned out by the thunderous noise created by hundreds of people as they paraded down the street. Horns tooted and drums banged, tin lids were slammed together, and Prue's ears rang with the sheer loudness of it all.

A young pretty teenager came up to her and placed another flower garland around Prue's neck to join the three she already had. The girl gave a yellow garland to Nina before darting away to give out more to the wedding guests.

The wedding ceremony had taken place that morning in warm sunshine and Prue had enjoyed observing a traditional Indian wedding. The mystic of the face-covered bride, the groom arriving on a white horse, the music, the prayers all filled her with a calming warmth.

She'd watched a ceremony take place that captured respect and family togetherness. She wished Millie and Cece had been with her to witness it with her too.

Now they were making their way down narrow cobbled streets and crossed wide squares towards a large building on the edge of the old fort area, which was to hold the feasting and dancing.

Boman had been with them for a while, before he'd gone to speak to other members of his family. During the ceremony he'd stood by her side, being attentive and informative. She enjoyed his happy company; the man was always smiling. He promised to dance with her later and might even sing on the stage just for Prue.

The jollity of the large wedding party carried other pedestrians along, whether they wished to go in that direction or not. They passed a band playing music on the back of a cart and it was a nice relief from the constant horns blaring and drums banging. Prue swung her arms in the air, wiggling her hips to the music as the women did in front of her.

'You're very good!' Nina laughed joining in. 'Move your hands like a snake, like this.'

Following Nina's movements, Prue gave herself to the music, laughing when she did something silly. In time with the rhythm, she stepped and pirouetted as Nina did, laughing and humming.

The sudden explosion of fireworks crackled the sky above. Despite it being daytime, the fireworks glowed fleetingly. People cheered. The streets swelled with people, the wedding guests alongside everyday workers and shoppers. The heat seemed intense, the smells of the streets penetrating. But the air pulsed with good vibes and surrounding them was a sea of smiling faces. Prue loved it all.

'I'm so thirsty,' Prue called to Nina. Her arms had grown tired. In fact, she'd been overly tired for the last few days and made a promise to herself to go to bed early more often. Too many late nights dancing at the Club and dinner parties were taking their toll. Grandmama encouraged her to go out at night for the atmosphere at home was tangible. Gertie remained quiet, Daphne over-bright and talkative and Hugo brooding and sullen. With Grandmama's contacts Prue was never short of invitations and accepted them all.

'I have money,' Nina shouted, indicating a small silk purse slung around her waist. 'We can find a drink stall down one of the side streets.'

'Yes, good,' Prue yelled back at the same time another explosion erupted.

Judging it to be more fireworks, Prue ignored it and looked for any water or tea suppliers down the side street as they passed.

She glanced back at Nina who'd stopped dancing and was frowning at something in front of the people ahead. More explosions erupted.

Prue searched the crowd and stopped still as she spotted Ajay Khan threading his way between the guests. He hadn't seen her. Prue watched him push his way through the people, an intent look on his face. She raised her hand to get his attention, but he didn't see her.

Another explosion shook the ground, and the rat-tat-tat of gunshots blasted through the air. Prue frowned. Did they shoot off guns at an Indian wedding?

Unsure of what was happening, Prue stared at Khan as he paused, looked back over his shoulder and then stopped to speak to a woman with a small child. He was indicating for them to return and go back the way they'd come.

Suddenly, screams rent the air.

Prue shuddered. Something was wrong. People started running back towards them, their faces full of panic and horror.

Nina called her name from the side of the street, but the abrupt stampede of the fleeing people swept Nina away. With each moment Nina was jostled and pushed further away from Prue.

An Indian man ran past her, bleeding from the head, his turban knocked sideways. Another had his shirt torn, wounds on his chest. Children were crying, adding to the mayhem and noise. A woman fainted in the street. Prue ran to help but was knocked down by a man, whose arm was bleeding.

Getting back up, Prue searched for Nina in the bolting crowd. Screams and shouts had replaced the music and drums. Prue thought she saw the top of Nina's head, but with so many black-haired people it was hard to tell.

'Nina!' she yelled, finally catching sight of her friend, but Nina was getting pushed further away by the press of the crowd.

More gunshots sounded. What was happening? Fear circled Prue's stomach, she had to get away.

Suddenly Ajay Khan appeared, he was carrying a child, its wailing mother following.

'Ajay!' Prue called to him, the noise escalating as more and more gunshots sounded.

Not hearing her, Ajay disappeared in the rush of people.

Alone, alarm and anxiety throbbed through her body. The violence seemed never-ending. She had to get home to Grandmama.

It was terrifying to Prue to push her way through men and women screeching for help. A woman hobbled by, her torn sari splattered with blood. She was crying, holding her head. A Brahma cow trotted through the crowd, the whites of its eyes showing its panic.

More shots were fired. More screams rent the air.

As if in a dream, Prue was crushed against a shop wall as another surge of petrified people raced through the street, yelling, crying, warning others to run.

She wanted to run, too, but where was Nina or Ajay? Should she go without them or wait?

A child stumbled to the ground in front of her before his father scooped him up one-handed and kept running. She noticed a few of the wedding guests hurrying past, one woman had lost her sandal. On the ground were flower garlands crushed into the dirt.

Through a cloud of dust, a horse and cart came charging down the street with men standing up shooting randomly into the scattering crowd.

Prue stared in horror. Before her eyes she watched men being shot and fall.

The crazed horse stumbled on the uneven road when a group of brave wedding guests caught its reins to halt it. The rebels fired on them, downing them all in seconds.

Shrieks and crying was all Prue could hear. She cringed at the distraught sounds, the gunfire, the blood-curdling yells of the rebels who were now on foot and firing indiscriminately into the people.

She stared, dazed. She was going to be shot at. She was next. Today she would die.

'Prue!' Nina was beside her, her dark eyes large in her beautiful face. 'Come! Hurry!'

Needing no second bidding, Prue lifted the skirt of her dazzling peacock-coloured sari and pushed her way through the frightened wedding guests.

A bullet nicked the stonework of the building next to them. They both ducked as shards of brick burst about them. Nina cried out and stumbled.

'Are you hurt?' Prue pulled her up.

'A little. A piece of stone hit me in the neck.' Nina touched the side of her neck and her fingers came away bloodied.

'We can't stop!' Prue shouted, shaking, fully expecting the next bullet to be in her back.

Amongst the screams and stampede, Prue held Nina's arm as they were jostled and shoved.

'Prue!' Someone called out to her.

She glanced over her shoulder and tripped over her sari, yet relieved to see Ajay running towards her, now free of the child and mother. She waited against a wall for him to catch up.

'What are you doing?' Nina cried at her. 'We have to go!'

'Are you hurt?' Ajay asked, on reaching her. Frantically, his gaze roamed her body as he clutched her arms.

'No. Are you?' She stared into his worried brown eyes.

'No.' He gasped for breath. 'Why are you here?'

'Attending the wedding. Why are you here? You aren't a part of all this, are you?'

'Is that what you think?' He looked incredulous.

'Well, I don't know,' she snapped, frightened. She hardly knew Ajay, he could be a rioter for all she knew.

'Who is he, Prue?' Nina demanded. 'A rebel?'

'No, I'm not!' Ajay glanced behind him as more shouts came. 'I was on my way home from visiting a friend.'

'What's happening?' Prue asked.

'I'm not certain. Riots, obviously, but this is more than just a few hotheads letting off some rounds. This was well-orchestrated from what I can make out and many men and petrol bombs.' He glanced around as more people ran past, bleeding and terrified.

'What did you see of the wedding party?' Nina begged him. 'My family have scattered. I must find them!'

'You can't go back there. I'll help you both to get home. If we find our way blocked, we might have to hide out until it's dark. Someone said that there are fires in the centre of town and down by the old fort area.'

'We go!' Nina screeched and pulled Prue's hand as rebels ran around the corner and fired randomly.

A man fell to his knees in the middle of the street.

A rioter, his dark eyes wild in his face, shot again, hitting a woman in the shoulder. He noticed Prue and sprinted towards her.

'Run!' Ajay yelled.

Prue turned to flee, but the rioter grabbed her, flinging her to the ground. She screamed, pain in her knee.

The rioter lifted his rifle and aimed it straight at her face. For what seemed an eternity she watched the rioter squeeze the trigger. She closed her eyes, waiting for the bullet to smash into her body.

'Prue!' Ajay knocked her out of the way.

The gun blasted.

She fell onto the cobbles, banging her head. In a daze she watched Ajay jerk, then slowly he fell sideways and landed with a thud on the road beside her.

Nina screamed while all Prue could do was stare in astonishment at the spreading red stain on Ajay's shirt.

Another bullet shot past them before the rebel ran off.

'Run!' Nina dragged Prue away.

'Ajay?' Prue yanked herself free from Nina's grip. 'He's hurt. We must help him!' She knelt by his side. 'Ajay?'

Blood covered his shirt, oozing out so fast it became a tiny rivulet on the cobbles, quickly soaking up the dust. She laid her hands over what she thought was the wound, blood seeped through her fingers, covering her hands in moments. 'Help me, Nina!'

'Leave him!'

'No.' Although he lay motionless, Prue couldn't move her hands from his chest. She had to save him.

'Prue!' Crying hard, Nina tried to pull her up. 'We must go. Leave him!'

'He needs help!' Angry at Nina, Prue put more pressure on Ajay's chest. 'We have to get him to a hospital. He needs a doctor!'

'No! He's dead. I want to go home,' Nina sobbed.

A door squeaked open behind them and an old Indian man wearing all white, crouched down beside Prue. 'I am a doctor. Get him inside. Quickly.'

Without caring for her own safety, Prue ignored the screaming, fleeing people rushing past and dragged Ajay towards the open doorway. He was heavy, and she needed Nina's and the old man's help to get him over the doorstep. She averted her eyes from the trailing stream of blood left behind.

The old man bolted the door and knelt over Ajay to examine him. How he did so in the murky dim light of the room, Prue didn't know. The windows were shuttered, filtering the sunlight and muting the outside chaos.

Nina collapsed onto a chair, her hands shaking as she covered her face. 'My family!'

'They may be safe. I'm sure they are.' Prue spoke woodenly, not taking her gaze off Ajay who lay unmoving and silent. Blood dripped from her hands where they hung by her side.

The old doctor's knees creaked as he stood and shuffled into another room. He was soon back, wiping his hands with a cloth. He took off his glasses and also wiped them with the cloth. 'I'm afraid your friend is dead. The bullet too close to his heart.'

'Are you completely certain?' Prue whispered, not daring to believe it.

'Yes.'

A whimper built up in Prue's throat. She stared, not able to comprehend the truth. She quickly knelt on the floor beside Ajay but couldn't touch his face with her bloodied hands. He looked more handsome than ever and only appeared to be sleeping. How could this be real? He couldn't die, not like that, not at all.

'I must get home!' Nina wiped her eyes. 'I have to find out what has happened to my family.'

'Then go,' Prue whispered, not wanting to leave Ajay.

'You both must go, but not yet,' the doctor spoke from the window where he was peeking out. 'It's best to wait until night falls.'

'I cannot wait until then.' Nina jerked to her feet. 'I must find out what has happened. They may be bleeding in the streets. I have to go. Now!' Her voice rose to an alarming squeal.

'You mustn't become hysterical.' The doctor shook his head. 'Calm is needed, or we will all die,' he whispered harshly.

Prue couldn't take in what was happening. How had this bright and cheerful day ended in such a tragedy? She became light-headed, wishing she could go back in time, be anywhere other than in this suffocating room.

'We have to go,' Nina repeated, tears rolling down her cheeks. The black kohl eyeliner she'd applied that morning was smudged and streaking down in ugly lines on her face.

'What about Ajay?' Prue asked, swaying at the sight of the blood on her hands, some of which was starting to dry and cake. She gagged.

'I will deal with him once it's quietened down. What is his name?' The doctor poured water from a jug into a bowl and placed it on the table with a towel. 'Wash.'

'Thank you.' She scrambled up from her knees to the bowl and scrubbed her hands, stifling a moan as the water turned pink. Did blood stain the skin? She was going to be sick.

'His name?' The Indian repeated.

'Sorry. It's Ajay Khan, he's a lawyer,' she murmured.

'Write it down and his address.' He passed her a writing pad and pen from his desk.

In a trembling hand, Prue wrote down what she knew of Ajay, which was pathetically little.

Yet, she had shared her body with him.

She stared down at him lying on the floor, gazed at his hands that had touched her so tenderly. She swayed.

The doctor poured them both a drink of water and then covered Ajay with a dark red blanket.

A sudden bang on the door made them all jump.

Nina's eyes grew wide. She stared at Prue. 'They are coming in. We'll all be murdered!'

The doctor held a finger to his lips as shouts sounded from outside in the street.

Quietly, the doctor beckoned them from the room and into a kitchen area. A pot of curry simmered on the stovetop. Prue smelt burning. She turned and vomited into a bucket by the back door.

When she had finished, the Indian opened the door and peeped out. 'In the alley, go left. Follow it until you reach the back of the temple. You can hide there.'

'Thank you,' Nina gushed and then ran ahead, and Prue had no choice but to follow her even though she felt it was very wrong to leave Ajay.

Without speaking, they ran as quickly as they could through the twisting alleyway for what seemed an age. They passed cowering people, crying children and dogs barking at the commotion, but the further they ran, the gunfire and screams grew less.

Finally, coming out into another street and at the back of an ornate temple, they stopped to catch their breath.

Prue could taste sick in her mouth and gagged.

'Come,' Nina urged.

Cautiously, they stepped out from the alley, but all was quiet. Here, birds tweeted and flew from tree to tree in the small compound surrounding the temple. Monkeys sat picking each other's fur searching for lice. An elderly woman sat on a bench, her face lifted to the sun and her gold sari shimmering. A child played in the gutter with stones and sticks.

'The rioters have not come this far,' Nina whispered, the top of her sari spotted with blood from the cut on her neck. Her long black hair was a tangle about her shoulders, and she'd lost an earring. 'Let us cross to the other street. There may be a rickshaw we can take.'

Nodding to each other, they hurriedly crossed to the front of the silent temple. Here, a larger road held more traffic, but all seemed normal. No one was fleeing in panic, there were no screams or gunshots, no one dying.

Down the road, Prue spotted several young men leaning against their rickshaws, talking and smoking. A bullock driver plodded along, his cart piled high with planks of wood. Two beggars sat in the gutter. A woman banged a rug against a wall.

It was as though they had stepped from one world into another. Gone was the mayhem, the carnage, and instead it was replaced by ordinary people going about their business.

Prue swayed at the suddenness of it. How did these people not know what was going on only a mile from this very spot? Why weren't they concerned? Why weren't they running to help? She wanted to rage at them, demand that they assist, but she couldn't speak. She had no words to tell them. Only images in her mind.

Once in a rickshaw and heading for Malabar Hill, Nina wouldn't stop talking and crying. Prue tried to listen, tried to offer comfort, but her stomach churned, and it took all her effort not to vomit over the side of the jangling rickshaw. She couldn't look down at her beautiful sari for it now had bloodstains on it... Ajay's blood.

Nina twisted the end of her sari between her fingers. 'As soon as I get home, I will find out if anyone has made it back, and if not, I'll send out runners to scout the city for my family.'

At the gates to the Patel's home, Nina alighted, paid the charge and with a swift farewell ran up the drive. Prue wondered if she should have gone with her, but the urge to be sick was stronger and she instructed to be taken home.

Her uncle's motor car was coming out of the drive as she reached it. In a daze, she climbed down from the rickshaw. Her knees wobbled.

'You are home early, Prue,' Uncle Hugo said. 'Is everything all right? You look pale.'

'Uncle…' She fell into Uncle Hugo's arms as he rushed out of the motor car.

'Dear girl!' He called for help.

She was aware of her aunt screaming for someone to fetch a doctor, her grandmama's gentle touch on her cheek and then nothing more.

Chapter Ten

Prue sat on the veranda in a wide cushioned cane chair. Beside her was a cup of tea she couldn't drink and a book she couldn't read. She kept her gaze on the drive, waiting for Uncle Hugo to return.

The screen door opened and Grandmama came out, holding a letter. 'Your mama writes that all is well at home. She's returned from spending a month with Millie.' Grandmama sat down in the chair opposite Prue. 'Is that tea cold now?'

'Yes.'

Grandmama spoke to Rama who stood by the door then continued perusing the letter. 'Apparently, Jonathan is growing like a willow. Isn't that wonderful? Millie will be so relieved. It's been another good summer for the grape vines. Violet mentions that she spent some time in Paris with Jacques.' Grandmama peered over her glasses at Prue. 'Your mama will end up marrying that fellow, you just watch.'

'Would that be a problem?' Prue asked quietly. Grandmama was repeating everything Millie had told her in a letter she'd received yesterday. She knew why her grandmama was talking, it was to keep Prue from thinking of the riots two days ago. But nothing would stop her seeing Ajay dying in the street, the blood, the screams.

Ajay had saved her life… and she had left him in a stranger's house…

'Prue?'

She blinked, focusing again. 'Sorry.'

'I said Hugo may not return again tonight. Bombay is in chaos and his office is overwhelmed trying to sort out the destruction the rebels caused. They have to get it all under control in time for the Prince of Wales visit in a few weeks. Sitting out here for hours, waiting for his return, will be in vain, my dear.'

'There's nothing else I want to do but sit here. Uncle Hugo said he would try to find out what happened to Nina's family. If I felt well enough, I would go myself.'

'You do look positively dreadful.' Grandmama reached for her hand in a rare show of affection, but Prue's attention was caught by Nina coming through the gate.

'Nina!' She went to the top of the steps but faltered going down as the sadness on Nina's face stopped her.

Nina brought her hands together in front of her chest and bowed to Grandmama and then Prue. 'Namaste.'

'Namaste,' Prue whispered, hands together.

'I've slipped out of the house. I thought I should come and see you.'

'Come and sit down, Miss Patel.' Grandmama bade them to sit at the table as a servant came with a fresh tea tray and Rama poured out three cups.

'I mustn't stay long. My family will be angry at me for leaving the house. We are in mourning.' Nina sat at the edge of her chair. 'But I wanted to speak to you, Prue, instead of writing a note.'

'I wasn't sure if you received my note yesterday?' Prue asked quickly. 'I've not been feeling well enough to visit you, I'm sorry.'

'Do not apologise.' Nina's small smile was fleeting. 'Your note was enough.'

'And your family?' Grandmama asked, pouring milk into the teacups. 'My son, Hugo has been trying to find out as much information as he can, but the government has been swamped with requests for help, the hospitals overrun.'

'Our dear cousins, Masood and Boman, were killed.'

Prue gasped. Boman, the talkative but kindly man who'd been so nice to her. 'Oh, Nina. I'm so sorry to hear that. Boman was a lovely man.'

'Also, many of my family and friends were wounded and hurt in the crush of the fleeing. They are in hospitals all around the city.'

'Your mother and father?' Prue asked.

'Safe and well.' Nina glanced down at her hands. 'They imagined I was dead. They are very sad for our family.'

'And the bride and groom?' Grandmama asked.

'Safe, but who could recover from such a thing happening on your wedding day? They believe they are cursed now. There is much crying. Much sadness. Now we must mourn.'

'Our sympathies,' Grandmama murmured.

Nina gazed at Prue, her dark eyes full of sorrow. 'I was not a good friend to you when your friend died at our feet. I am not worthy of your friendship.'

141

Grandmama's hand stilled over adding sugar to her teacup.

Inwardly, Prue groaned. She hadn't told her family about what had happened with Ajay only that she was there at the riots and had to flee with the other wedding guests. 'You've nothing to be sorry for, Nina. We were both very scared.'

'But a man died. Someone you knew. I am sorry. I was not in my mind. Forgive me.'

'I do, of course.'

Nina stood in the fluid way that Prue admired so much. 'I must go. You understand. I have much to do. My parents are very sad.' Nina bowed again.

'Yes, of course,' Grandmama said. 'If you need any assistance from us, please don't hesitate to ask.'

Prue walked with her down the drive. 'Thank you for coming. I was so worried about your family.'

By the gate, Nina took Prue's hands. 'My father tells me we are going away to Calcutta on business once the mourning is over. We shall be gone some time. He doesn't want to be in Bombay when the Prince of Wales arrives as he feels there will be more unrest and protests.'

'Yes, my uncle agrees. The Prince's visit isn't popular to some and there could be more riots.'

'You may have already left for Italy before we return. So, I must apologise again for my behaviour that day. I have your forgiveness?'

'Truly, there is nothing to forgive, Nina.'

'Goodbye, Prue.'

Prue watched Nina quickly walk up the road, head down, shoulders bowed. Nina's goodbye seemed too formal and final, Prue didn't like it. She hoped to see her friend again one day, but something inside told her she wouldn't.

With a deep sigh, Prue turned and walked back up the drive just as it started to rain.

Grandmama sat waiting, as Prue knew she would be. 'Tell me everything.'

'There isn't a lot to tell, actually.' Prue sat down, tired, her head aching.

'Then it won't take long in the telling, will it?' A frown creased Grandmama's forehead. 'I never thought you would keep secrets from me, but I was being naïve. If you had a man friend, then so be it. That is not what I am worried about. What does worry me though is that he *died* in front of *you* and you've not mentioned a word of it to any of us, *especially* to me.'

'Yes, he did die. He was shot and killed saving me.' Prue closed her eyes, reliving the moment. 'The bullet was meant for me... Ajay pushed me away. He saved my life.'

'Dear God. Why didn't you tell me!'

'I didn't think I could speak of it... It's like a nightmare I can't wake up from.'

'Prue, dearest girl.'

'I put my hands... on his bleeding chest... so much blood, Grandmama, so much...' A sob rose in her throat and caught. 'A doctor helped us drag Ajay into his house, but he couldn't help Ajay. He was already... dead.'

'Dearest.'

Hot tears burned behind her eyes, but she didn't cry. She hadn't shed a tear so far, and she was determined not to for she might never stop.

'What happened then?'

Prue took a deep breath. 'The kind doctor then told us how to escape. It all seemed like a dream, really.'

'A terrible business, my dear, shocking. I wish you had mentioned this two days ago. I could have understood your quietness more.'

'I don't know why I didn't.' She gazed out at the rain, which for a change wasn't the deluge of monsoon but a soft rain like they had back home in England. 'There was nothing I could do to save Ajay.'

'Of course, there wasn't anything you could do. It was a riot. Men had guns.'

'A man died for me, Grandmama. My mind can't cope with that knowledge. A good man gave his life for me. He didn't deserve to die.' It was the one thought that kept going around in her head, stopping her from eating, stopping her from sleeping.

'No, he didn't. But then, nor do you.'

'All I can think of is that I don't want to die, Grandmama, I've barely lived. Life can be so short. Here one minute and gone the next.'

'You're not going to die, stop talking such tosh!' Grandmama bustled in her chair with annoyance. 'We don't simper in this family. We face tragedy face on. We are strong, not weak. I can't abide feeble females. You have survived your papa's death with grace and dignity, and you will do so again in this situation, understand?'

'This is different. I had a gun pointed at me!' Prue snapped, daring to speak to her grandmama in such a way.

'And? I'm not denying that it was a terrible event, and it has shaken you badly, naturally it would. But do we fall into a quivering heap? No. Do you have vapours for the rest of your life and let the incident destroy you? No. You have survived it. That is what we do in this family. We survive and we get on with living. That is what sorts out the weak from the strong. Do you understand?'

'Yes.' Though she still felt fragile and swallowed the lump in her throat.

A leak in the veranda roof dripped into a brass pot in the corner. The noise irritated her.

Grandmama sipped her tea. 'Now, this man. Do I know him? Is he a soldier? Did you meet him at the Club? What was his full name? What does A.J. stand for? Are we to attend his funeral?'

'You don't know him. His name was Ajay Khan, a lawyer. He was Anglo-Indian, not British and lived down by the old Fort district.'

'Anglo-Indian?' Grandmama didn't conceal her surprise. 'I suspect he was devilishly handsome? Most of the half-castes are. Mixed marriages are frowned upon these days, but back in the seventeenth century the East India Company men often took an Indian wife. I'm sure there is a case of it in your grandpapa's bloodline somewhere.'

'He was handsome, yes.'

'Did you love him?'

'No.' A rogue tear ran down Prue's cheek and she hurriedly wiped it away.

'Did you share his bed?'

'Yes.'

'So, there's a possibility you could be pregnant.' It was a statement not a question.

'No. I had my monthly show three days after I... after we...'

The relief made Grandmama's shoulders sag. 'Excellent. That is one worry we do not need.'

Prue wiped her nose with a handkerchief from her pocket. The rain continued to fall as did her tears. 'Are you dreadfully disappointed in me?'

'No.' Grandmama picked up her teacup and put it back down again. 'If I did, I would be a hypocrite, and that is something I've never been. I cannot give you a sermon on sleeping with a man you're not married to, for I have done it myself.'

Prue stared at her. 'You did?'

Grandmama gave a small smile. 'I was young and beautiful once, and I loved life.'

'I know. I've seen your portraits. You were very beautiful. Did you tell Grandpapa that you weren't a virgin when he asked you to marry him?'

'Absolutely. We had no secrets between us. Edward loved me unconditionally, but that's not to say he fully accepted it. Men are strange creatures, they like to assume no one has touched their property before, a bit like how dogs pee on everything to show other dogs that is their territory.'

'And the other man?' Prue wiped away her tears.

Grandmama stared across the lush gardens as the rain fell softly washing away the dust of previous days. 'He was everything to me at the time. I was infatuated with him, but that is a story for another day.' She shook herself gently as though ridding the memories from her mind. 'All this will feel awfully hurtful now, of course it will, but you'll heal. It was a tragic incident and you'll never forget it, but you will, in time, regain normalcy, and it might be quicker than you expect because your heart wasn't affected, and that's nothing to be ashamed of, understand?'

'Yes.'

'Do you believe me?'

'I do.' And she did, for Grandmama would never lie to her.

~ ~ ~ ~

Later that evening, Prue sat curled up on the sofa reading the newspaper, or trying to, for her head ached dreadfully. Rain still fell and in the darkness of night the frogs and crickets were loud in the bushes. She blamed their noise and the constant dripping from the gutters and the odd leaks around the house as the reason for her banging headache.

She'd declined an invitation to join Uncle Hugo, Aunt Daphne and Grandmama for dinner at the Club, preferring to stay home and write some letters. However, with her head pounding, she felt listless and unable to concentrate. Her letters remained unwritten. Besides, what could she write to Mama? *Dear Mama, I was nearly shot and killed, instead my lover took the bullet...* No, she couldn't write that to her mama or Cece, and although she could confess it to Millie, something stopped her. Pride perhaps. She didn't want Millie to think badly of her.

Movement in the doorway made her look up, she winced at the effort.

Gertie stood there, her stomach large with child. 'Forgive me. I thought everyone had gone out.'

'I'm a bit under the weather and decided to stay home. Did you want something?'

'No.'

'Do you want to come and sit down?' Prue couldn't help but feel sorry for the ghost of a woman standing there. Gertie had no colour in her cheeks, her hair lank and, apart from her stomach, she looked gaunt and thin.

'I was going to walk the veranda. I do that at night when everyone is either out or asleep. I like to stretch my legs after being in my room all day. No one sees me,' Gertie spoke defensively.

Prue sighed. The woman was still so prickly. 'Gertie, please, come and relax.'

'I wouldn't wish to disturb you.'

'You do not.' Prue waved to a chair. 'I may have a bath in a moment, anyway.'

'I had one earlier. There was a snake in there.'

'A snake?'

'Yes, just a small one. It came up through the water drain.'

'How did you get it out? I never heard a scream.' Prue was intrigued.

'I didn't scream,' Gertie replied curtly. 'I simply threw my towel at it, and it slithered back down the drain and outside again.'

'That's brave.'

Gertie shrugged. 'I wouldn't care if it bit me and I died.'

'Don't say that.' Prue shivered. 'You might not want to live, but you have a baby that deserves a chance. It must be due to be born very soon.'

'It can't come quick enough for me, then I can leave this place and get on with my life.' Gertie walked to the window and pushed open the plantation shutters. The smell of rain and dampness came in on the air and also the scent of jasmine.

'What will you do in the future?'

Gertie stared into the night. 'I've applied to teach at a mission school. There are advertisements for teachers up in the Himalayan Mountains to teach in the village schools.'

'You won't go home to your parents?'

'No. I cannot face them yet. Perhaps in time.'

Prue uncurled her legs and sat up straighter. 'I can't imagine how you are feeling.'

'I don't feel anything for anyone or anything.'
Gertie spoke without emotion.

'But you and Uncle Hugo, there would have been
affection between you?'

Gertie's laugh was mocking. 'He had none for me,
he's proven that, hasn't he? He chose her, not me,
even when I can give him the one thing he wants, and
she can't. He could have had me and the baby, but he
caved to her demands when she decided to wrap all
this up in a neat little package. He can't live off the
money your grandmama gives him without also
spending Daphne's money she receives from the trust
her father set up when he died. Hugo likes money
more than anything.'

Suddenly Prue saw Uncle Hugo as a weak man, and
it saddened her. 'Why did you do it? With him of all
people, your cousin's husband?'

'I wish I knew. I suppose I was flattered. A good-
looking, smart man was showing me attention for the
first time in my life. I fell for his charms. *You* know
how it is,' she accused.

'I do?' Prue wiped the sweat from her forehead.
Perspiration seemed to seep out of all her pores.

'I saw you talking to that Indian man by the gates
weeks ago. He was the same one you met at the polo,
and I was walking the gardens the night you returned
home late and your grandmother was sitting on the
veranda. You had gone to meet him. I'm ugly, not
dumb.' Gertie's face twisted with spite. 'You're all
hypocrites, treating me like I'm something disgusting,
while you attract men like a dog on heat, and that is to
be applauded. At every occasion you flirt and tease all
the men and it's all a big joke!'

'I don't think—'

'You had poor Captain Lewis, a good decent man wanting you and you used him until he no longer entertained you.'

Prue's headache pounded her brain. 'That's not true. We were just friends. I gave him no encouragement.'

'Nonsense! Accepting invitations to dinners and morning rides is exactly the encouragement a man needs.' Gertie punched her stomach. 'Be careful, or you'll end up like me!' She fled from the room.

The need to be sick drew Prue up from the sofa, but her legs wobbled, not holding her weight. She stumbled, dizzily. Her head felt heavy and like it was about to explode.

Whimpering, Prue held onto the walls, trying to make it to her room. The dark corridor swayed before her eyes, a filtered light coming from a table lamp dazzled her eyes.

Why was she so hot?

Her bedroom door was an arm's length away, yet she couldn't reach it. Her knees hurt. How was that even possible?

'Gertie…' she called, but it was a feeble attempt. 'Gertie.'

Her legs gave out and she slid down the wall, hitting her arm on the hall table. Pain shot through her whole body like she was being stabbed a hundred times.

'Memsahib?' One of the Indian servants stood over her, wearing a worried expression. 'Memsahib?'

The vision of him blurred and then all went black.

Chapter Eleven

Prue dimly woke, shivering, but she had no energy to stay awake. The very act of shivering hurt. Her whole body ached. How was it conceivable to be so cold in India?

She was so tired…

She needed to get up and find more blankets, but the effort was beyond her. She must call for Mama.

A white haze shrouded her. What was that? Fog? Smoke?

She was so cold… Why was there a mist in her room?

The heat! Her body burned. Why was it so hot?

She kicked the coverings off her legs. Sweat soaked the sheets, sticking her nightgown to her body. Someone was touching her head with red-hot fingers, poking and prodding.

Stop touching me! She wanted to scream. You're hurting me!

There was no coolness to be found anywhere. She needed a bath, a drink. Where was Mama?

Suddenly, something cool was placed against her forehead, such bliss…

No… it was too cold! Icy shivers tingled down her skin. Tremors wracked her body, making her teeth chatter.

She cried out, scared. There was blood on her hands. She'd been shot. She was dying! Ajay had shot her… Help! Mama!

Soothing hands held her down.

She couldn't open her eyes.

Fireworks exploded.

Her head pounded.

Her body was on fire.

Was she being burned alive? Was this her funeral?

No, she wasn't dead yet!

Voices murmured to her.

Why weren't they helping her?

She called out, but no one was there ...

~ ~ ~ ~

Prue opened her eyes and took a moment to focus. Without moving her head, she gazed through the mosquito net around the bed and made out Grandmama sleeping on the chair next to the bed. Near the chest of drawers, Ganika was in the corner folding something.

'Gran…' she croaked, her throat was dry, her tongue felt thick in her mouth.

She closed her eyes. It was all too much effort.

When she woke again, she heard the rapid, frightened voice of Aunt Daphne and the quieter steady tone of her grandmama.

'No, she's not going to the hospital, Daphne. Do not mention it again,' Grandmama snapped. 'Doctor

Sawyer told me that we can look after Prue here. We can trust his judgement, I'm certain.'

'But it's been days, and she's not woken! We aren't nurses!' Aunt Daphne's wail set Prue's teeth on edge.

'Gran...'she whispered.

'Prue!' In an instant, Grandmama was beside her, throwing the net aside and clasping her hand. 'Darling girl. You're back with us!' Emotion made Grandmama's voice gruff.

'Oh, thank God!' Aunt Daphne burst into tears. 'Our prayers have been answered.'

'What... happened?' Prue moved her head but the ache in her neck made her wince.

'Stay still, my pet,' Grandmama soothed. 'You need to drink this now.' Grandmama placed a cup to Prue's lips, and she drank it thirstily though it tasted vile, but the exertion exhausted her.

'Well done, that's my girl,' Grandmama crooned. 'We'll soon have you back on your feet, my sweet.' She turned to Aunt Daphne. 'Send for Doctor Sawyer.'

Once Aunt Daphne had hurried from the room, Grandmama took Prue's hand again and smiled lovingly. 'Now then, that was a fright I'd not like to repeat, thank you very much!' Tears filled Grandmama's blue eyes.

It was hard to concentrate, and Prue's eyelids were extremely heavy, yet she was concerned that Grandmama had tears in her eyes, for it was a rare day when Grandmama cried.

'Gran...'

'It's fine, my petal, don't worry. The fever has broken. You can sleep now. The worst is over.'

'Stay...' Prue whispered, not able to fight the drowsiness.

Prue

A tear trickled down Grandmama's cheek. 'I'll not leave you for a minute.'

~ ~ ~ ~

A door slamming jerked Prue into wakefulness. Raised voices sounded from the hallway. Sunlight streamed in from the gaps in the plantation shutters and dust mites danced in the rays. Outside birds called in the trees.

Lying quietly, Prue listened for other sounds. There was the clip-whoosh of the hand-pushed lawn mower, the squeak of the wheelbarrow that Aunt Daphne complained needed oiling and none of the garden servants ever did it. Prue had laughingly watched her one day try to communicate to the old Indian gardener that he needed to oil the wheel, but it had all been lost in translation and the wheelbarrow continued to squeak.

The sound of another door opening and closing made her stare at the bedroom door, but it remained closed. Footsteps sounded and there was a smothered groan.

Prue frowned, trying to work it out.

The idea to get out of bed came and left. Her body ached and her limbs seemed too weighty to move. She wore only a nightgown and one sheet covered her, yet, she wasn't cold or hot.

Another groan reached her, louder this time, followed by murmurs.

The time on the clock showed five past one. Who was groaning? Was someone hurt?

The bedroom door opened and Grandmama came in, followed by Ganika carrying a tea tray, which she placed on the table beside the bed.

'Oh, dear girl, you are awake? I was just coming in to sit with you for a while and have a cup of tea.' Grandmama kissed Prue's forehead and then touched it with the back of her hand. 'And you're not hot in the least. Wonderful. How do you feel?'

'I can't seem to move properly, it's so tiring to do so.'

'Well, that's because we need to rebuild your strength back up. Drink this.' Grandmama held a glass to Prue's lips, and she drank all the queer tasting liquid. 'That's the quinine. Your medicine.'

'Quinine? What has happened to me?'

Grandmama took her hand. 'Malaria, dearest. Have you been taking your quinine daily as I instructed when we first arrived?'

'Er, yes, I think so.' Her mind was a little fuzzy, so she wasn't quite sure. 'Malaria?' Prue couldn't believe it.

'Yes, you've been unwell for four days. You got hit hard by the attack, but Doctor Sawyer has been brilliant and said you are young and healthy, and you'd pull through. I, of course, had no doubt.' Grandmama nodded in assurance. 'As if a case of malaria would take one of my family. Absurd.'

'I will get better though, won't I?'

'Absolutely! A strong girl like you? No problem at all. You'll be back dancing and flirting with handsome young men before you know it.'

Prue yawned. 'Good.'

She closed her eyes and welcomed the sleep.

When she woke again, the clock showed a quarter past three. Grandmama sat on the chair reading a letter.

'Grandmama?'

Putting down the letter, Grandmama smiled. 'That was a nice restful nap for you. Doctor Sawyer said you'd sleep a lot as you recover. Would you like something to eat?'

A loud groan came again from the hallway.

'What is that noise?'

Grandmama glanced over her shoulder. 'Gertie is in labour.'

Prue stared at Grandmama who didn't seem too concerned. 'Goodness.'

'Shall we sit you up for a bit? It's time you started eating and getting some meat on your bones.'

Prue, with Grandmama's help, sat up against three pillows, and Grandmama placed a pale green cashmere shawl around her shoulders.

'It's becoming colder this last week. We've had the fires lit each night. A real cold snap has come along. Not that you would have felt it, for your temperature was incredible at times.'

A high-pitched yelp sounded.

'Who is with Gertie?' Prue asked, finding it difficult to comprehend that across the hall Gertie was giving birth.

'Doctor Sawyer and his assistant, and Daphne is in there, too.' Grandmama straightened the sheet and then added a blanket at Prue's feet, before going to the door and instructing a passing servant that special food for memsahib was to be brought in.

'And Uncle Hugo?'

'He's taken himself off to the Club, or the office, I don't know which. Gertie has been in labour since last evening, and he was driving everyone mad with his never-ending questions. He was neither use nor ornament. I was tired of hearing him.'

'He's bound to be worried. It's his first child.'

'Yes, well that's his fault, isn't it?' Grandmama opened the shutters a little more to let in more sunlight. 'Does that hurt your eyes?'

'No. How long have I been sick for?'

'Four days. Rama sent a runner to find us when you collapsed, but the servants wouldn't touch you. They are a respectful lot. However, it was a shock to find you like that.'

'I'm sorry I scared you.'

'You couldn't help it, dearest. However, dealing with you being so ill and then yesterday Gertie going into labour, well, it's been a strain on Daphne's poor nerves.' Grandmama shook her head at the foolishness of such a thing. 'I had to give her a good talking to, of course, for she was near hysterical when we found you collapsed in the hallway. So, I made her do practical things and cancel all engagements. I've found that if she is kept busy, she is calmer.'

'Poor Aunt Daphne.'

'Hmm, well, *poor Aunt Daphne* is a little more in control of herself now, thankfully.' Grandmama folded some towels and put them away in the wardrobe. 'Gertie seems to have come early, we think, for it's only the beginning of November. Daphne hadn't arranged for a nanny, so I tasked her with that job. And just this morning she's employed an ayah for the baby.'

'An ayah?'

'A nanny to you and me. This ayah is an Indian woman, a relative of Jal's who is widowed and has a baby of her own to support.'

Prue yawned, watching Grandmama search her drawers and take out a clean nightgown. 'Why didn't Aunt Daphne employ a British nanny before now?'

'Who knows?' Grandmama sat back down beside the bed. 'I did ask, and Daphne's response was that unlike a British nanny, an Indian ayah knew their place and didn't gossip. Their devotion to their charges is unstinting. Apparently, this young woman will be able to feed her own son, who is about a year old, and also my new grandchild. A civilised arrangement if you ask me. I've heard only good things about ayahs. Some British nannies behave as though they rule the house.'

'I feel sorry for Gertie, to give birth and then hand over the baby straight away.'

'It is an uneasy situation, true. Yet, it is the plan. If Gertie wanted something different, she would have left weeks ago when it was all found out and taken her chances. Obviously, she doesn't want to keep the child and I believe she is doing the right thing.'

'I don't know if I could do it.'

'Then let us hope you never have to find out.' Grandmama nodded wisely as Ganika brought in a bed tray for Prue.

Grandmama took it from her and placed it over Prue's lap. 'You are to eat as much as you can. Doctor Sawyer doesn't expect it to be much. Eggs first and then in a few hours we'll have chicken broth and some rice.'

The delicious aroma of scrambled eggs, toast and tea made Prue's stomach rumble. 'I didn't realise I was even hungry.'

'Eat.' Grandmama instructed, sitting back down.

For a while they sat in silence. Prue started eating with gusto, enjoying the creamy eggs and hot buttered toast. However, after only a few mouthfuls, she tired. The physical act of bringing the fork to her mouth grew harder.

'Let me help.' Grandmama held the teacup for Prue to sip from.

Prue's eyes started to close. 'Sorry.'

'No need to be. You've managed some, and that's better than nothing.' Grandmama took the tray away and placed it on the drawers.

'I'm so weary.' Prue nestled back against the pillows.

'Sleep will heal you, and once you're better and fit for travel, we shall catch the first steamer home to England.'

'England?' Prue scowled, fighting sleep. 'We are to go to Italy.'

'We were, yes, but not now, you need to convalesce. Your mama is worried out of her mind. I sent her a telegram yesterday when you woke and told her you had caught malaria but that you are out of danger. She answered that you are to come home straight away.'

'What did you answer to that?'

Grandmama shrugged slightly. 'I didn't. The day my daughter dictates to me is the day I'm on my deathbed.'

'I can convalesce in Italy,' Prue said stubbornly.

Grandmama tilted her head to one side to study her. 'Is that what you want? I imagined you'd want to go home after everything that has happened.'

'Not particularly. I do miss Mama and Cece and Millie. But I will soon regain my health and there is no reason to return to England where it's cold.'

'Agreed. I wasn't looking forward to spending the winter in England, I'd much prefer to spend it in Italy, where it's warmer.'

'Please, Grandmama, let us go to Italy.'

Before Grandmama could answer, a baby's cry filled the air.

Chapter Twelve

Spring. Rome, Italy, April 1922.

Brandon Forster sat on the hotel's terrace sipping an icy limoncello while staring out over the River Tiber. The heat of the day was gently subsiding as though loathed to give up its power to the coolness of the night. Below on the river, boats rocked gently, and every now and then a new light would flare to join the other flickering bursts of gold as twilight descended.

He cradled the cold ceramic cup in one hand and rubbed his aching shoulder with the other. He'd overdone it today. Stupid of him really. His war wound, although healed, had left his right shoulder weak and why he had to keep pushing himself, he didn't know. Mountain climbing was exciting, and when the conditions were good, it was very exhilarating, like today. Yet, he understood the limits of his shoulder, so why continue when the ache became so bad he could barely hold the rope?

'There you are, my friend,' a voice came from behind Brandon and he turned to see his good friend, Vince Barton, stroll out onto the terrace. 'This hotel suite is vast. I got lost going from the bathroom to my bedroom. You've outdone yourself this time with this place.'

'I'm pleased it meets your with your approval.' Brandon poured Vince a cup of limoncello. 'How was your bath?'

Vince's black curls were still damp. He lit a cigarette and offered one to Brandon who accepted. 'Splendid. Hot and deep exactly as I like it to ease my aches. Now, what are we doing for dinner? I'm ravenous. There is a nice little restaurant a few streets away or we can dine at the hotel's restaurant?'

Brandon settled back in his cushioned cane chair and considered the options of a quiet night in or heading down to the piazza as they had done every night for the last week. Like Vince, after bathing he'd dressed in a black suit and white shirt ready for dinner and a night out, but he really didn't fancy it. 'Why don't we eat here in the hotel tonight?'

'Your shoulder pains you, doesn't it, old chap?' Vince sat opposite, the small table between them. 'We shouldn't have done the last climb.'

'I'm fine.'

'Liar. You allowed me to drive the motor car to the hotel. You never do that unless your shoulder pains you.'

'I don't let you drive because you're terrible at it.' Brandon grinned, drawing on the cigarette.

Vince scowled, then shrugged dismissively. 'Why you can't be honest with me of all people, eludes me. I know what's been done to your shoulder. You know I know the truth. I was the one running beside you

161

when we faced the machine gun fire. It was I who, and with no thought to my own safety, stopped in the middle of the battlefield and tended to you before carrying you under fire back to the first aid post.' He smiled smugly. 'I'm a hero.'

Raising an eyebrow, Brandon gave Vince a superior look. 'Well, it makes up for the amount of times I've carried *you* home from one place or another over the years, doesn't it?'

'You've never had to do it under gun fire though, have you?'

'You received a medal for it, didn't you?' Brandon laughed. 'A medal you have used to win over the ladies with ever since!'

Vince chuckled. 'Ah, yes, the ladies jolly well love a good medal story. Shall we repeat the good old times then? Let us get extremely drunk, my friend. We're not climbing until you've rested that shoulder, so we might as well enjoy what Rome has to offer now we are here.'

'We could go back to Milan for a few days?' Brandon said without much enthusiasm.

They'd done nothing but travel since the war ended over three years ago. Neither he nor Vince could settle at home in England, and after years being on the move with the army, it had been difficult to suddenly stay at home. He'd done it for a few months, but soon his mother's concerns that he was aimlessly wasting his days started to feel like a noose around his neck, not that any of it was her fault. His parents were patient and as sympathetic as possible, but in the end, he had to get out. He needed to breathe, to live.

By some stroke of luck, he had survived numerous battlefield injuries, and he had no wish to simply exist on his parent's estate as the weeks blurred into one another.

No, something drove him on to always look for a new adventure, his next escapade. Vince, feeling the same restlessness, was a perfect companion. Friends since attending Eton as boys they had an understanding, a bond. Fighting side by side in battle had strengthened that connection.

Brandon looked at him. 'Well?'

Vince gave a grin. 'I'd rather not venture back to Milan for a while. There's a certain Mama who is currently residing in my favourite hotel and you know she insists on cornering me at every function to offer up her daughter like a prized heifer.'

'It might have escaped your notice, but Milan is rather large.' Brandon laughed. 'I'm sure we can find an extremely lively bolthole to disappear into and swallow up a few days.'

'Sounds exhausting.' Vince yawned. 'Damn, I must be getting old.'

Gazing out over the river, Brandon sighed. 'No, we're getting bored with living this life.'

'What's the alternative? Shall we return home to England? Shall I spend the rest of my days trying desperately to keep the family estate running?' Vince swore softly. 'Bloody government. We fight for king and country and return home to find we're taxed to the hilt and when Father dies… Well, I don't know how we'll pay the death duties. We could lose everything. I'm in half a mind to sell the whole lot up and find a little cottage here in Italy to live out my days.'

'It's not that desperate, is it?' He looked at the worry sketched across Vince's face. 'You *can* pay the death duties, can't you?'

'Yes, if we sell just about every item we own. Hopefully, we will find enough ugly, yet valuable pieces of artwork in the attics.' Vince took a long drink of the limoncello. 'Unlike you, Forster, my family do not have a history of wise investments to keep us afloat.'

'I told you at the beginning of fourteen something was going to happen, a war of some kind. I told you to buy into industry. The days of farming, of political power, cannot keep families such as ours financial any more. We have to move with the times or die.'

'I know. I know. I'm sorry now I didn't listen to you. Those types of things bloody bore me senseless. And, unlike you, I didn't study history and economics and learn about such things at school.'

'You didn't learn anything at school. Too busy playing sport or chasing pretty girls in the villages.'

Vince gave him a cheeky smirk. 'And who had the better time?'

Brandon snickered, glad that the atmosphere had lightened. 'You did. It is acknowledged.'

'Yes, I did!' Vince nodded regally, snubbing out his cigarette in an ashtray. 'Come on, old chap. Let's go to the bar and get completely indelicate.'

Standing, Brandon placed his cup on the table and squashed his cigarette into the ashtray. 'I need to eat first, and so do you!'

'Fine. We'll eat and then drink until the sun comes up. Agreed?'

'Very well.' Troubled by Vince's situation, Brandon halted him by the door. 'Soon, we are going to sit down and discuss business properly and get our futures sorted out.'

'Like mature adults?' Vince smiled.

'Yes, at last. And you *will* let me help you.'

164

For a moment a serious shadow passed across Vince's brown eyes. 'Yes, my good friend. I will listen to your advice and act on it.'

Brandon closed the door and they walked to the lift. 'Don't let our sacrifices, and all the death we witnessed be for nothing. We must make it all worthwhile. We still have fight left in us for what is important.'

'Fighting taxes is important?' Vince pressed the button to take them down to the dining room. 'Gosh, who would have thought!'

'We're still fighting for our homes, our families. It's all the same thing. We fight for what is ours. It's purely a different battle.'

'I'm tired of fighting, Brandon.' Vince walked out of the lift, shoulders slumped.

Annoyed with himself for upsetting Vince, of reminding him of the troubles he faced at home, Brandon hurried to catch him up at the bar and jabbed him in the ribs. 'You know what to do then, don't you?'

'No, what's that?'

'Marry an heiress!' Brandon winked and signalled to the bartender. 'I'll look out for one for you. As your closest friend, it's the least I can do.'

'Thank you, but I can do that very well by myself. That's one subject I could always excel at. You, on the other hand, are extremely undeveloped in that matter.'

Brandon chuckled and ordered for their drinks to be taken through to the dining room. 'I manage quite well enough.'

'Really? I disagree. When was the last time you were taken with a lovely woman, and I mean the kind we could take home to Mother?'

'Ah, yes, well, those types are few and far between, as you well know.'

'But you have Claudia out of your system now, yes?' Vince gave him a sidelong glance. 'I mean, yes, she did a cowardly act, but it was years ago now. She's definitely not worth further thought or any lingering sentiment on your part.'

'I haven't thought of her for a long time, many months, in fact.' He frowned, realising it was true. His old love, the one woman he had wanted to marry, but who rejected him via letter hours before the Battle of the Somme, no longer featured in his everyday thoughts, and he was secretly pleased. He'd wasted enough time grieving for her. Last he'd heard, she was married with a baby.

They greeted fellow hotel guests as they followed the restaurant's host through the tables and headed for the smaller tables in the far corner. A new party were taking their seats as they approached, and Brandon assisted the elderly woman into her seat before the waiter could get to her.

'Thank you so much. Very kind.' She smiled up at him.

He guessed her age to be anywhere between seventy and eighty. Decked in pearls and diamonds, her gown a rich bronze silk, she had that softened magnificence which spoke of a long-held beauty that had faded gracefully into age.

'You are welcome, madam.' He bowed and politely turned to the other woman opposite whom Vince was holding a chair for. At the same time, she looked up at him and smiled. He felt an instant blow to his chest and startled, took a step back. He saw the same uncertainty reflected in her eyes and wondered what the hell just happened. Then, taking a sudden breath his mind understood. Here she was, the one he'd been waiting for.

Slowly he became aware of Vince and the older woman chatting and before he was fully aware of what was going on, they were moving to another larger table and the four of them were sitting down together.

'I'm Prue Marsh and this is my grandmama, Mrs Adeline Fordham.' Her soft voice reached through the fog of his befuddled brain as he savoured her name. Prue Marsh. She was English not Italian.

'It's a pleasure to meet you, Miss Marsh, Mrs Fordham. I'm Brandon Forster. How do you do?' His reply was instinctive and born out of years of being schooled in good manners, but all he could do was stare into her blue eyes and try to remember to breathe. She was stunning. Simply no other word described her better.

She turned away from him to answer something Vince asked, and her smile lit her face so beautifully, Brandon's stomach flipped.

In the blink of a moment he was lost, and would never be the same again. Another turning point in his life. Like going to boarding school, leaving home, joining the army, dodging bullets, seeing men blown to pieces, surviving, returning home to his mother's tears and warm embrace… They were all moments that changed him slightly, and they had all led him to this one special moment. They led to her.

He wasn't ready.

Shocked and appalled this had happened to him, he turned to the only person he could rely on, the one who had his back through every battle, every childhood scrape and adventure.

Vince's eyes widened in reply to Brandon's helpless look before he turned back to Miss Marsh and asked her about her opinion of the hotel.

'And you, Mr Forster, are you staying in Italy long?' the older woman asked.

He turned his attention to the grandmother, whose name, embarrassingly, had escaped him. 'Er, no, madam, well, that is to say, I'm undecided ...'

'We've been mountain climbing, you see,' Vince put in smoothly. 'And we are fast running out of mountains to climb in this region. We shall move on shortly.' He disarmed the women with a charming smile that never failed to please.

Brandon let out a pent-up breath and looked around for the blasted waiter, he was sorely in need of a drink. His gaze drifted to Miss Marsh and again his stomach clenched as she stared at him, a small smile playing on her lips and in her blue eyes he found a twinkle of mischief. For some reason, this relaxed him more than any amount of alcohol. He studied her openly, not caring that it was rude, or that she would see his interest. He was rewarded by her regarding him in return.

Prue Marsh was thin. Too thin. Her bones protruded from a skeletal frame like those who had suffered a recent illness. Stylishly dressed in a sheath of shimmering gold with lots of tassels and beads, she twirled a long string of pearls in her fingers. Her face was attractive, certainly, but there was something more.

In her blue eyes he saw a challenge, a fight within her. For what reason? Did she have something to prove? Her golden blonde hair had a slight touch of red in it when the light caught it. Cut short about her ears, it was straight and sleek, and he loved the sassiness of it.

She was the opposite to any woman he'd ever been attracted to. She held no claim to curves or decent sized breasts, no long hair or conservative dress. Prue Marsh simply looked as though she'd stepped from one of those lady's fashion magazines his sister was always poring over.

Somehow, without losing all credibility, he made it through the first course of their meal, a thin soup he barely tasted. Thank God for Vince, who, with extreme dexterity kept the ladies entertained throughout the meal without excluding Brandon. Not that he'd cared if he had, for admiring Miss Marsh more than compensated for the lack of conversation on his part.

'Yorkshire, is it, Mr Forster, where you hail from?' Mrs Fordham asked him. 'As my late son-in-law's family do. The Marsh family come from York.'

Brandon nodded to the grandmother, as their second course of prawn salad was delivered to their table. 'My family is from near Whitby, North Yorkshire.'

'I have visited there many times. Fabulous jet jewellery. Has your family always been there?'

'Indeed, for many generations and about four hundred years or so.'

'And yet we haven't heard of the Forsters.' She frowned as though this was a serious slight on someone's part, either his family or hers, he wasn't sure.

'Perhaps, in the past, our families did know of each other in some connection.' He tried to mollify her as his gaze strayed to her granddaughter once more, but Miss Marsh was listening to Vince.

A tap on his arm brought his attention back to the grandmother as she leaned in close. 'Madam?'

'Prue is unattached, Mr Forster, despite my best intentions to fix her up with some very agreeable gentlemen we met in Palermo over Christmas. If you are interested, and I can see you are, for you've not been able to take your eyes off her since we sat down, then I suggest a stroll on the terrace after our meal has finished. And, if you take the advice of an old woman, be bold. You've been a soldier, a British soldier at that, so you know how to take risks, unlike these Italians who are now scared of their own shadows, thanks to Mussolini.'

He hid a smile at this but listened closely as she continued.

'Prue needs a man who isn't afraid of taking action. She's not a quiet mouse, Mr Forster, who needs gentle handling. She's independent of thought, remember that. Strong women do not intimidate you, do they?'

'No, madam, they do not. I find them rather refreshing.'

'Excellent.' She relaxed back in her chair and started eating. 'We travel on to Switzerland in a few weeks.' She raised her voice to include the whole table. 'They have rather large mountains there, you know, to climb.'

He chuckled. 'Yes, I hear the Alps are extraordinary to climb.'

'You've not attempted them?' Miss Marsh spoke to him directly for the first time.

'Not yet. We started in Spain, then travelled to Morocco, and now to Italy. The Alps are on the list.'

She forked a small amount of prawns into her mouth. 'Perhaps, you might be inclined to travel with us?' She looked to her grandmother. 'Would you agree, Grandmama, that having the gentlemen accompany us would be rather jolly?'

'A very merry party indeed,' Mrs Fordham agreed, a small grin on her face. 'But that is for the gentlemen to decide, my girl. After all, they may have other plans.'

Vince leaned back in his chair. 'We have none, do we, Brandon?'

'No, not really. We thought to maybe head out of Rome in a few weeks, for as summer progresses it'll get too hot here in the city.'

'We are considering travelling to the coast, aren't we, Grandmama?'

Mrs Fordham dabbed her mouth with a napkin. 'Yes, and hire a villa on the east coast. After spending months by the water in Palermo, we miss seeing the ocean every day.'

'Well, that is something we can perhaps organise together?' Brandon spoke directly to Mrs Fordham.

She nodded serenely. 'I'm sure that will be suitable. If you can tolerate an old woman in your party, then I can tolerate two spoilt men.'

Brandon laughed. He liked her.

'If you come from North Yorkshire, Mr Forster, you may know of Sir Jeremy Remington?' Miss Marsh asked him. 'He is my brother-in-law and was also an officer in the war.'

Pleasantly surprised, Brandon paused in his eating. 'I do know of him very well. We met during the war quite a few times. We were officers in the same brigade, but different battalions. Vince and I think him a fine fellow, don't we, Vince?'

'You'll go far to meet a braver man, that's for certain.' Vince sipped his wine. 'And he married your older sister? I'm pleased for him. He endured a lot. He deserves happiness.' A glimmer of sadness passed over Vince's face and Brandon knew he was recalling war memories, and not good ones.

Refilling everyone's glasses with more wine, Brandon tried to steer the conversation to a lighter topic. 'We were, in fact, invited to his wedding, but the invitation was late finding us in Spain. So, unfortunately, we missed the occasion. I am doubly sorry I did now. I do hope they had a wonderful day.' If only he had gone to that wedding. He'd have met the lovely Miss Marsh so much sooner!

'It was a beautiful day, wasn't it, Grandmama?' Miss Marsh lifted her glass. 'Everything went off perfectly. They have a baby boy now.'

'Excellent. Lucky man.' Brandon sipped his wine.

Miss Marsh finished her prawns. 'I'm so happy we have met some friends of Jeremy's. It makes it more intimate, doesn't it?'

Mrs Fordham turned to Vince. 'And you, Mr Barton, do you also hail from Yorkshire?'

'No, madam. I'm from the southern counties. My family's estate is outside of a small village called Mayfield, East Sussex.'

'A delightful area, indeed. My late husband had a cousin living in East Sussex.'

'How did you two meet?' Miss Marsh asked. 'Was it in the war?'

'No.' Brandon shook his head. 'We met at Eton, as boys. When the war broke out, I was determined to join up in one of the Yorkshire regiments.'

'And I, Miss Marsh,' Vince butted in, 'could not let the poor fool go on his own and get shot at, so while I was visiting him, we decided to join up together.' Vince drank the last of his wine.

'Honourable.' Mrs Fordham raised her glass to them both.

'I believe, madam, on my part a lot of alcohol had been consumed.' Vince chuckled.

'Well,' the old woman sighed, 'it wouldn't be the first time alcohol has been the cause of dubious decisions and I doubt it'll be the last. Yet, you stayed together to watch out for each other and in my book, that is the best kind of friendship.'

The conversation turned to other topics and Brandon relaxed more. Good food, fine wine and Miss Marsh's engaging presence and attractive face across from him put him into a pleasant mood. For now, it was enough.

'Forgive me, will you?' Mrs Fordham wiped her mouth with a linen napkin. 'As much as I've enjoyed this evening, I am old and in need of my bed.' As she rose, Brandon stood to assist her. 'Thank you, Mr Forster. No, Prue, stay. You've no need to turn in, too. The night is young, and I am sure our new friends will look after you for me, won't you?' She turned to stare at Brandon.

'Absolutely, madam.'

'Thank you. Goodnight all.' She kissed her granddaughter's cheek.

Vince stepped forward. 'Allow me to escort you to your room, Mrs Fordham. Miss Marsh might enjoy a stroll on the terrace, Brandon?'

Brandon looked at Prue expectantly, hoping she'd agree. 'Would you, Miss Marsh?'

'I would, thank you.' She collected her silk wrap, and he helped her put it around her shoulders.

She looked up at him from under her lashes and he had a strong urge to kiss her. No, not yet. Too soon. Take it slow. You've time.

Gathering his wits, he guided her out of the dining room and through the opened doors to the terrace.

A small set of steps led down to another level and the paved area gave way to lawns and gardens. A path snaked between tall palm trees and garden beds full of roses in new bud. At intervals, torches spread golden circles of light, enough for them to see by as they sauntered.

Pausing at a railing overlooking the water below, Miss Marsh stopped and leaned against it. For a moment she simply stared out across the water and Brandon was content to watch her, memorise her loveliness.

'It is a beautiful night,' she said. 'I do love Italy.'

'You don't miss England?'

'I do, yes, a little, but the charm of Italy has captivated me. We've spent the last three months in Palermo, and it was fabulous. I'm not sure I ever want to return home.'

'I understand what you mean, but at some point, I must return and take over the running of my family's concerns.' For some reason he was starting to come to terms with the idea of being at home. He couldn't climb mountains forever.

'In Whitby?'

'Our country estate is there, yes, and where my parents wish to live permanently, but our main home is in London. Only my father is tired of London and prefers the country now. He wants me home so he can retire from politics and enjoy his passion of raising sheep.'

'Grandmama's house is in Mayfair.'

'We are in Belgravia.' He smiled. 'Where were you before coming to Italy?'

She glanced away. 'India. Bombay, actually.'

'That sounds exciting.'

'It was…' her voice drifted off.

He felt he'd touched a nerve and didn't press for information about India. 'So, you spent the winter in Palermo and now you are in Rome.'

'Yes.' She instantly brightened. 'I am eager to explore this wonderful city.'

'Perhaps we could do some exploring together?' The words were out of his mouth before he realised. 'If you want to, of course.'

Her eyes widened, but she smiled. 'I'd like that.'

'Vince and I arrived here just a week ago, and I've not seen the city's delights during the day for we have been climbing and trekking in the hills to the north and south. I'm eager to see the history.'

'Yes, we are surrounded by such splendour. And once I've seen Rome, I'd like to go to the coast and swim in the ocean. I have seen photos and heard much about the Amalfi Coast. My papa travelled there on his Grand Tour when he was a young man and always spoke of it. Apparently, it is most beautiful. I'm eager to see it, but Grandmama isn't too keen. She knows it to be very mountainous and not easy to reach by motor car. A lot of travelling in one day tires her now.'

'I, too, want to see that part of the coast. Vince and I have heard there are good climbs there. Perhaps we can work on your grandmama together and suggest we go there before you leave for Switzerland?'

She smiled cheekily, which curled his insides in a delicious way. 'I think that is a perfect idea, Mr Forster.'

Chapter Thirteen

The following morning, Prue craned her neck to look up at the vast ceiling of the Sistine Chapel. The beautiful colourful paintings of Michelangelo enthralled her. She took photos while the guide talked of artists and design. Although the photos would never be able to show the bright colours of the paintings, she would still have evidence of being there.

'It's incredible, isn't it?' Brandon Forster whispered beside her, looking up.

'Yes. It amazes me that it's so old, and yet it is so striking.' Her skin prickled at his closeness. He was too good looking for her liking, and after her experience with Ajay Khan she was wary of giving away too much of herself. That twist in her stomach when he glanced at her, didn't bode well, as it was the same kick of desire she felt for Ajay Khan and look where that got her.

She didn't regret sleeping with Ajay, but on reflection he wasn't the best person to give her virginity to, but then who was? She might never marry and if that was the case, why should she wait for the perfect man to come along when he might never show up?

Prue moved on to gaze at another part of the paintings on the vaulted ceiling. She needed an excuse to keep her distance from Mr Forster. Her senses came alive when he was around, and she couldn't trust herself. 'Are we not very fortunate?'

'How so?'

'We are lucky enough to see such wonderful works of art and so many people in the world will never visit here.' She walked on, glad that he followed her.

'That can be said for many places. I know I will not see everything I would wish to, but perhaps my children and their children will see parts of the world I never will?'

She gave him a quick smile. 'That is a lovely way to think of it.'

'Miss Marsh.' Vince found them amongst the other tourists. 'Your grandmama wishes to find a café and have some coffee. She says if another American tourist treads on her toes, she'll not be responsible for her actions.'

'Oh dear. Yes, we'll find a café. I'd hate to have to break up an argument between Grandmama and an American.'

'Mrs Fordham would win!' Vince grinned.

'Undoubtedly.' She smiled warmly at Vince, liking him very much. He was funny and witty and in the short time of their acquaintance she knew he'd be the kind of friend she could have forever. She felt no sexual tension with Vince and so he received all of her attention and meaningless flirtations.

Prue and Mr Forster followed him outside where Grandmama sat on a bench in the Vatican Gardens.

'I'm sorry to drag you away, my dear,' Grandmama said as they approached. 'But I needed to sit down for a moment.'

'Are you feeling all right?' Prue worried.

'Absolutely. But the crowds!' Grandmama stood and took Prue's arm. 'It just became so busy in there.'

'Well, there is a new pope, and people travel far in the hope of seeing him.'

'Pope Pius XI,' Grandmama grunted. 'As if he'd be wandering around here like a normal person? Why are people so stupid to imagine they will see him? The best they might get is him appearing at a window and saying a blessing.'

'Perhaps that is all they want, a blessing.'

'Good luck to them. Most of the tourists here just want to want to say they've been to such a holy building, not everyone is here for religion. One fellow, I think he was a German, spoke so loudly I couldn't hear the guide and he preceded to tell everyone the history of the chapel himself. Disgraceful. As if a German would be more knowledgeable than the Italian guide? Someone needs to remind them that they lost the war, and no one is interested in what they have to say. They should have the common decency to keep quiet.'

'Not all Germans are bad, Grandmama,' Prue whispered as they walked along the path and back into the circular Piazza San Pietro. Sometimes it was difficult to stop Grandmama speaking her prejudices.

'I know that. I once had some very good German friends. Very intelligent, but we lost touch during the war. They weren't the kind to shout their mouth off at every occasion.'

'Where shall we have some coffee, Mrs Fordham?' Vince asked jovially, but Prue saw the slight twitch at the corner of his eye. Did the talk of Germans upset him?

'The nearest place you can find, my good man, if you please?'

'Certainly, madam. There's a lovely little café we passed this morning, and it's only along the river a short way, once we cross the bridge.'

'That will do, thank you.' Grandmama took his arm, and Prue knew she, too, liked their new friends.

However, Prue watched her grandmama closely as they walked slowly along the Ponte Vittorio Emanuele II. Of late, Grandmama seemed to be slowing down. Their lengthy stay at a friend's villa in Palermo had been for Prue's recovery from the malaria but it also gave Grandmama a long rest as well. Naturally, she'd never admit to it, but Prue understood the signs now. Grandmama needed longer to get going in the mornings and frequent rests during the day. The emotional goodbyes when leaving Uncle Hugo and the baby had upset Grandmama more than she let on. Grandmama felt she'd never see Hugo again and Prue believed her. He and Aunt Daphne were moving to Ceylon, and they had no intentions of returning to England.

Halfway along the bridge, Prue paused and took some photographs of the Castel Sant'Angelo. The sunshine was warm on her face, but there wasn't the cloying humidity of India to cope with.

'Shall I take one of you?' Mr Forster stopped to ask.

'No, thank you.' Prue put the camera away.

'Shame, you would be an extremely suitable model.' He walked off.

Annoyed that she'd rebuffed him instead of laughing and joking as was her way, Prue stared down at the flowing water and wondered why she couldn't treat him the same way as she did with Vince. It really would make life so much easier if she could. Any kind of tension irritated her.

Prue hurried up to Vince and Grandmama and joined in their conversation about Italian food. Mr Forster strolled behind, whistling. She was aware of his presence too much.

Last night, she had returned to her room and lay in bed for hours thinking of Brandon Forster. During dinner, she'd learned a little about him. An ex-soldier like Jeremy, Forster and Vince seemed to have some wealth, or they'd not be staying in such a luxurious hotel. They spent their time roaming countries mountain climbing and partying, a decadent life. Vince told her they were all about having a good time, and Prue admired that. Surely, they deserved it after years of war. She, too, wanted to live life to the fullest, especially after the wedding day massacre, when she easily could have died as Ajay did. The images of that day still made her shudder. It was one memory that wouldn't fade.

By this morning she had made up her mind that at twenty-three she had a few years to be free and impulsive, before she became serious with getting married and having children. Life could be short, and she wanted to make the most of it.

~ ~ ~ ~

'Where are we going again?' Prue asked as she held Vince's hand and they ran through the rain to a doorway.

'Balla's Bal Tic Tac! The only place to be in Rome at night, apparently.' Vince told her as Forster pushed open the door.

'How did you come to know about it?'

'We met some people in Milan who are from Rome,' Forster said, as they walked down a staircase radiantly painted in red and yellow. 'They told us to come here for night-time entertainment.'

At the bottom, Vince groaned as a queue had formed along the long corridor, its pillars painted white and red. 'It looks popular, that's for sure.'

'It's very… bright,' Prue murmured, staring at the colourful interior and they were only in the corridor.

Eventually they made it to the entrance of a large room, where they were greeted by a middle-aged man dressed in a blue linen suit. His black moustache was twirled at the ends and he wore a monocle, whether he needed one or not, Prue wasn't quite sure. When she looked back, he was gone.

'Was that the owner?' she asked.

'Yes, Giacomo Balla, the artist,' Forster answered.

As they moved through the tables, Arabian belly dancers were on the stage. Prue was in awe of their movements, the quick shimmy of their hips, bangles jangling, gossamer outfits with veiled faces, then the slow rhythmic turns and hand gestures.

Vince clapped Forster on the back. 'We struck it well, tonight, old chap.'

'What do you want to drink, Miss Marsh?' Forster asked Prue over the loud Arabian music and cheering.

'A gin and tonic, please?'

He nodded and made his way to the bar as Vince guided her to a vacant table by the wall decorated in garish blue and red. 'There is a jazz band on later.'

'That is perfect. I love jazz.' Prue sat and watched the dancers, their supple bodies mesmerising. She must learn to belly dance properly not like the silly hip twists she used to do when messing about with Cece and Millie.

Suddenly, as if the dancers knew they had their audience captured, they jumped off the stage and circulated through the tables choosing random guests to dance with them.

One pretty young woman, her eyes heavy with thick make-up, grabbed Prue's hand and pulled her up on to the stage.

Laughing, Prue squinted in the spotlights, unable to see the audience cheering. The music changed again as each dancer instructed their pupil on the ways to move.

Glad she'd worn a short metallic emerald dress shot through with gold thread, the tassels on her legs swished with every movement she made. Carefully, she watched her instructor, mirroring her movements. Dancing was one of her loves, and Prue forgot the audience and kept her focus on the belly dancer's instructions, eager to learn and do well.

In time with the music, Prue felt the rhythm and gyrated her hips the same as the dancers. She picked up the movements quickly and was soon confident enough to look out into the darkness of the crowd. She could pick out a few people, one being Forster as he sat at the table with Vince drinking.

When the music stopped, Prue thanked her partner and when back to the table, hot but elated.

'That was fantastic!' Vince applauded.

'Thank you,' Prue puffed. 'I've not danced in months, not since India.' Reminded of dancing in the street at the wedding parade, Prue quickly sat down and sipped her gin and tonic, pushing the Indian dancing to the back of her mind. 'Thank you for getting me this.'

'No problem,' Forster replied, switching his gaze from her back to the stage as a band set up their instruments.

Tables were pushed further to the sides of the room and a dance floor was made in front of the stage. The band tuned up for a few minutes, but when they started in earnest, Prue's feet tapped, and her body bopped in her seat.

'Care to dance, Miss Marsh?' Vince stood and held out his hand.

'Only if you call me Prue.'

'Prue it is then and I'm Vince, and that is Brandon. Who needs to be formal on a night like this?'

'Agreed.' Prue grinned and took another sip of her drink. 'I'll not sit down once I start dancing, I'm giving you fair warning!'

'Let us see how long we last then!' He winked.

Other couples joined them on the dance floor, all young and eager for fun as Prue was. She danced with uninhibited joy. The beat of the drums and the jazz sounds of the saxophone made her body move of its own accord and she gave into the delicious feeling of just dancing to the heady music.

As the beat grew in pace, Vince twirled her around before letting her go so she could dance alone. In the next moment a young lean Italian man, dressed in a black suit, his dark hair slicked back, grabbed her hand and whirled her. He could dance better than anyone she'd seen.

His feet tapped out a rhythmic sequence and then suddenly he'd do a hop and a twirl and glide back to Prue and spin her around his body. She followed his movements, never having done such a dance before but loving it all the same. Vince was partnering another young woman on the edge of the dance floor, but Prue and her unnamed partner only had eyes for each other as they shimmied and twisted to the beat.

'You are a great dancer,' Prue shouted to him over the music. 'Where did you learn to move like that?'

'America.' He leaned closer to whisper in her ear. 'Down south in Louisiana. It's all the rage, sweetheart.' His Italian accent was entwined with an American accent.

'You've been to America? How fascinating.'

'You're the best-looking woman here.'

'Thank you.'

'Want to know more about my time in America?'

'I would yes. What is your name?'

'Alberto.'

'I'm Prue.'

'Let me get you a drink, Prue.' Effortlessly, he guided her to the bar.

The pink light of early dawn was coming over the horizon when Prue wearily left the club with Vince and Forster. She had her arm linked through Vince's as he was very drunk and with Forster on the other side of him, they managed to walk along the wet roads back to their hotel.

'That was quite a night,' Forster murmured.

'One of the best in my life.' Prue sighed happily. Now she had stopped dancing her feet throbbed and her ears rang, but she couldn't stop smiling.

'You certainly enjoyed it.' Forster raised his eyebrows at her over Vince's bent head.

She stiffened slightly. Was he censuring her? 'The night was there to enjoy. So, I did.'

'You certainly know how to dance and had many willing partners. That Italian fellow was a bit of a show pony though, wasn't he?'

'No, I don't regard him as so. He was an excellent dancer and why should he hide the fact?'

Between them Vince burped loudly.

Forster heaved him up a bit more. 'Perhaps next time we can find somewhere else that has music a little slower to dance to, then maybe I could have a turn with you around the dancefloor?'

'Yes, I'm sure we can.' Prue stared ahead, not sure if she wanted to be in Forster's arms. Her skin tingled at the thought of him holding her. He'd watched her all night, but declared jazz dancing wasn't his style, unlike Vince who danced with her and several other women for hours before he gave up and sat down. When she wasn't dancing with Vince, she was with Alberto.

'I'm surprised we got you out of there without fending off several Italians intent on taking you home.' His grin made a joke of it but something in his green eyes said the opposite.

She laughed softly, glancing up at the night sky now clear of rain clouds. 'I was only interested in the dancing.'

Vince burped again and straightened a little. 'I thinks... we... we... should 'ave another drinks...'

Prue giggled at his slurring.

'We've had more than enough, old chap.' Forster hoisted Vince up further as he began to slip.

Vince's head swayed when he gazed at Prue. 'He's... a spoilsport... You and me... sweet girl...'

'We have to get you to bed,' Prue soothed, getting a better grip of his arm.

'You coming to beds... withs me?' One eye squinted up at her.

'No!' Shaking her head, she heaved up a bit more on her side.

'A drinks then?'

'No.'

'Tomorrow then?' he asked sleepily.

'Maybe.' She struggled with his weight.

'I… I'm going to be sick.' Vince abruptly turned and vomited into some bushes at the front of the hotel.

Forster sighed. 'He never can hold his liquor.'

Thankfully, the streets were quiet, and no one witnessed their disgrace. The doorman of the hotel came down to the steps to help Forster half-carry half-drag Vince up into the foyer.

'A drink!' Vince shouted.

'No, and be quiet,' Forster demanded.

Prue crossed the marble floor to the lift, where the lift-operator opened the doors for them. She bit her lip to stop from grinning as Vince began to sing loudly.

'Vince, shut up, you fool.' Forster manhandled him into the lift.

Prue told the lift-operator the floor number.

'He'll wake the entire hotel,' Prue chuckled as the annoyed doorman left them to return to his post.

Once on their floor, Prue and Forster encouraged Vince to go with them into their suite instead of going back down to the bar. The lift-operator helped Forster assist in getting Vince upright and out of the lift.

'Brandon…' Vince leaned drunkenly against the corridor wall as Forster put the key in the lock of their room door. 'Brandon… isn't she wonderful?' Vince waved in Prue's direction.

'Yes, very,' Forster answered, pulling Vince away from the wall. 'Come on, let us get you inside.'

Embarrassed by Vince's comment, Prue helped Forster get Vince to the sofa where he collapsed and instantly started snoring.

'I don't know why I put up with him at times.' Forster shook his head, then preceded to take off Vince's shoes.

'Because he's your best friend.' Prue found a blanket from one of the bedrooms and placed it over Vince. 'Will he be all right?'

'Definitely. I've lost count over the years of the amount of times I've brought him home in such a state. He's been worse since the war, but that can't be helped.'

'My brother-in-law, Jeremy has issues, too. Nightmares and such,' Prue murmured.

'For some people the war doesn't always end with the armistice.' Forster stepped away and tiredly wiped his hand over his face. He undid the top button of his white shirt, exposing his suntanned neck.

Prue watched his fingers and her stomach clench in awareness of him. 'I'd best go to my room.'

'I enjoyed tonight,' Forster said as she reached the door.

She turned and gave him a glimmer of a smile. 'I did too.'

'I liked watching you dance.'

She didn't know what to say to that. 'Thank you, Mr Forster, for taking me along.'

'I thought we were on a first name basis now? I'm Brandon.' His intense gaze sent shivers over her body.

They stared at each other for a moment then she fled down the corridor to the safety of her own suite.

Chapter Fourteen

Reclining on the brocade sofa in the suite she shared with Grandmama, Prue tucked her legs up under her and opened Millie's letter which had just been delivered.

Dearest Prue,

I'm so pleased you've arrived safely in Rome. Was the journey terribly tiring? Are you fully recovered from the malaria now? In your last letter written from Palermo you said you were back to normal, but it is a worry when this horrible affliction can come back at any time. You must take care of yourself.

Grandmama keeps insisting that you are fine, as you do yourself so we, Mama and I, and Cece, of course, must believe it. I do long to see you though. It's been forever.

Mama and Cece have returned to York after another visit here. Mama spent some time in Paris with Jacques. It wouldn't surprise me if they got married within the year. Cece spent most of her time with

Jonathan, which was so helpful to me. He loves her dearly. With Cece's help we were able to let Nurse Allard take some much-needed holiday time.

You asked me if I could come out and visit you while you were in Italy, but dearest sister, sadly I am unable. You see, I am having another baby! You are to be an aunt again!

Jeremy and I are so pleased, worried too, naturally, with Jonathan arriving too soon. This baby is due in October, but with my history who can rely on that? We really don't want to take the risk and travel. I'm so sorry. I really wanted to go to Italy and see you. I hope you understand?

Prue put down the letter and gazed out at the small balcony where rain fell at a steady rate. She was going to be an aunt again. Emotion built behind her eyes at the wonderful news of Millie having another baby. It'd been over a year since she last saw Millie and she missed her sister terribly.

It also upset her that Cece was spending so much time with Jonathan. The darling baby wouldn't even remember Prue. Was she doing the right thing by engaging in all this travelling when she could be spending time with her family?

Your photographs are simply amazing, Prue. I show them to everyone here at the chateau and friends who visit. I'm so pleased you are documenting your travels. Do keep sending them to me.

We read in the newspaper recently that Gandhi has been jailed for six years in India. There has been more rioting as a consequence. I am pleased you are no longer there. I do hope Uncle Hugo and Aunt

Daphne can find some peace now they have moved to Ceylon.

What is this about a man named Mussolini creating problems in Italy? Jeremy says that some parts of Italy have given over to Mussolini's regime as though he is already in power, but he's not yet. There is no violence in Rome, is there? Or are you too busy partying to notice? Ha!

I'd better close this letter now for we have a dinner party to attend tonight and I need to wash my hair. I'll write again in a few days. Enjoy the Italian sunshine and don't flirt with too many Italian men! Ha.

All my love,
Millie x
Chateau Dumont
Epernay, France. April 1922

Getting up and walking over to the writing desk, Prue took a fresh piece of paper and began to write.

Dear Millie,

Thank you for your letter. I'm so pleased to hear that Jonathan is to be a big brother! I'm extremely excited for you and Jeremy and you must not even think to travel while pregnant. I've decided that I shall come to you before the baby is born, as I don't want to miss seeing my new niece or nephew come into the world.

Grandmama and I don't need to go on to Switzerland after our stay in Italy is over. I would much prefer to spend time with you. I miss you very much and I want to see the new baby far more than I want to travel to Switzerland. I miss our chats.

Prue paused. She hadn't told Millie or anyone other than Grandmama about what happened in Bombay with Ajay Khan. Each time she tried to write about it to Millie the words wouldn't flow and so she gave up. Yet she wanted to talk to Millie about Ajay, and what she had done with him, about the massacre that killed thirty-four people and how Ajay died at her feet, saving her. Perhaps she could share with Jeremy how she had such nightmares where she had his blood on her hands, a gun pointing at her.

She wanted to talk to Millie about leaving Bombay two weeks after Uncle Hugo's baby boy was born, and how Gertie fled in the night after giving birth and hasn't been heard of again. None of what really happened in India could be written in a letter.

Prue took a deep breath, banished the memories and continued writing.

We have met the loveliest two men, who are staying in the same hotel as we are. Two men who Jeremy will know! Mr Vince Barton and Mr Brandon Forster, both were officers in the same brigade or battalion — I can't remember which – with Jeremy.

Jeremy invited them to your wedding, but they were in Spain, or somewhere, mountain climbing. Mr B and Mr F are most charming and very social. We went out two nights ago to a jazz club. I had a fabulous time. Today we were going to do some more sightseeing, but it is raining, so we decided against it. Instead, Grandmama is having her hair done in the hotel's salon and I am recovering from a long dinner

last night with Mr B and Mr F in which a lot of
drinking was involved.

There is a splendid restaurant here and a piano bar.
We stayed in the piano bar until the hotel staff very
politely asked us to leave about three o'clock this
morning. Mr F plays the piano beautifully and asked
if he could play when the pianist had finished his
shift. He was granted permission and his playing
entertained us for another hour or more.

Prue stopped and remembered the delight in
listening to Mr Forster, Brandon, play the piano last
night. His fingers, long and supple, drifted over the
keys as though he was part of the piano, the music
flowed into the empty bar and she believed Brandon
forgot the world as he played.

She and Vince were content to sit and drink,
listening to the enchantment of the music.

Mr B and Mr F may come to the coast with
Grandmama and I for a while after we've grown tired
of Rome. However, after that, Grandmama and I shall
come to you in France. I can always go to
Switzerland another time. As I mentioned above, I'd
much prefer seeing you and Jonathan and the new
baby.

After the upset of leaving Uncle Hugo and the baby,
I think Grandmama would like to be with family, too.

Prue looked up from the letter as Grandmama
entered the room, her grey hair washed and softly
curled. 'You look lovely.'

'Thank you, dearest.' Grandmama patted her curls.
'I must say it was a unique experience. Having a

stranger touch one's hair in such an intimate manner is rather disturbing.'

'I'm delighted you attended the salon. You're never too old to try new things.'

Grandmama gave her a cutting glare. 'That saying is worthy when one is sampling foreign foods for the first time, not when a woman of my age is having her scalp massaged by an Italian woman in the basement of a hotel.'

'It's a luxury, Grandmama, it's modern. You enjoyed the session, didn't you?'

'I will grudgingly admit that the manageress of the salon, Senora Bianco, was very attentive and most knowledgeable, so much better than Mavis at home.'

Prue smiled. 'Mavis is over sixty and needs to be retired. You're being stubborn about not pensioning her off and employing a younger lady's maid.'

'Tosh!' Grandmama placed her black leather handbag on the table and slipped off her gloves. 'Did I not allow Mavis to stay in London and not accompany me on this journey?'

'Only because you have me, who can act as your lady's maid, or have splendid Indian servants as you had at Uncle Hugo's house.'

'As good as you are, it's not the same. I prefer having Mavis with me. She knows my routine.'

'Mavis has to take care of her health, too, Grandmama. She wasn't up to this trip.'

'The woman puts it on, always whining about her aches and pains. I'm well over seventy and have I retired from life? No, I have not. Mavis has it very well in my service, and I'll not hear anything different.'

Prue rolled her eyes and put away her letter.

'Who are you writing to?'

'Millie. I received a letter from her this morning. She is to have another baby.'

'She is?' Grandmama smiled contentedly. 'That is wonderful news. I must buy them a present. Though I did talk to Millie about spacing apart the arrival of children. She obviously didn't listen.'

'Jonathan is over a year old. He'll be nearly two when the baby is born.'

'Yes, but Millie is a very busy woman. She has no time to be pregnant. Perhaps if they have a girl, they'll stop. Copious amounts of children is so Victorian.' Grandmama sat down on the sofa. 'I have ordered tea to be brought up. The rain is too heavy to go out. I'm not wasting my morning having a stranger touch my hair only for it be flat with rain the minute I step outside.'

'I'm happy to stay indoors today. We have the theatre tonight.'

Grandmama picked up one of Prue's discarded fashion magazines and then put it down again. 'Oh, the talk of the new baby nearly made me forget to tell you something which I believe you'll be most happy about.'

'What is it?'

'There was a lady in the chair next to me at the salon, a Mrs Grandwell-Smith, we introduced ourselves sans cards, how very bohemian of us!' Grandmama chuckled. 'Anyway, Mrs Grandwell-Smith hails from Manchester, her father made the family money in mills. We can't hold that against her, of course.' Grandmama waved her hand dismissively. 'Her husband, long dead, bought a villa along the Amalfi Coast some time ago and she visits it for the first three months of the year to avoid the worst of the winter in England. Entirely sensible, if you ask me. I mentioned your wish to travel to that part of the coast. Now hasn't this Mrs Grandwell-Smith been the best of acquaintances and offered us her villa for the summer?'

Astonished, Prue jumped up from her chair. 'She has? Why would she do that? She doesn't know us.'

Grandmama frowned. 'And what is wrong with her offer? Do I look untrustworthy?'

'No, I didn't mean that.'

'That is what it sounded like. Do I have the appearance of someone unscrupulous?'

'No. I simply meant that you don't know each other. She isn't a friend, yet she has offered us her villa.'

'I've stayed in the houses of many an unknown person, Prue. Back in my day, staying at someone's house while the family were in residence was considered discourteous! The homes of friends of friends was the *only* way to procure excellent accommodation you could trust.' Grandmama shook her head sadly. 'For all your modern ways, girl, you haven't lived.'

Prue dismissed the last comment. 'Well, this Mrs Grandwell-Smith sounds like a very nice lady.'

'Incredible, isn't it? She met me only an hour before and there she was offering her villa to us over a cup of coffee and a biscotti!'

'That is so generous.'

A knock on the door interrupted them. Prue opened it to allow a male hotel staff member to wheel in a trolley full of tea, bread, cheese and cakes.

Grandmama tipped the man and closed the door on him. 'So, we are able to have the villa from next Saturday. Is that suitable for you? I think that makes it May second. Are you happy with that?'

'Yes, very happy. Where is the villa?' Prue couldn't believe their luck. Excitement thrummed through her.

'Positano, not Amalfi as you wished. But the chances of meeting another lady with a villa on the Amalfi Coast while I'm having my hair washed is highly unlikely, I'm afraid. Positano will have to do.'

'I do not mind Positano at all.'

'The villa is up high, with excellent views, but it's quite a walk down a great many stairs to the beach I was told. I say walk but it's more of a trek of fortitude.' Grandmama tutted as she mashed the tea. 'I shall need a lot of books to keep me occupied, for I shan't be rambling up and down the cliff side. I'm not a mountain goat.'

'We'll work it out, Grandmama.' Fit to burst with enthusiasm, Prue sat at the table, took a plate and selected a slice of fresh crusty bread, cheese, prosciutto and dried tomatoes. 'How long can we stay?'

'The whole summer if we wished. Mrs Grandwell-Smith doesn't like to rent the place out in summer unless it's to friends, people she can trust. She tried it one time before the war and a group of young Greek men had it after finishing university and they nearly destroyed the place with their wild parties.' Grandmama gave Prue a knowing look. 'You can never trust the Greeks, remember that, especially handsome young Greek fishermen from the islands. They are all soft words and white teeth and have a woman in every port.'

Prue hid a smile. 'I will remember.'

'Mrs Grandwell-Smith also mentioned that the whole area was full of wealthy American tourists, especially Sorrento. It seems a great many Italians emigrated to America and made money, so their descendants come back and buy up ruins in various villages. Terribly vulgar. So, we will have to endure that and hope they don't join us on our side of the coast. They seem to seep into every nook and cranny like lice.'

'Grandmama, *we* will be tourists as well.'

Grandmama looked affronted. 'The British aren't tourists, girl. At one point we owned most of the world. When we travel, we are simply revisiting old territories.' Grandmama popped an olive into her mouth. 'I passed Mr Barton and Mr Forster in the foyer and mentioned the villa to them.'

'Oh?' Prue tried not to be affected by the response whatever it turned out to be.

'They graciously accepted the invite. I did not think it would harm us to be in the company of two fine gentlemen such as them. Mr Barton makes me laugh and Mr Forster is intelligent and has good conversation. Are you in agreement with them joining us?'

Prue's heart somersaulted. 'Yes. I'm happy you asked them.'

Grandmama added sugar to her tea. 'I thought you might be.'

~ ~ ~ ~

In the hot crowded streets surrounding the impressive Colosseum, Brandon stood with Vince and Prue. They were searching for a restaurant that Prue had been given as a recommendation. However, she didn't know where the restaurant was or remembered its name, only that it was near the Colosseum.

Vince eyed a pretty woman who walked past before turning back to Prue. 'I deem we have hit a dead end, my dear friend. Without a name or street how will we ever find it? You've been into four different places now and no one knows your Indian friend.'

Brandon watched Prue's reaction. She had been cagey about her mission today. After shopping all morning, she'd suggested lunch would be on her. She wanted to try to find a place recommended to her, but she had little details and wouldn't speak of the person who gave her the recommendation. It intrigued him.

'Perhaps if you were to write to your friend in India and ask them?' Vince said, lighting a cigarette.

'No. I can't do that.' Prue's blue eyes turned dull as she glanced away.

'Why?' Vince quizzed. 'Was he a former lover?'

Prue's laugh was forced and brittle, Brandon could tell. 'Not at all. He was the cousin of a friend of mine.'

Brandon straightened, picking up on the past tense of her sentence. The man was dead. 'Shall we go to that place over there on the corner?' he suggested. He wanted her to smile properly and bask in her sunny nature again. He didn't like to see her sad. 'We could do with getting out of the sun.'

'Yes, thank you.' She seemed relieved by his idea.

Once they were seated outside the front of the restaurant under the awning, Brandon ordered a jug of iced water and coffee for the table. Light salads, pasta and bread was added to the order and then Vince sauntered off to the bar inside.

Brandon leaned back in his chair and observed Prue watching the tourists file past. She'd brought her camera and contentedly captured some photographs of the famous gladiator arena.

'We can go inside the Colosseum after lunch if you wish?' he asked her.

'I'd like that, thank you. Grandmama has been before and said it is worth a visit.'

'I'm imagining that Mrs Fordham is enjoying her lunch with Mrs Grandwell-Smith. I suspect she'd rather do that than mingle with so many tourists.'

'Yes, Grandmama wanted to discuss last-minute details with Mrs Grandwell-Smith before the lady leaves for England tomorrow.'

'I'm looking forward to staying at the villa. I think we'll make a merry party.' Brandon said no more as the waiter came with a carafe of water, and another of red wine, which had been ordered by Vince at the bar.

Prue raised her eyebrows. 'If I drink red wine during the day and in this warm weather, I'll have a headache and be asleep before dinner.'

'Vince. He can't be trusted. You don't have to drink any.' Brandon poured out the water into their glasses.

The thought of spending months with Prue Marsh thrilled and confused him. He was deeply attracted to her, but she gave him such mixed signals he didn't know whether to press his cause or not. She was beautiful, polite, charming and funny, but she never gave him flirtatious looks as she did to Vince. It was all harmless with Vince, he knew. Vince treated her like a sister and best friend all rolled into one.

Whereas he always seemed on the outside. She held him at arm's length and never fully relaxed in his presence. She wouldn't hold his gaze or would move away if he accidently got too close. He'd never experienced that before with a woman. Most either wanted sex as he did or treated him like a brother. Funnily enough he wanted to have more than just sex with Prue Marsh and would hate it if she treated him like a sibling.

He found it amazing that she had managed to get under his skin so swiftly. He wanted more than a holiday romance and that realisation frightened him more than he could say. He hadn't felt that way since Claudia.

Vince returned all smiles and waving a card. 'Luca, the owner of this fine establishment has given me the card of his cousin, Antonio, who has a bar and restaurant in Positano. Isn't that fortunate?'

Prue grinned at him, tucking her short blonde hair behind her ear. 'Typical that it is a bar.'

'What would you prefer?' Vince asked innocently, pouring glasses of ruby red wine.

'Oh, I don't know. A nice jewellery shop?'

'Ah, the lady wants diamonds and gold, Brandon, did you hear?'

'And why not?' Prue slapped Vince's arm. 'A girl always wants pretty things.'

As the food was brought out, Brandon sat back and listened to Vince and Prue chatter about nothing important. He liked it when they talked for he could openly watch Prue without query, but he wished she would speak so freely to him. He was envious that Vince got all her smiles and jokes. He noticed that Prue spoke easily about her family and her home in York, but always changed the subject of India if it was brought up. It intrigued him. He couldn't help but to keep digging to find out why India was such a touchy subject.

He smeared roasted garlic onto his bread and dipped it into the olive oil. 'Are you to give up on searching for this particular restaurant?' he asked Prue.

She put down her glass of water and tilted her head to one side in thought. 'It seems I have to. Without any proper information I'm stuck. In the end, it was a passing fancy of mine to try to find it. Silly, really. The man who told me about it said it was a good restaurant to frequent, but it isn't such a big deal.'

'Never underestimate a good recommendation!' Vince drank some of his wine. 'Tell me about India. I long to visit there.'

Brandon silently praised Vince for the question.

Prue drank more water. 'It's a wonderful place to visit. It's colourful, aromatic…' She looked away to the Colosseum. 'It has its own charms.'

Vince forked up some pasta. 'Exotic, too. All that heat and spices, beautiful women wearing those thin veils and bright saris. Heaven.'

Commotion at the end of the street made the diners pause in their eating.

Brandon leaned back in his chair to get a better view of what was happening.

'Has an auto bus broken down?' Vince asked, eating his pasta.

Brandon squinted into sun as shouts became louder. 'I'm not sure. An argument has broken out. There's a lot of people about.' He turned back to the table and noticed a stillness about Prue.

'The Italians are passionate people,' Vince said.

The sound of breaking glass cut above the talk of people.

Prue screamed. Vince and Brandon jumped and stared her.

More glass shattered.

Vince dropped his fork. 'What the hell is happening?'

Shop windows were being smashed by men wearing black. Shouts and yells filled the air as another truck of men dressed in black arrived and filtered out along the street.

A woman cried out and ran from one shop, her head bleeding from a cut.

The word Mussolini was whispered on the diner's lips. Many tables started to gather their belongings and throwing money on the table, they quickly disappeared into the crowds.

'I have to go!' Prue slammed back her chair. She looked terrified.

Brandon touched her arm. 'Prue, it's all right. It's nothing to do with us.'

'No, it's not safe! I have to go!' Her camera bag strap was wrapped around the bottom of the chair leg. She cried, trying to yank it free.

Suddenly, a fire took hold in a shop window, which has been smashed. People fled the scene heading towards the café where they sat, and behind them marched angry looking black-shirted men brandishing batons, some even held a rifle or pistol.

'Blackshirts! They are coming this way!' Brandon jerked up from his chair.

Prue moaned, her eyes wide in her pale face.

He grabbed Prue's arm and dragged her behind him. 'Hurry, Vince! They are Fascist Blackshirts, Mussolini's men!'

'But we are British,' Vince argued, downing a mouthful of wine as he rose. 'They won't hurt us.'

'Please!' Prue begged, already edging out of the confined area of tables and out into the street, pulling on Brandon's arm to go with her.

'Come on!' Brandon yelled at Vince, gripping Prue's hand.

A wave of violence followed them as every window in the street was smashed by a team of livid Blackshirts. Women screamed, children cried. One man was pulled out of his shop, his arms flailing, and was beaten.

Serious men intent on causing damage shouted as people scrambled to get away from the destruction and hide.

Brandon had seen enough. There were no police nearby to stop the devastation, and he wasn't sure if they would, anyway. The Italians were afraid of Mussolini's men, and that included the police.

He ran down the street, weaving himself and Prue through the running pedestrians. When a side alley appeared, he turned and signalled Vince to follow them away from the Colosseum.

Prue's sobbing upset him. She was as white as a sheet and shaking. He held her hand and was grateful she could keep up with him. Vince was behind them, warning others who came out to stare at the commotion to go back inside.

They crossed a main road and headed into a grassy park opposite. Here, people sat in the sun or strolled about the ruins oblivious to the havoc being created down the other street.

Brandon slowed to catch his breath.

Clutching her camera, Prue bent over, breathing heavily. She shook so badly her teeth chattered.

Vince leaned against a stump of a Roman statue long gone. 'That was crazy!' He snorted a laugh. 'What an escape! Those damn Blackshirts! We outfoxed them!'

'Are you all right?' Brandon stepped closer to Prue. She shook her head, tears ran down her cheeks. Then abruptly she spun on her heel and vomited behind the statue.

Brandon stared in confusion. Her reaction was extreme.

Vince was beside her in seconds. 'Prue?'

Wordlessly she gazed at them, her big blue eyes awash with tears and haunted.

'Let us get back to the hotel.' Brandon put his arm around her. 'Vince, go wave down a passing taxi.'

On the drive back to the hotel, Brandon kept his arm about Prue's shoulders. She was so thin he could feel her bones through her blue linen dress. With her hands folded in her lap she kept her head bowed, the shaking didn't stop.

No one spoke the entire trip or even in the hotel lift. At the door to Prue's suite, she couldn't get the key out of her bag and ended up dropping it.

Brandon retrieved the key and opened the door. 'Mrs Fordham?'

'Yes, I'm here.' Mrs Fordham came out of one of the bedrooms, but her happy demeanour changed when she saw the state of Prue. 'What has happened?'

'A raid by the Blackshirts near where we were having lunch,' Brandon explained. 'Prue is pretty shaken up by it.'

Mrs Fordham took Prue into her arms even though Prue was much taller than the small old woman. 'Thank you for bringing her back. We'll see you both tomorrow.'

'Is there anything we can do?' Brandon persisted.

'No, nothing at all. Thank you.' Mrs Fordham started to close the door, forcing them out.

'Poor Prue,' Vince said, staring at the closed door. 'I thought she had more pluck than that, to be honest.'

'As did I,' Brandon murmured. Something wasn't right.

'Prue is really shaken. We were never really in great harm.' Vince frowned. 'I'm rather surprised. Until I saw her face, I considered it all a bit of a joke. The rush of fleeing, it was exhilarating. I expected Prue to be the type to see the fun side of that, too.'

'Obviously not.' Like Vince he expected Prue to laugh off the encounter, to joke about running away and how it would become a story to tell her grandchildren. She seemed the kind to find such things exciting. Her reaction was the opposite and reminded him of the soldiers in the war who had survived a battle without injury, as though it was all a dream. Yet, when you looked into their eyes, another story was told.

Vince stuck his hands his trousers pockets. 'I need a drink.'

'I'll join you.' Brandon fell into step with him.

Chapter Fifteen

Prue's first sight of Positano had been exactly what she hoped for. The dark green mountains surged up from the bay, creating secluded coves and jagged landscapes of sheer cliffs. Little villages like Positano clung to the cliff sides in steep terraces, their coloured stone houses packed in tightly and sprinkled with trees and cobbled streets and alleyways.

The closer the boat motored into the bay, the more defined the town became. In the dazzling sunlight, Prue could make out all the terraces belonging to the houses, some had vines growing along the balconies, the colours of blue wisteria, purple and red bougainvillea were punctuated with the yellow of plump lemons growing on rich green foliage.

Docking at the jetty, Prue smiled at the local fishermen. Along the street next to the grey pebbled beach, market stalls selling fresh fruit and vegetables took precedence. She noticed a gelato vendor standing under a red and white striped awning and he was shooing young children away who were bothering him for tastes of his gelato.

The slight breeze of late afternoon helped to cool the temperature, but it was still very hot for early May, and many people were swimming in the tranquil aqua water. The salty sea air and the humidity did nothing for her hair but squashed under her hat, she didn't care.

After travelling from Rome to Naples, they'd bought tickets on the ferry which left Naples and sailed to Sorrento. They'd then travelled by a smaller motor boat from Sorrento around the headland and down the coast to Positano.

While she and Grandmama supervised their luggage being taken off the boat, Brandon and Vince organised the cart to take them up the steep alleyways that blanketed the cliff sides.

Sitting on the back of an old cart being pulled by an equally ancient horse, Prue breathed in the salty sea breeze as it drifted up from the bay below. She was surrounded by their belongings and every bump over the cobbled road she felt as though she'd be toppled out of the cart, but she didn't care. She was here, in Positano, on the Amalfi Coast, following the footsteps of her dear papa.

On the seat next to the elderly cart driver, Grandmama chatted away in broken Italian to him.

Brandon and Vince were still down by the beach, negotiating the best price for a sad little motor car, which appeared like it had received one too many scrapes on these winding roads. But as Brandon said, a little automobile would be the best way for them to get about the coast and it would help Grandmama not be a prisoner in the villa.

At last the horse was halted and Prue jumped off the back of the cart. A stone wall higher than her head stretched along the road interspersed with wooden gates. There was number fifty-two — a green wooden gate which squeaked when Prue unlatched it.

She helped Grandmama down from the cart, and as the old man started unloading their luggage, Prue and Grandmama walked through the gate and along a short path bordered by vegetables and clumps of lavender.

Producing an enormous iron key, Grandmama unlocked the black wooden door, and they stepped inside a cool entrance with terracotta tiles on the floor. The first door on the right led into a good size kitchen, and on the left was a storage room. On the table in the kitchen was a basket of fresh bread sticks and other salad ingredients.

Going through a short corridor they entered a large white painted room with a long timber table and ten chairs and two sofas. Large windows let in the sunlight and French doors led out on to the wide tiled balcony, which held sun loungers and low tables.

The view from the room and the balcony took Prue's breath away. The entire town of Positano folded out like a fan beneath them stepping down to the grey sandy beach at the bottom. The blue-green dazzling bay reached out to the horizon. Not a cloud was in the blue sky and on the soft warm currents, birds swooped and dived.

'Do you like it then?' Grandmama asked, coming out onto the balcony.

'It's perfect.'

'Good.'

Prue ran inside and found two large bedrooms and two smaller ones, plus a tiny bathroom. The entire villa was painted white with the rust-coloured terracotta floor. Tubs of red geraniums dotted the balcony and lush green palms were placed in the living area around the plump yellow-cushioned sofas.

She gave the old man a tip as he brought in the last of the luggage. 'Which bedroom do you want, Grandmama?'

'The end bedroom is fine by me.'

Prue grabbed Grandmama's suitcase and another bag and hauled them into a large bedroom at the end of the corridor. The villa was wide, wrapping itself along the cliff. Two of the bedrooms had ocean views, while the other two faced the small walled garden and the road.

Grandmama joined her in the bedroom. 'You'll be all right here. I hear the Fascists aren't prominent in this area. It's too small and sleepy for them to worry about as yet. They don't care about fishermen and the odd tourist.'

'I'll be fine.' Not wanting to ponder about Fascists and the Blackshirts, Prue opened Grandmama's suitcase and took some dresses out and hung them in the wardrobe. 'It's good that the beds are made up. I assumed I'd have to make my first bed.'

'Leave that.' Grandmama touched Prue's shoulder. 'You've been quiet for days since the incident in the street. It's understandable that it would upset you, first India and now Rome, it's unfortunate that trouble has struck you twice, but dwelling on it won't undo what is done. You have to get on with your life and not let the bastards win.'

'Yes, I know.'

'Vince and Brandon are worried about you. They don't understand why seeing the Blackshirts smash up those shops affected you so badly. You either need to tell them what happened in India or paste on more

smiles than you are doing. You don't want to ruin
their holiday here with an awkward tension, do you?'

'No, not at all, but I don't want to tell them. I
couldn't cope with questions about India and Ajay.'

'If that's what you want.'

'It is. The past is better left alone. I need to forget it,
and I was doing so well. The quiet months in Palermo
helped greatly in that sense. I hope to recapture that
tranquillity here.' She paused in placing nightgowns
in the drawers by the window. 'I feel much better
already just by being on the coast and not in Rome.
It's quiet and peaceful.'

Grandmama gazed out of the window at the
dazzling view. 'How could anyone be unhappy here?
It's paradise.'

'And I'm eager to explore.'

'At the end of climbing up and down these streets
you'll have leg muscles on you like a weightlifter!'

Noise at the back door had them going out to meet
Brandon and Vince in the sitting room.

'Did you strike a deal?' Grandmama asked.

Vince waved a piece of paper in front of him. 'All
signed and sealed. We have transport, Mrs Fordham.
Shall I take you for a spin?'

'Absolutely not! If I wanted to die, I'd find a better
way to do it than have you drive us straight over the
cliff side!'

Vince laughed. 'You break my heart, madam.'

'I'd rather break your heart than you break my
neck.' She gave him a cutting stare before taking
notes out of her handbag and reading from them.
'Now a local woman, called Maria, will be here each
morning to cook us breakfast and bring fresh
supplies. She'll cook one main meal for us to have
either midday or in the evening, but we must let her

know. I will mention to her that we shall be eating out quite a lot. There is another local woman, Lola, I think she is called, who will come twice a week to clean and take the washing away.' Grandmama looked at them all. 'Is that satisfactory?'

They all agreed in unison.

'Good. Let us unpack and then we can decide where we shall eat this afternoon.'

In the flurry of getting luggage to bedrooms and making themselves at home, Prue was able to relax for the first time in a week.

'Where's the lav?' Vince asked from the hallway.

'Outside!' Prue chuckled, stacking her shoes into the wardrobe. 'Good job it's not the middle of winter.'

'How provincial.' Vince leaned against the doorjamb. 'Shall we go for a swim?'

'Yes! I'll get changed.' Prue shut the door on him with a laugh and quickly changed into an all-in-one swimming costume of navy blue. She pulled over it a thin white cotton coverall and donned white sandals. With a towel in her bag and grabbing her straw hat, she was ready.

In the sitting room, Brandon and Vince waited for her, both wearing swimming trunks and striped vest tops.

Prue glanced away from Brandon's broad chest with its sprinkling of dark hair just visible above the top of his vest. His legs and arms were well muscled, probably from all the mountain climbing he did. Everything about him set her senses alive and she had to quickly squash any feelings towards him. Desire would get her in trouble. She'd escaped being caught before, she couldn't risk doing it again. Also, Brandon was not Ajay. Ajay was someone who had piqued her interest, but then was quickly forgotten between visits. With Ajay she was curious, and he was forbidden, which made the hunt all the more exciting.

However, Brandon was in another league. Brandon would not allow her to call the shots. He would want to be in control. Instinctively, she knew she wouldn't be able to walk away from Brandon as easily as she had done with Ajay.

Besides, he was also living in the same villa so there would be no escape from her embarrassment should she do something silly.

'We're going now, Grandmama,' Prue said, heading for the door.

Grandmama, sitting out on the balcony, was reading a letter. 'Stay safe, and while you're out, find somewhere we can go to for dinner tonight,' she called as they left the villa.

'What is that?' Prue laughed when once through the gate she looked at the beaten-up motor car.

'Hey, be nice!' Brandon smiled, patting the dusty cream bonnet. 'It's a Vauxhall C10 Prince Henry.'

'She doesn't care what it is, Brandon,' Vince scoffed. 'It's nothing special.'

'That's not true. This would have been a good little motor when new.'

Prue was doubtful as she took in its damaged and dented bodywork. 'It looks like it's been sent over the side of the road on more than one occasion.'

'With some repairs, it could be restored to a grand beauty.' Brandon sighed lovingly.

Vince groaned, climbing over the back seat. 'Ignore him, Prue. He loves motor cars. Such a boring topic if you ask me.'

Brandon opened the passenger door for Prue. 'That's because, old chap, you're uneducated in the science and workmanship that goes into building these beauties.'

'This thing doesn't even have a roof. What if it rains?' Vince grunted. 'Waste of money.'

Prue turned to Vince as Brandon started the engine. 'I thought you liked the motor car?'

'I like that it saves me from walking.' Vince grinned. He tapped Brandon on the shoulder in front of him. 'Drive, dear boy, drive!'

Brandon shook his head and with a smile at Prue drove off down the road.

'I'd like to take it out onto the open road and see what this baby can do,' he shouted as they negotiated a sharp bend.

'That'll be fun,' Prue replied, enjoying the sun on her face and the openness of having a motor car with no roof. She could touch the buildings on either side of the narrow roads and often had to duck as overhanging vines of bright pink or red bougainvillea swept over their heads. With each curve of the road they had a new view, either of the bay or quaint little houses hugging the mountainside.

Closer to the beach, fisherman huts and cottages became more frequent, side by side with cafés and the dominating dome of the Church of Santa Maria Assunta which Prue had read about in a guide book on the train journey down from Rome. At present it was having restoration work done to it.

At the beach, Brandon parked the motorcar and they climbed out. Some sun worshippers were sitting on canvas chairs in front of little cafés and the more adventurous were lying on towels on the gritty sand, a few swimmers were in the water.

Prue ran down the sand and slipped off her sandals, hat and cover-all. She stepped into the gentle lapping waves that reached no higher than her calves. The cold water shocked her, but it was a delicious sensation to have her toes dig into the shingle and feel the coolness of the water about her feet.

'Not going in?' Brandon asked coming to stand beside her.

'I will, in a minute.' She stared out to the numerous boats on the water.

'We could hire a boat for the day and sail along the coast. What do you think?'

'That would be lovely.' She glanced over her shoulder. 'Where's Vince?'

'He's gone to the café to see if they have any wine or limoncello.'

'Oh. Typical Vince.'

'Yes.' Brandon sighed. 'It's becoming a habit.'

'The drinking?'

'He's worse than ever. It is getting out of control.'

'Oh.'

They stared out into the water for several moments until they heard Vince holler from behind. He came running down to them and with a yelp tackled Brandon into the water.

Prue squealed as she was splashed. The two men tussled and wrestled in the water, laughing and trying their best to drown the other.

Thinking she had escaped the madness, Prue squealed again as Vince picked her up and threw her into the water.

She sank down under the waves laughing and came up spluttering. 'I'll get you!' she yelled at Vince and proceeded to chase him through the shallows. He was too quick for her and giving up, she landed with a thump on the sand beside Brandon.

Sighing happily, Prue lay back on the sand as the trickle of tiny waves came up to her waist and then receded back. The three of them lay together, eyes closed to the sun above and content to be quiet and relaxed.

Prue turned her head and gazed at Brandon's profile. His wet hair had turned from its normal dark brown to black. With his eyes closed she could watch him without anyone noticing. She'd spent two weeks in the company of this man, and she only knew him a little, but the urge to touch him, kiss him was so strong it took all her effort to not lean over and kiss his lips.

'Are you a good swimmer, Prue?' Brandon suddenly murmured.

Shocked that she might have been caught staring, Prue sat up. 'Not bad.'

Brandon reclined onto one elbow. 'Shall we swim to that buoy out there?'

'No, that's too far.'

Vince also sat up. 'I'm starving. Can we eat instead?'

'Yes, good idea.' Prue collected her cover-all, hat and sandals and put them on. 'I'd like a coffee.'

'I thought you wanted to swim in the ocean?' Brandon said not moving. 'Come on, let's see how far we can get.'

'You go, Prue,' Vince encouraged. 'I've already booked us a table, so I'll go and order some food and drinks.'

Reluctantly, Prue stripped off again down to her bathing suit and stepped further into the water. They had to walk out quite a way before it was deep enough to swim properly. Prue watched Brandon cut through the water as though he was a fish. She tried to keep up but after a while he was over twenty yards away, so she flipped onto her back and floated, staring up at the blue sky.

Floating, letting the rock of the gentle swell move her, she relaxed. Although she wasn't a great swimmer, she was not scared. If she stood up, she'd not be in over her head. Birds flew above and she watched them, imagining what it was like to be so free.

Hands around her waist jolted her upright. She whipped around to stare at Brandon who was smiling back at her.

'Did you imagine I was a shark?'

'No!' She swam away, breaking the contact between them. She'd enjoyed the touch of his hands on her bare skin. Glancing back at him, she wished she could simply swim up to him and kiss him. Groaning in dismay at the fierce desire that filled her, she kicked her legs and moved further away. Did she never learn?

Other swimmers came closer to them. One young woman, her long dark hair floating in the water like a mermaid's, smiled at Brandon and he returned the smile and spoke to her in Italian. The woman laughed and replied, which made Brandon laugh as well.

Prue glared at them both and began to swim back to the beach.

'Race you back!' Brandon challenged, coming alongside of her.

Annoyed at her reaction to his touch and her own thoughts, Prue swam as fast as she could and managed to stay side by side with Brandon until their knees scraped the sand. She was elated that he'd not easily beaten her.

Brandon grinned, wiping the water out of his eyes. 'You're better than I thought.'

'And not just at swimming!' she replied tartly, and giving him a loaded look, walked up the beach to her belongings. That would show him!

Chapter Sixteen

Prue stood in the garden at the back of the villa and listened to Maria as she spoke in broken English about the vegetables growing in the plot.

'Look at these tomatoes, Grandmama. Aren't they brilliant?' Prue lightly touched the plump red tomatoes growing up the trellis.

Grandmama, sitting on a canvas chair under the apple tree, glanced over from reading her letters. 'They'll look better on a piece of bread for my lunch.'

Maria bent and snipped off cucumbers from another trellis and popped them into her basket.

Prue wandered over to the small lemon tree growing by the fence. The sun was hot on her head despite wearing her straw hat. She longed for a swim, but Brandon and Vince had taken the car and gone out for the day to visit some friends they'd met at university before the war. They'd invited Prue to go, but she'd declined. After a week at the villa she needed a break from being with Brandon.

It was becoming harder to deny the attraction that consumed her. From morning until bedtime, she was constantly aware of his presence. She felt him staring at her sometimes, he would listen to her when she spoke with Vince and Grandmama. She knew he wanted to talk to her properly, but she couldn't bring herself to be open with him.

In return she would watch and listen when he wasn't aware. She was beginning to understand his ways. He liked his coffee black with no sugar, his toast lightly buttered but heavy with jam. He preferred fried eggs to boiled and bought English newspapers from the little shop two streets down, which he would pore over and discuss articles with Grandmama. He laughed at Vince and equally could be annoyed with him. He treated Grandmama with utmost respect and loved chatting with her well into the night. His interests and conversation were stimulating, but she couldn't pay him too much attention or she'd be lost.

The gate opened and a woman with a long face and on an old hat on her head came in. 'Good day to you all,' she said in a strong American accent.

Prue left the lemon tree and walked towards her as Grandmama frowned from her chair.

The American closed the gate behind her and stood on the path, staring about the garden. 'I decided I'd come and introduce myself since we are going to be neighbours.'

Prue heard Grandmama's groan and quickly held out her hand to the American. 'How lovely to meet you. I'm Prue Marsh, and this is my grandmama Mrs Adeline Fordham, and this is Maria, our cook.'

'Charmed to meet you all. I'm Lesley Larkin, call me Lesley. Two villas down.' The woman was taller than Prue and shook her hand with the strength of a man, before sitting down next to Grandmama uninvited.

Grandmama's eyebrows shot up to her hairline at the boldness of the woman.

'Do you own this place or rent it? I've decided to rent mine for a few weeks until I decide this is where the family should want to be. There's no chance for errors when you live so far away. You need to make good judgements, so you feel secure when you leave the place. Do you agree, Mrs Fordham?'

Grandmama opened her mouth to speak but Lesley Larkin carried on talking.

'Is this your whole family, just your granddaughter? I've come on my own this first time. I've left my dear ole father back in the States with my brother and niece. Brought my niece up myself, yes, I did. Her mother died having her and of course my brother was needed on the ranch.' Lesley Larkin jerked up from the chair and strode around the garden in her long black skirt from another decade. 'Mighty fine vegetables you grow here. I'll be planting similar myself. Like to eat my own grown food. My late husband was a keen gardener. Dead these last three years, God rest his soul. I don't have a lot of land where I'm staying, about the same as you. Don't you find it incredible how these old places cling to the cliff side as they do. Remarkable engineering, or sheer luck, who knows?' Lesley Larkin laughed loudly.

Grandmama peered down her nose at her.

'What brings you to Positano, Mrs Larkin?' Prue managed to get in.

Lesley Larkin scratched behind her ear. 'My late mother was Italian, you see. Her family are from along the coast here, all were fishermen, and all long dead. My father said he'd bring my mother back one day, but he never did, so I'm doing it now. Got her ashes in an urn. I thought I might as well buy a place here and then we, my brother and I, and my niece no doubt, can come back from time to time. We should, shouldn't we? Seeing as we are half Italian. My niece is getting married next year, and a villa here would be a nice wedding present. Mighty fine lemons you have there.' She peered at the lemon tree before opening the gate. 'I'll drop by again tomorrow. We'll have a drink as the sun goes down. Best go unpack first or I'll be sleeping in the clothes I'm wearing on a bed not made, not that I care. I've slept on the dirt under the stars more times than I care to remember. Cheerio!'

Then she was gone.

Grandmama was lost for words. Her mouth opened and closed several times, her eyes wide in her face. 'What the bloody hell was that?'

Prue burst out laughing until she couldn't breathe.

~ ~ ~ ~

Reading a letter from Mama, Prue frowned when she heard Grandmama grumbling as she came out onto the balcony. 'What is wrong?'

'That American!'

Prue sighed. In the two weeks since 'that American' had moved in down the road, she'd done nothing but be a kind neighbour. However, the over-friendliness was very different to what Grandmama was used to and she couldn't handle Lesley Larkin coming into the villa at all times of the day and night to chat. 'What has she done now?'

'She's given me a chicken!' Grandmama fumed as though a horse's head on a spike had been thrown over the wall.

221

'And that is bad because…?'

'I don't want a chicken! Live or dead!' Grandmama spat. 'The woman is hopeless. She doesn't take a hint. I don't want to be her friend. I have plenty of friends and none of them are a loud American from the middle of nowhere in some god-forsaken state no one has ever heard of!'

'She comes from Kentucky.'

'And she needs to go back there as quick as she can.'

'Lesley is very nice, and you know it.'

'She is making me be totally ruthless in my rudeness to her and still she comes along talking a hundred words a minute. She's like a machine gun, never stops.'

'Grandmama, you like her.' Prue grinned.

'I do not. It's not to be borne! I don't care if she's bought eight chickens to be fed up for the pot. If I want to eat chicken, I'll go to a reputable restaurant and order it!'

'She's being neighbourly.'

'Neighbourly? I have neighbours on either side of me in London and have done my entire life and not once have they felt the need to give me a chicken!'

Vince and Brandon returned from inspecting a suitable mountain cliff to climb and came out onto the balcony.

'Why is there a dead chicken in the kitchen?' Vince rubbed his hands together joyfully. 'Is that for dinner?'

Grandmama stuck her finger out at him. 'One more word about that chicken and you'll be joining it in its current state!' She marched from the room.

'What did I say?' Vince asked innocently.

'Lesley.' That's all Prue needed to say for the men to understand the situation.

'We've not been out dancing in weeks,' Vince said, changing the subject. 'I fancy it, don't you, Prue?'

She nodded. 'I do, actually.'

'Excellent. There's a place I've found on the other side of the bay. Do you remember me getting the card from that place near the Colosseum? He told me it was his brother's or cousin's restaurant? Well, I found it. A nice little restaurant overlooking the water. Shall we go tonight?'

She smiled at him, not wanting to recall that day by the Colosseum. 'Since it's my birthday tomorrow, why not?'

Vince jumped up. 'It's your birthday? Why hasn't anything been mentioned before now?'

'Because I didn't want a fuss, and because my grandpapa died on my birthday and it's a difficult day for Grandmama.'

'That's tragic indeed,' Brandon murmured.

Prue folded away her mama's letter to read later. 'Tomorrow I shall spend the day with Grandmama to help her through a difficult day. I thought we might help her escape Lesley and go for a drive somewhere, if you two wish to come as well? We could take a picnic?'

'That would be grand.' Brandon leaned against the railing. 'Will Mrs Fordham want us to be there though? She might want you all to herself?'

'Of course, I would,' Grandmama answered for herself as she came back out onto the balcony. 'We should have a picnic and toast Prue's birthday and to my darling husband who would have loved to be here with us. It's not a day for sadness but a day to remember how much we loved and are loved.'

Vince took Grandmama in his arms and waltzed her around the balcony. 'But tonight, dear lady, tonight we dance!'

Grandmama giggled like a young woman. 'Get away with you, you soft lump. No, I'm not going out dancing tonight.'

'Why?' Vince cried heart broken.

'Because I've promised that stupid woman two villas down that I'd drop in and have a drink with her.' Grandmama's face was a picture.

Prue hid a laugh behind her hand. 'Are you sure you don't want to come with us instead? I'm sure Mrs Larkin wouldn't mind.'

'I'm British, Prue, we do not break promises unless there's money to be made. No, I shall go and sit with her for I know she is extremely lonely and missing her family. I'm doing my duty as any decent person would and suffering her company for her benefit.'

'You are a saint, Mrs F,' Vince declared dramatically.

'I agree. I've always said it.' Grandmama gave him a superior look. 'And I'll take your bottle of whisky for my pains, too, and while I languish under that woman's onslaught, I want you three to go out and celebrate Prue's birthday for tomorrow. Wine and dine and dance until morning. Yes?'

They could only agree with her.

Later that evening, as the buildings of Positano glowed with golden lights that reflected on the water, Brandon pulled 'Henry' as the motor car was nicknamed, to a stop beside a lone building situated high on a part of the jutting headland.

'I've asked around in town and I've heard only good things about this place,' Vince said, taking Prue's arm. 'Great food and a band who tours the country.'

'Sounds perfect!' Prue pulled her silk wrap closer over her bare shoulders. Tonight, for her birthday, she'd worn a fine satin slip dress in soft pink. A long strand of pearls hung about her neck and she wore a headband with three pink feathers on the side. Long satin gloves in white and heeled sandals completed the outfit.

Happily, Maria, a lover of fashion, had returned to the villa to wash and style Prue's hair into a straight bob, which ended below her ears.

Prue hoped she looked amazing, and the way Vince had whistled at her when she entered the sitting room told her the answer. From Brandon she'd received rare praise, and in his eyes, she perceived a subtle message that he also liked what he saw.

Inside the restaurant they were greeted warmly by a handsome Italian waiter, who said that his brother owned the restaurant. He gave them a table by the window over-looking the bay and Positano below. With candles and flowers on the white-clothed tables and soft music playing from a violinist, the atmosphere was subtle and high-class.

'Champagne is in order,' Brandon told the waiter. 'Your best bottle, per favore?'

'*Si, signore.*'

Vince rubbed his hands together, a habit he did when he was excited. 'I've just seen my future wife. The dark-haired one.'

Prue and Brandon looked to where he was staring. Another table was being seated, an older couple with two young women with them.

'Vince,' Brandon warned. 'Not tonight. It's Prue's birthday celebration. I don't want any fighting.'

'Why would I fight? Two beautiful young girls out with their parents and once the dancing starts, they'll be wanting a partner, will they not?'

'Can we not enjoy our dinner before you prey on any women, please?' Brandon mocked.

The waiter returned and with dramatic flair opened the champagne and poured it into their glasses.

Another man all dressed in black came to the table, a little older than Brandon Prue guessed, for his hair was dark grey and there were small lines at the corners of his grey eyes. He bowed and took Prue's hand to kiss it.

'Buongiorno. I am Antonio Bonito, owner of this establishment.'

'Miss Prue Marsh.'

'Is it a special occasion we are celebrating tonight, *signorina*?' He only had eyes for Prue.

'It is my birthday,' she announced.

'Your birthday, *signorina*? Ah, then it is a very special night indeed!' He still held Prue's hand and ignored Vince and Brandon. 'For you, tonight, will be no cost. Eat, drink whatever you like, and it is on me.' He bowed gallantly. 'But! Only if I have a dance with you?'

Flattered, and a little overwhelmed by his debonair charm, Prue blushed slightly. 'I would like that very much.'

'I shall return later!' Antonio bowed and left them.

'Go you, girl.' Vince nudged Prue with his elbow. 'Excellently done. Free food and you've caught the eye of the owner. Wherever we go, you attract attention.'

'Well, I'm ready for some fun, aren't you?' Prue winked at Vince.

'I love this woman!' Vince cheered.

Prue grinned and toasted Vince with her champagne flute. Brandon leaned back in his chair, a thoughtful expression on his face, but she didn't care if he approved of her or not. Tonight, she was going to have a blast.

The food was sublime. Course after course came out to their table: risotto, fish, pasta, salads, bread and cheese. The champagne flowed bottle after bottle and Vince and Prue waltzed around the dance floor between courses, laughing and having the best time.

Brandon watched from the table, happy to converse but didn't offer to dance with her, which irritated Prue more than she cared to admit.

Prue was talking to Vince about the beauty of Palermo when Antonio and one of his staff wheeled out a trolley and on it was a large cake with candles.

'Oh!' Prue clapped. 'I love cake.'

'Happy birthday to *signorina* Marsh.' Antonio's gaze didn't hide his interest in her.

To a round of applause, Prue blew out the candles. A bittersweet happiness filled her. She was celebrating her birthday for the first time with not one member of her family with her.

The band began to play, and Antonio held out his hand to her. Prue placed her hand in his and walked to the dance floor. In time with the music, they waltzed around the dance floor.

'*Sei bellissima, signorina.*' Antonio whispered sensually by her ear.

Prue shivered. 'Grazie.'

'I would like to spend the day with you. Tomorrow?'

Leaning back in his arms, Prue stared at him. 'You do?'

'*Si*. I take you somewhere special. Tomorrow?'

'No, not tomorrow.'

'The next day.' He moved elegantly, turning her effortlessly. 'I treat you like a *principessa*.'

Biting her lip in delight, Prue leaned closer to him. 'I've always wanted to be a princess.'

The music stopped and Antonio stared into her eyes. Prue felt a tingle of awareness and a frisson of desire as she had with Ajay and Brandon. What on earth was wrong with her? Was it normal to feel this way with different men?

He brought her hand up and softly kissed the back of it. 'I shall pick you up at ten o'clock.'

Prue told him her address and walked away, knowing he watched her every step.

Back at the table Vince was missing, and a quick glanced showed him to be talking to one of the young women he had spotted earlier.

'You have gained an admirer,' Brandon said, sipping a whisky.

'So, it seems.' Prue sat down and sipped the last of her champagne.

'Be careful.'

'Why?'

'Men like him eat ladies like you for breakfast, and that's after a night of passion.'

'What are you implying?'

'I'm simply saying, he'll want more than conversation, dear Prue.'

'And what if that is what I want too?' she challenged.

'Then more fool you.'

'Why?' She was ridiculously hurt by the comment. 'Aren't I allowed to have fun?'

'You are an innocent in the ways of men. You've no idea what that man wants.'

'I'm not stupid or a child, Brandon. I sense what he wants.'

'And you still want to spend time with him? I thought better of you.' Brandon strode to the bar.

Annoyed that Brandon had burst her bubble, she reached for the champagne bottle herself and poured a large glass.

Vince returned, all smiles. 'The lovely young lady has agreed to a dance, lucky me. The papa isn't so impressed.' He paused and peered at Prue through bloodshot eyes. 'What's wrong?'

Prue took a large swig from her glass. 'Brandon. He's such a... such a...'

'Prig?' Vince finished for her. 'Yes, he is. What did he say to upset you?'

'That Antonio only wants me for one thing.'

'I hate to break it to you, sweetheart, but he does.' Vince slumped onto his chair and poured another drink. 'He's a man and you are beautiful. Why wouldn't he? Every man wants to sleep with you? I'd sleep with you if you weren't my friend, and I have a strong code to never sleep with friends.' He nodded earnestly.

She shook her head at him. He was incorrigible. 'Would it be so bad if I wanted to sleep with Antonio? If men can have those needs and wants why can't women?'

'Go for it.' Vince shrugged. 'It doesn't bother me, but most men frown upon it. Double standards, I know. To be honest, I prefer a woman to have some experience, it much more fun than bedding a nervous virgin.'

'I'm going to go out with Antonio for the day. I want to experience things.'

'Good girl. Have a ball. He'll treat you like a—'

'*Principessa.*' Prue chuckled, drinking more champagne.

'Exactly, and why not?' Vince lifted the champagne bottle and found it empty. With a snap of his fingers, he ordered another bottle. 'Now, I'm going to go dance with that delightful young lady over there, who is far too pure and delicate for me. So, then I'll come back to you and we'll drink that bottle out under the stars, yes?'

'Yes.'

'And to hell with Brandon and anyone who dares to stop us from having a good time.'

Prue raised her glass in silent cheers to that. Damn Brandon and his disapproving glares.

Chapter Seventeen

'What are you reading, Brandon?' Mrs Fordham asked, peeling an orange.

Lifting his head up from his position on the blanket, he turned the book around to show her the cover. '*This Side of Paradise* by F. Scott Fitzgerald.'

'Are you enjoying it?'

'It's good, yes.'

'What is it about?'

Brandon sat up, squinting against the sun. 'A young man, Amory Blaine, from America, and how he fails at love despite his best intentions.'

'Oh, a bit like yourself then?' Mrs Fordham popped an orange segment into her mouth.

Chuckling Brandon reached for the bottle of cider and poured himself a drink. 'You could say that.'

'I did.'

He leaned back on his elbow, his gaze going to Prue where she was walking through the olive grove with Vince and Lesley Larkin, who'd been invited to the picnic by Mrs Fordham, despite her earlier protests.

'I told you back in Rome that Prue was the one for you. Yet, you've not acted on it at all. Why?'

'I don't know.'

'She won't wait. Prue usually goes after what she wants. Tomorrow she's off with that Italian restaurant owner, and who knows who will come along next? She's always had a string of admirers following behind her. If the war hadn't happened, she'd be married by now. Are you not interested?'

'I am.'

'You've a funny way of showing it. You've been hurt before, haven't you?' Mrs Fordham peered at him, it was as though she could read his mind.

He sighed and looked out over the water. From their vantage point up on the top of a mountain he could see for miles across the bay.

'You told me you had never married. I don't take you as a liar, so I'm guessing you were engaged?' she enquired.

'I was.'

'What did she do?'

'She married someone else while I was fighting in France.'

'Despicable.'

'Vince tells me I should move on. He is correct, of course, and I will, I am.'

'But you don't want to be hurt again. That makes sense.'

'I can usually trust my instincts. In the past they have saved my life, but with women…'

Mrs Fordham laughed, a light laugh that was joyful to hear. 'Darling Brandon, women will always tie men up in knots. It's nature. Desire becomes mixed up with rational thought and in the end all that is left is confusion. Sexual desire and rational thought aren't everything. At times, one must take a gamble. The heart usually knows best in my opinion.' She glanced down at the orange in her hand. 'I've flirted with men all my life, even when it was completely frowned upon, and I loved every moment of it.'

She stared at him, her voice soft. 'However, in the end, my heart found its soulmate before my head even realised. Edward was the love of my life. Ours was a love that defied any obstacle, and there were a few. When he died, I considered my life to be over, I would have been happy to join him. Yet, here I still am, years later, filling my days with travel and family so I can get by with this great big hole in my heart. Don't waste your time, Brandon, on being frightened of getting hurt.' She shrugged one shoulder. 'Otherwise, you might as well have died in the war.'

He watched an ant crawl over the edge of the blanket. She spoke the truth, and he knew it. He'd survived the war, and he'd survived the pain of Claudia leaving him.

Prue's laughter drifted on the breeze. He liked the sound of it.

'How do you feel about Prue spending the day with this Antonio fellow?' Mrs Fordham finished eating her orange and wiped her hands on a napkin.

How did he feel? Jealous. Irritated. The man had danced with Prue, flirted with Prue and was now going to spend the day with her tomorrow and likely kiss her…

'I hate it.'

Mrs Fordham chuckled. 'You poor man. You're already in love with her!'

He groaned. He wasn't ready.

As the others returned, Mrs Fordham leaned over to him. 'Do something about that Antonio fellow!'

'Like what? Prue is excited by the outing. It's all she's talked about all morning. Who am I to stop her from having a good time? I'm not even sure Prue likes me.'

'Good Lord, you men are true simpletons.'

Vince moaned sitting down on the grass. 'Pass me some water, Brandon, my head pounds like it is about to burst.'

'Me too,' Prue added. 'Gosh, I don't think I'll ever drink champagne again.'

Brandon poured them both a glass of water and then a third for Lesley Larkin.

'Moonshine,' Lesley Larkin declared.

'What on earth are you talking about now, Lesley?' Mrs Fordham tutted.

'Alcohol. White spirits. We make it at home. Have our own distillery. It'll take the paint off the walls, and likely start an engine but it sure helps you forget a bad day, that's for certain. Like the young ones here, it'll give you a bad head the next morning, too.'

'Well if you're anything to go by, Lesley, it addles your brain, too,' Mrs Fordham sniffed with disapproval.

Lesley Larkin snorted. 'Ah, Adeline, you are a funny one.'

Mrs Fordham glared at her. 'No, I am not. Here, have an orange, and sit further under the tree, you silly woman. You'll burn to a crisp.'

'I'm in the sun all day on the farm back home.'

'That's why your skin is like leather,' Mrs Fordham mumbled. 'I'll not have you fainting on me with heatstroke just because you're stubborn.'

'I like the sound of having my own distillery,' Vince piped up. 'We should look into such a thing, Brandon.'

'Are you mad?' Brandon bit into an apple. 'You drink more than enough without making it yourself.'

'Spoilsport.'

'What kind of farm do you have in Kentucky, Miss Larkin?' Brandon asked.

'Horses, mainly, a few crops for the horses, and some cattle as a sideline. But our passion is breeding good horse stock.'

'Sounds like a good size farm,' Brandon said.

'We've ten thousand acres.'

Mrs Fordham's eyes widened. 'That's enormous. You never said it was that big before when we've talked about it,' she accused. 'When you mentioned your farm, I thought it was a few sheep and some hens.'

Lesley wiped the orange juice that was running down her chin. 'It's a bigger ranch than we used to have which was only six thousand acres. My brother and I manage the ranch, but I have to spend some time in Oklahoma as well, that's where my late husband's family are.'

'Kentucky. Oklahoma. They sound amazing places.' Prue sighed. 'I so wish to go to America.'

'Then you must!' Lesley announced. 'You can come and stay with me. Can you ride a horse?'

'I can.'

'Well, then. You'll enjoy the ranch. Come next May and go to the Kentucky Derby. It's not to be missed.'

'You breed *race horses*?' Mrs Fordham nearly choked on her cider.

Lesley frowned at her. 'Do you not ever listen to me?'

'I try not to. After an hour with you I'm tone deaf.'

'I've heard of the Kentucky Derby,' Vince said, scouting through the picnic basket for something to eat.

'Best damn horse race in the world,' Lesley championed

'I doubt that,' Mrs Fordham countered. 'Epsom Derby is legendary.'

'I've been to that, yes, but nothing beats the Kentucky. My brother has bred many a horse that has run in it. This year's race is the first I've missed in ten years. It has affected more than I considered it would, which is why I'm leaving on Thursday to return home.'

'You're leaving on Thursday, as in two days' time?' Mrs Fordham frowned. 'Why didn't you say before now?'

'I thought I had.'

'You certainly did not.'

'Well, now you know.'

'You have bought chickens!' Mrs Fordham was outraged.

'You can have them.'

'I don't want your chickens. You are being irresponsible.'

Lesley drank some water. 'Yes, well I was going to stay longer, but I miss my family and want to go home. I've put an offer on the villa and the family who own it have accepted it.'

'You've bought the villa?' Brandon asked, surprised. 'That was quick work.'

'What is the point in waiting? I like Positano, I like the villa. I made an offer, and they accepted it. I've visited what's left of my mother's distant relations and scattered her ashes. I've done what I set out to achieve and now I can go home.' Lesley turned to

Mrs Fordham. 'Do you and Prue fancy coming back with me?'

'To America?' Prue jerked up, her expression one of surprise. 'Grandmama can we? I've always wanted to go to America.'

Brandon's heart twisted at the mention of Prue leaving to go to America.

'And put up with more people like Lesley? I think not. One Lesley is enough for me, thank you.' Mrs Fordham scowled. 'But you'll come to London, won't you, Lesley, and visit me? I'm too old to be travelling to America now.'

'I told you, Adeline, I'm coming to spend Christmas with you.'

'Christmas? No, you're not. I didn't agree to that. I assumed you were joking! I don't want you for Christmas with all your American ways. You'll ruin it. Come another time.'

Lesley laughed. 'I want to experience an English Christmas with church bells ringing and city streets full of shops and people buying gifts, the old grey buildings and the fog.'

'I don't live in a Dickens novel, woman.'

Brandon chuckled at that.

Lesley's laughter grew louder. 'I'm coming for Christmas, Adeline.'

'I hope you do, Lesley.' Prue smiled, encouraging her.

'I don't go back on my word, and you must come to me in Kentucky. You'll have the best time.'

'Thank you. I'd like that.' Prue smiled.

Lesley turned to Brandon and Vince. 'My invitation extends to you both as well.'

Vince knelt and kissed Lesley on both cheeks. 'We accept!'

'Thank you,' Brandon said, happy to be included. One could never have enough friends.

'You might find an American wife, Vince,' Prue teased.

'A very rich one will do, and we must get you a handsome horse breeder, perhaps?'

'No, I'd much prefer an actor like Rudolph Valentino. He's divine.' Prue sighed dreamily.

Brandon pretended to read his book as they chatted about America and movies. The words on the page made no sense to him as his mind dealt with many other things. He believed he was in love with Prue. Was it something he wanted to act on? Would she rebuff him? How the hell was he going to stop her from seeing Antonio, and more importantly how was he going to show her that he cared?

~ ~ ~ ~

Prue sipped her orange juice and thanked Maria when she placed a plate of eggs and bacon in front of her. Although hungry, her stomach churned. Antonio was to arrive soon, and she was both excited and apprehensive. She wanted to spend the day with him, but at what cost? Would he take no for an answer when he tried it on with her? Or in the spur of the moment would she want to sleep with him? She didn't trust herself around handsome men.

She'd tossed and turned all night worrying about how she'd react to his advances, and she was in no doubt that he would try to kiss her and more. The way they danced so closely, and the way he'd held her, his whispered words clearly spoke of his intentions and she couldn't deny the spark of attraction between them.

But then what?

Did she want another sexual encounter with no meaning? The guilt she'd feel afterwards was bound to make her annoyed.

'Good morning, dearest.' Grandmama came to the table.

'Morning. There's post there.' Prue indicated the pile of mail on the side of the table. She'd received a letter from Millie and from Mama, which she wanted to read but didn't have time. She glanced at the clock again. Nine thirty-five. Antonio said he'd collect her at ten o'clock. She wondered where he'd take her.

'*Grazie*, Maria.' Grandmama opened her letters as Maria poured fresh coffee for her and added toast to the table. 'I'm most disappointed that Lesley is leaving today. So rude of her to become my friend and then suddenly leave. I thought she was here for the summer.'

'She misses her family. It must be hard when she's on her own.'

'Very inconvenient if you ask me.' Grandmama sniffed. 'And I've been lumbered with her bloody chickens. What am I to do with them? How inconsiderate.'

'You offered to take them,' Prue argued.

'Yes, well…' Grandmama read her first letter. 'It's from your mama. She says Cece is not going with her to Paris and is staying in York with your cousin Agatha.'

'I've not received a letter from Cece in months, actually nothing since we were in Palermo and she sent Christmas greetings.'

Grandmama finished reading and put the letter to one side and buttered a slice of toast. 'Cece hasn't forgiven me for not asking her to come with us.'

Prue snorted. 'Can you imagine if Cece had come to India with us? Cece and Gertie together in the same house? It would have been unbearable.'

'Cece isn't as uptight as Gertie, but, yes, I see your point.'

'My sister wouldn't have enjoyed it, so don't feel guilty.'

'I never feel guilty.' Grandmama bit into her toast. 'Cece is a strange one. Too quiet and easy to judge others… I am sorry for her though.'

'Good morning, ladies.' Brandon joined them at the table, but they knew Vince wouldn't rise for another hour or so.

'Good morning,' Prue murmured, her heart skipping a beat at the sight of him. He was clean-shaven and smelled of soap.

'I don't believe it.' Grandmama was reading her second letter.

'What now?' Prue ate some bacon and contemplated if she had enough time for another coffee.

'This cannot be happening!' Grandmama fumed.

'What?' Prue asked.

'This letter is from Kilburn.'

Prue turned to Brandon. 'Kilburn is Grandmama's butler in London.'

He smiled. 'Thank you for filling me in.'

'Well, this is a dilemma.' Grandmama tapped the letter. 'Wyatt has resigned. She's been my cook for twenty-five years.'

'Heavens! Why has she resigned?'

'She's received an offer to work in Lord Pendridge's establishment. How dare he steal my cook! I'll never speak to Derry again, you see if I don't. Nasty little ferret. He's offered her more money and a sensible pension. She's taken it without even discussing it with me. I knew the last time he came for dinner he praised her food too enthusiastically. Snake!'

'That is a shame.' Prue always liked the jolly Wyatt and the little cakes she'd let Prue and her sisters sneak between meals when they visited Grandmama during school holidays.

'And if that's not disaster enough, Potter has left. Went and got married last week. How selfish. Do they not consider me at all?'

'That's nice.' Prue recalled the parlourmaid who often sang while cleaning Grandmama's rooms.

'It's not nice at all.' Grandmama banged the table. 'I have no cook or parlourmaid and Kilburn writes that he fell down the back stairs and has broken his arm. A butler with a broken arm. What is the world coming to?'

'Poor Kilburn.'

'Poor me!' Grandmama snapped.

'Yoo-hoo. It's only me,' Lesley called from the hallway as she came through. 'I've brought the chickens. I've let them run free in your garden. They laid four eggs this morning.'

'Stuff the chickens and their eggs.' Grandmama glared at her.

Lesley smiled. 'Good morning, Adeline. Isn't it a fine day?'

Grandmama pushed up from the table. 'No, it is not. I have to return home.'

'Home?' Prue gasped, her forkful of eggs halfway to her mouth. 'Why?'

'To sort out my household.'

'But Kilburn can arrange for new staff.'

'Not with one arm he can't and how will I know if the cook he hires is any good if I'm not there? I'm not paying wages for someone who might be too stupid to boil cabbage and I'm not there to judge.'

'I'm sure he has the experience to hire a suitable cook to your standards,' Prue argued. 'He's been your butler for nearly his whole life. I don't wish to go home yet.'

'I'm sorry, dearest, I am, but I shall need to return to London and sort this out. We can always come back in a few weeks.'

Even as Grandmama said the words, Prue knew it wouldn't happen. Such a quick turnaround would be too much for Grandmama and she'd want to stay in London, and once she started seeing her friends again, she'd be loathed to make another journey.

She caught Brandon's gaze and saw his disappointment. The thought of leaving him suddenly was too much. 'I wish to stay, Grandmama. Send word to Mama and she can go to London.'

Grandmama tapped the first letter. 'Violet is on her way to Paris.'

'But—'

'Prue,' Grandmama warned. 'I haven't time to discuss this. We need to go home.'

'*Buongiorno!*' Antonio arrived, looking smart in a white linen suit. In his arms, he carried a large spray of flowers wrapped in paper and ribbon. He gave them to Prue.

'*Grazie*. They are beautiful,' Prue said, and although Antonio had acknowledged everyone else in the room, his gaze remained on Prue. She felt he would devour her if he got the chance.

She glanced from him to Grandmama and back again. 'I'm sorry, Antonio, but I can't spend the day with you. Forgive me. Something has happened and my grandmama wishes to return to London.' She indicated to Grandmama who held out her hand to Antonio, and he kissed it.

'Ahh, that is no good, *signorina*.' His expression was concerned. 'May I be of help?'

'There's no need, thank you,' Brandon spoke up, dismissing him. 'I'll see you out.'

With Brandon walking from the room, Antonio had to follow, his eyes imploring Prue to stop him.

'*Arrivederci*, Antonio.' She waved to him, relieved that he was a situation she didn't have to deal with any more. As much as she might have enjoyed the day with him, it may have become more than she could handle. Besides, the fact she'd have to go home was all that concerned her.

'I need to go home and sort this mess out. I'm sorry.' Grandmama came to stand beside her and put her hand on Prue's shoulder. 'I cannot leave you here alone, dearest.'

'I understand.' Crushed, Prue pushed away her breakfast.

'If I'm being totally honest with you, I'm rather glad to be going home. It's time I slept in my own bed for a while. I overestimated my abilities to travel at my age.'

'I understand.' Yet emotion built in her chest.

Lesley, who'd been unusually quiet stepped forward. 'You can travel with me to Naples, Adeline. I'm booked on a ship to take me from there to New York. You might be able to buy tickets for a steamer to take you to London?'

'Yes, that sounds a sensible plan. At least in Naples there are plenty of hotels to stay at until we sail.'

Lesley got up from the sofa. 'Brandon said he'd drive me down to the jetty as I've secured a boat to take me to Sorrento, and from there I'm catching the ferry to Naples. I'm sure you'll be able to join me.'

'Thank you.'

'I'll go finish packing,' Lesley said, leaving the room. 'The boat leaves at twelve.'

'We'd best get a move on then, Prue.' Grandmama left to go to her bedroom to pack.

Brandon returned and sat at the table next to Prue. 'Do you want to stay?'

'Yes, but it's not possible.' She couldn't meet his eyes for fear of starting to cry. Suddenly faced with the knowledge she wouldn't see him again hit her like a sledgehammer.

'It would be if Vince and I move out. We can go to a hotel. Ask Maria or Lola to move in here so you are not alone. Then everything is respectable.'

A flicker of hope replaced the despair, then it died just quickly again. 'I cannot let Grandmama travel to London on her own. It's unthinkable.'

'No, it's not,' Grandmama said coming back into the room, carrying a small bag. 'Brandon's idea is totally acceptable. Thank you, Brandon.'

'Grandmama, I don't want you travelling alone.'

'Stuff and nonsense, girl. I'm old, not senile. I'm quite capable of being on a ship by myself. I'm only going from Naples to London, not discovering new worlds.'

'Yes, but—'

'No, buts. I was being selfish. Of course, you want to stay and finish your holiday until you're ready to return home. Your mama won't like it, but I'll talk her around.'

Brandon poured a cup of coffee. 'If it helps, I'll send a telegram to my sister and ask her to come and visit.' He glanced up at Prue. 'She's very nice.'

'Your sister?' She'd heard him mention her briefly before. 'Isn't she married? Would she want to come here?'

'Alice is widowed, and yes, she loves to travel.'

'Excellent,' Grandmama declared. 'That's all sorted and above board. I'll be far more relaxed knowing another woman was here with you, Prue. I'll go pack.'

Prue left the table and stood at the French doors; worried Brandon's sister might be another Gertie. 'Does she have children to care for?'

'No. Alice's husband was killed in battle before they had a chance to have children. They were married on one of his leaves and he returned to his regiment three days later. He was killed within a month.'

'How tragic.' Prue stared into the distance.

'You don't seem convinced this is a good idea?' Brandon asked, as Maria brought him a plate of bacon and eggs.

'I need someone who will allow me to do as I please. Would your sister be willing to do that? I don't need a nursemaid.'

Brandon laughed. 'Alice will never play the role of a nursemaid.'

'I'll pay her expenses, naturally.'

'My sister is quite able to pay her own way, she is Lady Mayton-Walsh.'

Shock made her turn to him. 'Lady Mayton-Walsh? Oh. Oh dear.'

'You've heard of her, then?'

'Er… yes.' Prue couldn't believe that his sister was one of London societies most sought after guests. She'd read about her in the newspapers. Lady

Mayton-Walsh was at all the best parties, balls and restaurants and linked to every scandal around town.

'My sister is not as bad as the newspapers and gossips like to make out. I promise you that. Do you still want her to come out?'

'I'm sure she wouldn't have the time or inclination to even consider it.'

Brandon shook his head. 'Not true. Alice is a good person, decent and kind and when you're her friend, it is for life. Yes, she is wild, imprudent, notorious for being late, outspoken and opinionated, and has made many mistakes, but she is loyal, caring and has a soft heart. She will, if she likes you, make you laugh until you cry and give unconditional love.'

Prue's resolve melted a little at his devotion to his sister. 'You make her sound like the friend I need.'

'I'll go and send a telegram to her now, shall I? I understand she is in Paris. Knowing Alice as I do, she will drop everything and likely be on the first boat out here. Always one for excitement is Alice.'

'She doesn't know me. She is an important woman with a wide circle of friends. Will she not think it outlandish that I'm asking her to come, a stranger?'

'You aren't asking her, I am, and she is always complaining we don't see enough of each other. In fact, I've not seen her in two years. I did receive a telegram from her last week saying she was in Paris if I was close by.'

'If you're sure she won't mind?'

'I wouldn't lie to you.'

Prue returned to the table and impulsively kissed Brandon's cheek. 'Thank you.'

'I had to stop you from leaving somehow.'

Her heart fluttered at his whispered words. She gave him a lingering look before going to help pack Grandmama's things.

Two hours later, Prue stood on a wooden jetty watching the owner of the little ferry and his two teenage sons load Lesley and Grandmama's luggage onboard. It was the same boat they'd arrived on three weeks earlier.

A warm breeze lifted her hair and fluttered the skirt of her lemon-coloured dress. Excitement pitted her stomach, but she tried to control it. Soon she would be alone in the villa. She could spend her days doing exactly as she wished, and although Grandmama wasn't a stickler for rules or ordered Prue about, it would still be the first time she'd ever been truly on her own. The sense of freedom was heady.

Lesley shook Prue's hand for she wasn't one for demonstrations of affection. 'Goodbye, Prue. Take care of those chickens. Maria makes good use of their eggs with her pasta. Now, you've got my address and I will expect letters and photographs from you. I'll see you at Christmas.'

'No, you won't,' Grandmama argued, pushing her to one side, but her blue eyes were soft with laughter and everyone knew that she and the loud American were the best of friends.

'Goodbye, Grandmama.' Unexpectedly emotional, Prue hugged her grandmama tight. 'I'll miss you.'

'I expect you will.' Grandmama nodded. 'But there'll be other things to keep you occupied.' Grandma glanced at Brandon who stood with Vince behind Prue. 'Keep safe and write often. The villa is paid up until the end of August.' Grandmama kissed Prue's cheeks. 'Remember, you've only got one life. Make it count.' She winked and turned away.

Vince came up beside Prue and put an arm around her shoulders. 'Just the three of us now, kiddo. We'll look after you.'

Prue grinned as she waved to her grandmama. 'You can barely look after yourself.'

He shrugged. 'Then *you* can look after me.'

Brandon joined them and gazed at Prue. 'I'm so pleased you are staying.'

'Me too.'

'You will be all right. You're safe with us, and Alice will be here in less than a week,' he added.

'I'm not worried. Maria is going to live in until Alice arrives. I'll be fine.' Prue believed it. Brandon had sent a telegram to Alice straight after breakfast and an hour later he received a telegram in reply saying she'll catch a train from Paris and travel to Naples. 'It's a shame you two have to go to a hotel though.'

'Speaking of which, shall we go see what we can find?' Vince suggested.

With a last wave to the boat, which grew smaller as it sailed into the distance, Prue turned and linked arms through Vince and Brandon's. She felt this was a new stage of her life.

Chapter Eighteen

Prue tapped her fingers together and paced the balcony. Waiting for Lady Mayton-Walsh was wearing on her nerves. Birds flew overhead, gliding on the warm air currents drifting up from the bay. Maria appeared and took away Prue's empty glass she'd left on the small table near the sun recliner. She smiled at her but looked beyond her shoulder into the sitting room, hoping to see Brandon or Vince returning with the notorious lady.

Brandon.

With startling ease, he had become important to her. Together with Vince they had spent the last few days enjoying trips out to nearby villages, afternoons on the beach, lazy mornings sunning themselves on the balcony or playing cards, talking and generally learning more about each other as May slipped into June.

As each day rolled into another, Prue was becoming more attached to Brandon. She'd never been in love before and wasn't quite sure if this was love, but she knew that it was something more important than mere flirtation, or even desire. She flirted with Vince, but not with Brandon, it was much more intense with him. It frightened her.

What did he feel though? Sometimes she caught him looking at her as though she was something to marvel at, and then at other times, he frowned, lost in his thoughts and his emotions masked. Should she examine it closely, or leave it well alone?

Over the last couple of weeks, they had learned so much about each other and grown closer, but what would come of it? Yes, he was handsome and from a good family. She couldn't deny the pull of attraction and she sensed it was returned by him, but was it enough? He made no move towards her. And more importantly, did she want to start a relationship with him? He seemed as unsettled as she was.

Did she really want to settle down to marriage and children if he were to ask? Or did she want to roam the world, free as a bird and unconcerned of anything but where to travel next? She didn't have an answer.

Sighing, she began to pace, nibbling a fingernail.

'Well, I declare you are a fine-looking woman! What a relief!'

Prue jerked at the loud statement and the woman who uttered it. Lady Mayton-Walsh was tall, refined, and utterly elegant in a white trouser suit with a red scarf. An enormous red straw hat flopped in waves about her head and in her fingers, she held a cigarette fitted into a long black holder.

On high sandals, she stepped towards Prue, smiling widely and reaching out to her. 'Darling, Prue. It is a pleasure indeed to finally meet you.' She kissed both of Prue's cheeks with gusto. 'You are simply delightful. The boys have nothing but praise for you.'

'I'm so pleased to meet you, Lady Mayton-Walsh and thank you for coming.'

'Oh, sweetie, think nothing of it. Sit. Sit.' She ordered Prue into a recliner next to her. 'To be truthful, I was desperate to get out of Paris. I've been aching to visit Italy all summer, for business, you see. So, your charming invitation came at the perfect time.'

'I hope you don't consider me terribly rude, or peculiar to ask you to come live with me in this villa, as a stranger?'

'Lord, no, darling.' She puffed on her cigarette. 'Besides, my dearest Brandon insisted I come out here, and I see him so rarely I couldn't resist his plea.'

'Thank you.'

Alice blew out a ring of smoke. 'So, I'm to be company for you, and allow you to be, how do we say it, respectable, which is all nonsense of course, you're respectable anyway whether I am here or not. I don't know why old women assume that younger ones cannot control themselves and must be watched constantly. As if a chaperone can ever truly stop someone from doing what they want? Don't you agree? Well, you must do, otherwise you wouldn't be here by yourself wanting adventures without family.'

Prue simply nodded.

'I'm so relieved to meet another person who thinks like myself. It is such an uncommon occurrence. Brandon is going to have his hands full with the both of us! How hilarious!' Her peal of laughter finally stopped the flow of words and Prue just stared at this amazing woman before her.

'And before we go any further, I insist on no formalities. I loathe how some people hide behind formalities. I refuse to. So, I'm Alice and you are Prue. No Lady this and that. Agreed?'

'Yes, very well. If you insist. My sister is Lady Remington and she is of the same opinion.'

'Titles can be so cumbersome. They create walls for people to hide behind and I refuse to succumb to such an idea.' She drew deep on her cigarette. 'Now, I've decided we should go simply everywhere and do everything until we are utterly exhausted. And the minute we say no, we *cannot* do that, then we absolutely *must* do it. What say you?'

Prue grinned. The woman was a force to be reckoned with. 'That sounds perfect to me.'

'You are divine! We can't let the men have all the fun, now can we?'

'Certainly not.'

'Excellent.' Alice tilted her head to peer closely at Prue. 'So, are you in love with my brother yet?'

Prue gaped as Alice started to laugh.

'Darling, everyone falls in love with my brother. Why would they not?'

'Indeed…'

'Only this time, seeing you now, I have a feeling my brother might actually allow someone to break through the armour he donned after Claudia. If you weren't important to him, he'd never have sent for me.'

'Claudia?' Prue repeated, confused.

'The love of his life or was.' Alice stood and stretched widely like a man. 'Travelling is exhausting. I'll go lie down for an hour if you don't mind. I brought my own maid, Bridget, so you won't have to share yours. Is yours English or French?'

'Er… I don't have one. Grandmama and I helped each other, as Grandmama's lady's maid couldn't come with us. In India we had servants, so we didn't bring someone with us from England.' She couldn't think about maids at the minute as the name Claudia kept repeating in her mind.

'Oh, don't bother with any of that. Bridget is wonderful and does everything, I'd be lost without her. She will be able to go between the both of us.' She paused at the doorway. 'And I insist you tell me all about India, I long to go there.'

Prue blanched. She had no wish to talk about India. 'Very well.'

'Brandon and Vince dropped me off and have gone to inspect a cliff face to climb tomorrow. I'm sure they'll tell us all about it later. Brandon's shoulder has been rested enough, so he says.'

'His shoulder?'

'Yes, the damaged one.'

'I was aware he'd injured it. Was that from his last climb?' Why hadn't she been told?

Alice stilled. 'No, not from climbing. He nearly died from a bomb blast. Vince saved his life. It was all very ghastly.' She sniffed and straightened, as though to shake off bad memories. 'Will you be all right for an hour?'

'Yes. Absolutely.' Why hadn't Brandon mentioned it, or Vince? It seemed she didn't know as much about him as she thought.

'A little nap will fix me up and then we'll drink champagne and talk long into the night and really get to know each other, yes?'

'Sounds lovely.' As she spoke the men joined them.

'Oh, that didn't take long,' Alice joked with Vince.

'No, it looks good. We plan to go first thing in the morning. Care to join us?' He returned inside with her, their laughter floating back out through the doors.

Prue

Prue looked at Brandon as though seeing him properly for the first time. He stood at the railing on the edge of the balcony, gazing out to sea.

From where she sat, she admired his handsome profile, his athletic body, but also noticed his aloofness. There were times over the last couple of weeks when he became distant, especially with her, and as she watched him, she realised she didn't want to hold him at arm's length any more.

Why did the knowledge of him nearly dying and of this unknown woman Claudia change her thoughts? Why hadn't he mentioned any of it during their many conversations? She knew of the survivor's guilt that some returning soldiers suffered. Hadn't she seen it first hand with Jeremy? And what about her own guilt surviving the wedding massacre? Wasn't that similar? She knew of the nightmares, the flashbacks.

Is that how Brandon felt? Is that why he risked his life still by climbing mountains, to drown out the images?

And who was this Claudia woman who had hurt him? Did he still love her?

She had so many questions to ask him. It was time she stopped hiding herself away. *Grab life!*

Standing, she took a deep breath and gathered her courage. She had never been one to wait patiently, or the type to let things roll by. Grab life, that's what Grandmama always said. That was precisely what she was going to do and damn the consequences. Since the wedding day massacre and Ajay's death, she'd been hiding, not really living. She'd survived all that and malaria, it was time to take some chances.

She went to stand beside him at the railing. 'You look lost in your thoughts.'

He turned with a ready smile. 'I was.'

Looking into his eyes, she saw them narrow with that intense gaze he often gave her. 'May I ask what they were?'

He was silent for a long moment. 'You, mostly.'

'Me?' Surprised that he'd admit to it, a warm glow spread through her. 'I hope they are good thoughts.'

A wry smile broke his sombre expression. 'Yes.'

'I'm pleased.' Excitement made her heart beat faster, but she acted calmly, resting her elbows on the railing. Despite wanting to throw herself at him, she needed to be sophisticated. 'Tell me what you've been thinking.'

'How lovely you are. How much I would like to spend more time with you, just the two of us. We are never alone. Now Alice is here, she can keep Vince occupied.' The penetrating stare returned, but desire showed too. 'And I was thinking how much I would like to kiss you.'

'Right now?' she teased, delighted.

'Right now.' He gathered her into his arms before she could speak and when his lips touched hers, she gripped his shoulders to keep upright. She sighed against him as he held her closer, tightly. His kiss didn't disappoint. It was perfect. She felt alive, he was real, solid. It was a moment suspended and for her to remember forever.

Eventually, he drew back, but still held her. 'You're a wonderful woman, Prue Marsh.'

'Thank you.' She traced his jaw with a fingertip and he shuddered softly. 'I hold you in high regard, too, Brandon Forster.'

Noise from within broke them apart reluctantly. They shared a tender look before Vince joined them.

'Brandon, old chap,' Vince threw himself on a sun lounger, 'Alice believes we should hire a boat tomorrow and go for a jolly sail. I told her we would, I can never deny her anything, so we'll have to postpone our climb.'

On legs that were a little wobbly, Prue walked over and sat beside Vince. 'A sail would be delightful.' She kissed his cheek, happiness overflowing from her every pore.

He curved his arm around her waist. 'How the hell am I going to cope with two beautiful women in my life, ordering me about?'

Brandon walked past and scuffed up Vince's hair. 'I'm sure you'll cope. I'll drive down to the beach and see if I can organise a boat for tomorrow and I'll book us a table at a restaurant for tonight, while I'm at it.'

'Can I come with you?' Prue asked.

Brandon held out his hand. 'Always.'

With joyful abandonment, Prue couldn't stop smiling as they travelled down the winding roads towards the beach. Everything seemed brighter, the white of the buildings they passed, the colour of the flowers, the scent of lemons and the sea. She loved it all and at that very moment she was the happiest she'd ever been.

Parking the motor car down a side alley, Brandon turned in the seat and pulled Prue into his chest and kissed her deeply. 'I can't tell you how many times since meeting you how much I've wanted to kiss you,' he whispered against her lips.

'You can kiss me whenever you like,' she whispered back, running her hands through his hair and bringing his head down for another long kiss.

Eventually, Brandon sighed and unwillingly released her. 'We've got a task to do and if we don't leave now, I doubt we ever will.'

She laughed and bit her lip as desire throbbed within her.

He groaned. 'Don't look at me like that, woman…' He kissed her again. 'Come on.'

Hand in hand, they walked the rest of the way along the path hugging the beach. With a few inquiries they were sent further up the street where again they were directed further up and had to walk up numerous steps, until they finally found a young Italian man, wearing nothing but trousers, sleeping in a hammock behind a house.

'Stefano?' Brandon enquired to the sleeping form.

Opening his eyes, the man, who Prue thought to be her own age, lifted his head. '*Si*?'

'We were told that you hire out a boat?'

'*Si.*' Stefano swung his legs down and expertly leapt off the hammock. His black hair tussled, Prue noticed his handsome features and lean body. Where all Italians so gorgeous?

'Tomorrow?' Brandon asked.

'*Si.*' Stefano turned and pointed out in the bay. 'The wooden one with the white hull, *Rosa.* She'll be waiting at the jetty. Ten o'clock?'

'Si. *Grazie.*' Brandon shook his head. 'We'll want her all day, *per favore*?'

'*Si.*' Stefano gave Prue a long lingering look. 'I be your *capitano.*'

Brandon took Prue's hand. 'See you in the morning. *Addio.*'

'I'm going to have to spend all day tomorrow fighting him off you,' Brandon joked as they strolled back to the motor car.

'Italian men leave you in no doubt when they are interested, unlike British men,' Prue replied saucily.

Laughing, Brandon stopped and gathered her into his arms. 'I was a fool to wait all these weeks. I accepted back in Rome that I wanted you.'

Arm in arm they took their time reaching the motor car. Prue tried not to think too far ahead and forced herself to only enjoy the present and not ask the questions she needed answers to. She had a wonderful man by her side and a summer in Positano to enjoy. What happened after that, who knew? She'd think about that later.

~ ~ ~ ~

With the sun warm on her body, but the sea breeze making it bearable, Prue, wearing a yellow and white striped swimming costume, lay on the blanket on the deck of the *Rosa*. Above her the sails flapped, while the soft sound of the boat cutting through the water was rhythmic and soothing. It complemented Stefano's younger brother, Gino, who sat on the deck, strumming a guitar and singing in Italian. He had a lovely voice, and although officially he was Stefano's deckhand, he also provided entertainment. She didn't understand what he was singing, but that didn't matter.

She turned her head and watched Brandon standing at the wheel, learning how to steer the boat from a bare-chested Stefano. Behind them on a cushioned bench seat Alice and Vince sat chatting and drinking wine.

Prue closed her eyes, recalling last night when the four of them had gone out for dinner. It had been a great night. They'd eaten and drank and talked for hours. Under the table, Brandon had held her hand, his thumb constantly rubbing her skin, sending delicious tingles up her arm.

Just a touch from him, or a simple smile sent her into a pool of longing. She couldn't control it. What's more, she didn't want to. She wanted him, not only physically but in every way. She wanted his heart, his soul. She wanted his every thought to be about her. And she wanted to be beautiful for him, clever and witty. To make him proud she was his.

Was this love? It had to be. This was so very different to how she felt about Ajay Khan. With him all she wanted was his body and to satisfy a curiosity. With Brandon it was different and so much more.

A sudden thought made her flinch. What would Brandon say when she told him she wasn't a virgin? Would he be disgusted? Would he care? Yes, he would care, but would he understand that she'd been inquisitive, caught up in the exotic romance of India?

'Are you asleep?' Alice asked, coming to sit beside her.

'No.' Prue sat up and noticed they'd sailed into a small cove.

Stefano and Gino were busy pulling in the sails, with help from Vince.

'What's happening?' Prue wrapped a white cotton skirt around her waist and reached for her straw hat.

'We are stopping for lunch.' Alice gazed at Stefano, his muscles rippling as he heaved on a rope.

Prue smiled but made no comment and got to her feet. They'd bought a picnic basket crammed with food, and another basket filled with bottles of wine, limoncello and water.

'Shall we have a swim first?' Brandon asked, leaving the wheel as Gino lowered the rattling anchor with a splash.

'I'm not swimming,' Alice declared. 'I'll set out the picnic instead.'

A loud splash made them turn and stare over the side of the boat.

Vince had dived over and came up grinning. 'Come on. It's great in here.'

'Want to?' Brandon asked, stripping off his shirt.

Prue gazed at his bare chest, liking that he'd not worn the swim suit as he had done previously. Instead, he wore shorts as Stefano and Gino did and nothing else. Prue admired his strong chest and arms, developed over years of climbing.

She quickly slipped off her wrap and put it and her hat on the bench seat. 'Last one in is a rotten egg!' she shouted and jumped off the side of the boat.

'You cheat!' Brandon yelled, jumping in.

The cold water shocked Prue at first, but she soon became used to it and swam over to where Vince was treading water. He was encouraging Alice to come for a swim.

Hands snaked around Prue's waist and she spun into Brandon's chest.

He kissed her. 'You cheated.'

'And you're a rotten egg!' she laughed.

He quickly pushed her under the water. The surprise attack made her splutter. She broke the surface coughing and intent on pulling him under the water.

Chuckling at her feeble attempts, he quickly pushed her under the water again.

All she heard was Brandon and Vince laughing.

Needing a moment, she swam away a few feet to plan her revenge. Perhaps if she attacked Vince first? She turned to him but the expression on his face made her falter. He was watching Alice flirting with Stefano, and clearly not liking it.

'Poor sap,' Brandon whispered, coming up beside her and wrapping his arms around her waist under the water.

'I don't understand?' Prue frowned, holding Brandon's shoulders as they trod water. 'He treats her like a sister.'

'They've known each other since we were kids and Vince would come to our house sometimes in the school holidays. He has always loved her, but she doesn't love him, not like that. She loved her husband very much. She only regards Vince as a brother.'

'Poor Vince.'

'He'll be fine. He'll find a woman or two to seduce and forget that his heart is broken.' Brandon kissed her. 'Let us swim to the beach.'

Prue peered towards the rugged cliffs. 'There's a beach there?'

'Only a tiny one between the rocks. I saw it from the boat.'

A few minutes later they reached the grey-pebbled beach and sat to catch their breath.

'Come on.' Brandon pulled her up to her feet.

'Where are we going?'

'Away from prying eyes.' Brandon led her behind a large rock and in the shade of the overhanging cliff, he rested his back against the rock and cradled Prue against him.

Their kiss was passionate and demanding, Prue pressed into him, eager to explore not only his mouth but his whole body. She ached when his hands cupped her breasts through her thin swimming costume.

'God, I want you,' his voice was muffled as he kissed her neck, licking the salt water from her skin.

Prue trembled, knowing what she wanted and knowing she wanted it from him now. She could feel his need for her against her belly. 'Brandon…'

'I know.'

With an enormous strength of will they broke apart.

Without speaking they walked hand in hand back into the cool water and swam out to the boat.

Chapter Nineteen

As the sun slowly descended, Prue sat at the table and started to open the large pile of mail while Alice was having a nap. She and Alice had just returned to the villa after spending the last week in Naples while Brandon and Vince had gone mountain climbing on Monte Faito.

Ridiculously, she had missed Brandon incredibly, but the week apart gave her time to reason things out, which seemed impossible to do whenever he was around her. She couldn't deny that she had been attracted to him since she met him but now it was so much deeper than mere physical magnetism, she liked him as a person. She knew him to be kind and generous, considerate and funny. From out of nowhere he had entered her heart and was lodged there. But where would it go from here? What did he want? A summer romance or something more? She was full of questions and doubts, not daring to hope for something meaningful.

Days of shopping and exploring Naples with Alice had been pleasurable and distracting from her own thoughts. Alice's charm and never say die attitude made every day an adventure. They shopped until their feet hurt, purchasing armloads of goods, which Alice had shipped back to England. Alice was thinking of starting a new business in women's fashion and often asked for Prue's opinion on her choices.

Prue also bought items for her whole family as well as a suitcase full of elegant clothes and sandals, colourful scarfs and hats of all shapes and sizes for herself.

A guided tour took them up half way up Mount Vesuvius before Alice declared it was not worth the effort and decided they needed to find a bar and order champagne, which they did.

They stayed at the best hotel, Alice insisted, and ate at the best restaurants. She was modest enough to admit that she and Alice drew attention wherever they went and often were asked to join one table or another for drinks. Yet, despite all the attention that at one time she would have adored, now she thought that none of the men stood up to Brandon.

Focusing on her letters, and in mild surprise, she opened a short letter from Cece. Her younger sister rarely wrote to her.

Dear Prue,

Thank you for sending me a birthday present. The shawl is beautiful. I really like all the different shades of green. I'm writing this letter from Grandmama's house, as she sent for me to come down to see her and help her interview new staff. We are all shocked that Wyatt has gone. Poor Kilburn is struggling to cope with one arm, not that he'd admit it, but the broken arm will heal soon.

Mama is still in Paris. She lives there more than at home. If she's not in Paris, she's with Millie.

Prue stopped reading, suddenly aware that Cece had no one. Millie had Jeremy and Mama had Jacques, she'd been with Grandmama until recently and the whole time Cece was alone. For the first time, Prue felt remorseful for how her sister had been treated. Everyone went about their lives without giving a thought to Cece. She needed to make it up to her in some way. She wasn't exactly sure how she'd do it, for she and Cece had no common interests. But she had to make more of an effort with her.

Agatha is well and Uncle has recovered from a bad chest. I understand Agatha has written to you recently, so I'll not repeat her words about my time staying with them. We did the same things we always do and saw the same people at the same events. Nothing exciting at all.

I'm thinking of staying here with Grandmama for a time and see if I can be of use to her and perhaps help with some charity works here in London.

Many of our acquaintances have gone to the country for summer, obviously, but Grandmama doesn't want to go to York without Mama there, so we are staying in London. Grandmama is busy catching up with friends and the house is as busy as a train station with many people coming and going from morning until night. Still, I prefer it than the quietness of home.

I hope you are appreciating Positano very much and not simply getting drunk each night and sleeping all day.

Take care,
Your sister, Cece.
Mayfair, London.

Maria entered the villa carrying fresh produce. '*Signorina.* You return?'

'Yes, we are back from Naples, Maria. Did you miss us?' Prue smiled, folding away Cece's letter. 'Are the chickens well? I saw two of them as I came through the gate.'

'*Si*, all good. Many eggs. I make you dinner tonight?'

'*Si, per favore.*' Prue opened the next letter, her mind on Brandon. She didn't know if he would be calling by the villa tonight. She wasn't sure if he had returned from whatever mountain they'd gone to.

Her next letter was a short note from Mama saying she was leaving Paris to go to Millie at Chateau Dumont and would be staying there for the rest of the summer as Millie had been told by the doctor to take it easy during the pregnancy and Mama wanted to make sure she did.

Prue put the letter away. She suddenly missed her mama and Millie dreadfully. She wanted to hear their voices.

Commotion at the doorway made her look up as Vince could be heard telling Maria she was a vision of loveliness.

Brandon came into the sitting room and Prue leapt up from her chair.

'I'm so happy you're back.' Prue kissed him soundly.

'I missed you,' Brandon replied, kissing her back.

'Put each other down, you can't be sure where the other has been,' Vince joked, plonking himself down on the sofa.

'Did you enjoy Naples?' Brandon asked, sitting at the table next to Prue.

'Yes, we had a great time. Lots of shopping and sight-seeing. Alice is having a nap. We had a late night last night and a long trip home today. Did you get back this morning?'

'Midday.' Brandon held Prue's hand. 'We've cleaned and checked our gear, washed and shaved and are ready to be wined and dined by two beautiful ladies.'

'I need a bath first,' Prue murmured as Alice came through from the bedrooms.

'I thought I heard you both.' Giving both her brother and Vince a kiss on the cheek, Alice stretched and yawned. 'What a day. Did Prue tell you our ferry from Naples to Sorrento was delayed an hour? Then the little boat that was meant to take us to Positano failed to materialise. Luckily, we saw Stefano in Sorrento, and he brought us back to the villa in his boat. But the sea was choppy around the headland, not fun.'

Brandon rubbed his thumb on the back of Prue's hand. 'Rough day?'

'A little, yes.' Prue rose, tiredly. 'I'll go run a bath. We can either eat here or go out, which do you prefer? I'll need to let Maria know.'

'I'm voting here.' Alice started to make everyone a gin and tonic. 'I need a night doing nothing at all. We've had such a hectic week, haven't we, Prue?'

'We have. It was nonstop all week, yet I loved every minute of it.'

'Suits me to stay in.' Vince put his feet up on the small coffee table. 'We can play cards after dinner, if you fancy it?'

Prue kissed Brandon and left them arguing about what entertainment to do after dinner and went into the bathroom to run the bath. Letting the water fill the tub, she crossed the hallway to her bedroom.

Grabbing clean underwear from her drawers, she gasped as Brandon came in.

He stared around the room, smiling. 'Every night when I slept in the room right across the hallway, I'd lie in bed thinking of you wearing your silky nightgown…' He came and pulled her into him. 'I wanted to creep in and make love to you quietly, secretly.'

'I wish you had,' she murmured, running her fingers through his hair.

'I doubt your grandmama would have agreed,' he chuckled. 'Besides, I'm a gentleman, and sneaking around isn't my style.'

'It would have been fun finding out.' She stroked his face, knowing that she loved this man.

'I respect you too much to participate in a quick fumble with your grandmama sleeping in the next room. That's not how I behave.' He kissed her deeply, demanding the same urgent response from her.

She gave it willingly. 'Stay tonight then. No Grandmama,' she whispered between kisses.

He reared back, astonished. 'Really?'

Nodding, Prue continued kissing him. 'Oh yes. It's what we both want, isn't it?'

'Yes, of course it is, but it's a big step, especially for you.'

'Why especially for me?'

'Because… because you're innocent. I want your first time to be special. Wouldn't you want us to be married first?'

'Brandon, I'm a modern woman.' She tried to say it lightly, to erase the seriousness in his eyes. 'It's nineteen-twenty-two, not the Victorian age.'

'Modern or not, there are standards. I want you to know that you are special to me. I wouldn't take advantage of you.'

'You won't be.' Her heart did a flip in her chest. 'But there is something I need to tell you.'

'Oh?'

'I'm… I'm not… The thing is… I'm not a virgin.' She swallowed as he frowned.

He became very still. 'You aren't?'

She shook her head. 'No.'

'I don't understand. You are telling me you've shared another man's bed?'

'Yes. There was someone in India.'

Taking a step back, Brandon turned from her slightly. 'Do you love him?'

'No! No, I don't. I didn't.'

As though he was seeing her for the first time, he stared, confused. 'You didn't love him? He wasn't someone you were at least engaged to?'

'No.' Her stomach clenched at the look on his face.

'I know you to be adventurous and fun-seeking, but I never imagined you would have done such an intimate act on a whim.'

'It wasn't a whim,' Prue defended, a coldness entering her heart. 'We were friends and—'

'You sleep with all your friends?' His voice was hard.

'Of course not.' Anger started to build. 'Why are you so annoyed? I was curious.'

'Curious?' he mocked.

'Yes, damn you, curious. There is nothing wrong with that.' Rage was quickly replacing the anger. 'I presume you aren't a virgin?'

'I'm thirty years old, Prue, and a man. It isn't expected for me to be innocent on my wedding day.'

'But I am meant to be, of course?'

'As a lady from a decent family, yes, yes, it is expected. Naturally!' His voice rose to match hers.

'I'm sorry I've disappointed you!'

'Who was this person?' he demanded.

'What does it matter? It's in the past.'

'It matters to me. Are you still in contact with him?'

'No.'

'What is his name then?'

'Ajay Khan.'

It took a moment for him to register that the name wasn't British. His expression changed from anger to bewilderment to incredulous. 'An Indian?'

'Yes, an Anglo-Indian. Does that make a difference?'

Brandon stepped to the door. 'I'm beyond shocked. I never thought the woman I wanted to marry would have first had an Indian lover!' He slammed the door behind him.

'Brandon!' She ran after him, appalling Vince and Alice who were sitting drinking on the sofa staring at them.

'Brandon!' she called again.

He strode straight out of the villa and through the gate, ignoring her calls.

'Brandon!' Prue stood at the villa door, so angry she wanted to scream. The roar of the engine and skid of the tyres told her he had gone.

'What the hell just happened?' Alice came to her as she finally returned inside.

'I told Brandon I wasn't a virgin.'

'Oh, you silly fool.' Vince gave her a hug. 'I told you that some men don't like to know such things.'

Alice rounded on him. 'Why should Prue keep it quiet? Why is there one rule for men and another for women? We should be allowed to have some fun, too. Why can't women have the right to explore as men do?'

Vince raised his hands. 'Hey, don't blame me. He's *your* brother!'

Fuming, but also terribly hurt by Brandon's reaction, Prue stormed out onto the balcony and stared at the shimmering bay as the sun set. She should have mentioned to Brandon that Ajay was dead, but her stubbornness refused to let her. How dare he judge her! Had he told her about Claudia? Actually, had he told her anything that was deeply personal in all their time together? No, he hadn't!

'He'll come around,' Alice said, coming to stand beside her.

'I didn't want any secrets between us.'

'He's the biggest fool.'

Prue replayed the conversation again in her mind. 'He said he wanted to marry me, but I don't think that is the case any more. I'm tainted in his eyes.' Up until that moment she wasn't aware just how much she wanted to be his wife.

'He's a stupid pig-headed fool. I'll talk to him tomorrow when he's calmed down.'

'It won't change anything. I cannot undo what I have done.'

'No, but he needs to realise you are not a saint. He never learns. He did the same with Claudia, put her up on a pedestal. He thought her to be perfect and treated her as such. Only, she was simply a normal woman who wasn't perfect and had flaws, as we all do. Brandon didn't see any of that, but I did. I knew she wasn't right for him.'

'What happened between them?' Prue asked the question she'd been longing to know the answer too but too frightened to bring up the subject.

'She married another man when Brandon was fighting in France. She sent him a letter after she got married. Broke his heart, the soulless witch! I liked Claudia, but she shouldn't have done what she did. You don't send such a letter to a man facing machine guns. That's cruel.' Alice took a deep breath. 'He's not trusted any woman since, or ever loved anyone. You are the first after Claudia. I guess that's why he's reacted so badly. He thought you to be perfect, too.'

'I'm not.' Prue cringed at the mention of Claudia. She was jealous of a woman she didn't even know. This Claudia had been Brandon's first love.

'No one is perfect, dearest.' Alice hugged her. 'I'll talk to him.'

'Is it so wrong for me to find other men attractive?'

'No. Some women are prone to wanting to explore their feelings and urges, others not so much. It doesn't make you a bad person, Prue.'

'I bet you were a virgin on your wedding day?'

'I was, yes. But I've not lived like a nun since my husband died. For a while I went a little crazy. Some of the gossip about me is true, not that Brandon or any of my family would believe it, of course.

Nevertheless, I did behave wildly for a time, and I shared men's beds without a care, simply to assuage my own pain at missing my husband. I told no one because they wouldn't understand, but I think you do.'

'Thank you for telling me. Selfishly, I feel better now that I know it's not just me who has acted this way.'

'Society puts labels on people, it will always be that way. Single women should be pure for their future husbands, that's what people expect. Reality is very different. You aren't the first and you won't be the last, trust me.'

'You don't think less of me?'

Alice hugged Prue to her side. 'Not at all. I'm the last person to cast aspersions.'

'I would be loyal to Brandon, you must believe me.'

'I do.'

~ ~ ~ ~

In the pale light of a lantern hanging on a hook above his head, Brandon threw back another glass of grappa. The strength of which burned his throat and all the way down into his gullet. But it was deadening the pain.

He sat at a small wooden table, its blue paint chipped and faded. The chair was in the same state, in fact the whole bar was nothing more than an old fisherman's hut repurposed for the locals to visit to relish a cool drink and a plain decent bowl of pasta or whatever the old woman cooked behind the bar.

There was nothing fancy to the place to draw anyone here, but locals and the only other patrons were two old men smoking and chatting in the corner of the veranda. The one redeeming factor of the hut was its location, right on the water, secluded from prying eyes and unless you were a local, you'd never know it existed and that was exactly what Brandon wanted. To be left alone.

He'd found the place by accident. In his crazy dash from the villa he'd driven way too fast and recklessly. He'd rounded the bends too sharply, too quickly and yet, once out of Positano he'd driven as fast as the old motor car could go along the narrow dirt mountain roads. Stupidly, in fading light, he'd sped round a bend and nearly crashed into a herd of goats. He'd avoided a collision by swerving down an even narrower dirt lane that was nearly vertical.

Alarmed, he'd slowed down but unable to turn around without careening over the side of the cliff, he'd continued down the bumpy lane until he reached the secluded cove and the fisherman's hut.

Shaking slightly from his wild drive and the anger still simmering from Prue's admission, he made his way to the ramshackle bar and ordered a drink.

That was four hours ago.

Night had fallen, and although he couldn't see any houses before, a few lights twinkled in small buildings further along the curve of the cove. In the bar the old woman had been joined by a few more people and more lanterns were lit and strung along the veranda.

'We close soon, *signore.*' The old woman, dressed all in black announced, stepping out onto the veranda. 'Stay. Sit,' she added as Brandon rose to leave. 'You no drive. Over cliff.' She smashed her hands together. 'Die.'

Through eyes that were becoming increasingly difficult to see out of, Brandon watched the old woman return with a blanket. She threw this over a hammock that was strung in the corner of the veranda behind the two men who still sat, smoking and chatting.

'*Signore?* Sleep.' She indicated the hammock.

'*Grazie.*' Brandon had no wish to go anywhere right now. His head was fuzzy from drinking a lot of grappa for hours on an empty stomach.

She brought him out another bottle, and he paid her handsomely.

Resting back in the chair, he stared out over the black water. In the distance lights on a couple of fishing boats twinkled. A full moon was visible and the breeze coming off the water was cool but not unpleasant. The day had been so hot, it was a refreshing change.

'*Signore?*' one of the old men called to Brandon with a smile. 'Trouble? *Signorinas?*'

'*Si!*' Brandon raised his glass in their direction. Yes, trouble with a woman.

They laughed in return.

Brandon didn't join in. He didn't want to laugh or even joke. He was annoyed, frustrated and damn jealous that Prue had slept with another man. It was unreasonable to think this way, a small part of his brain argued, but he couldn't help it.

After Claudia broke his heart, he didn't care about women. For the last few years since the war ended he'd been happy climbing with Vince and visiting the odd lady of the night when in a strange town. Most times, he and Vince found willing partners when out drinking and no questions were asked as they sated their physical needs. He was never looking for a wife.

When the time came to marry, he wanted a woman who he could trust to be his ideal, someone who was solely his, untouched and who loved him in return, unlike Claudia. He didn't want a woman who had been with another, who had explored another man's body, who had let another man touch her so intimately, to be her first.

Some other man had felt Prue's touch on his body and Brandon couldn't cope with the jealousy that coursed through him. Another man had given Prue pleasure and had taught her what it was like to be sexually aroused and ache for more than mere kisses.

How was he to contend with that? Would she always compare him to her Indian lover? Would he match up?

No! He wasn't putting himself through it again. Claudia had found him wanting, obviously, for she'd given him no thought when she'd gone off and married another. He hadn't been worth waiting for and he was damned if he was going to play second best again. He didn't give a fig for modern ways or that women wanted to express themselves now. Is this what he'd fought for, nearly died for? To let women sleep with whoever they wanted and hang the consequences? Claudia hadn't cared about him as he faced bullets. She'd only concerned herself, her wants and her needs. Was Prue going to be the same?

He finished another glass of grappa, his mind and body slowly becoming numb and he welcomed it. He rose unsteadily from the chair, taking the bottle with him. Weaving between the few tables on the veranda, he headed for the hammock.

The two men laughed at his swaying, mismatched steps. Brandon tried to concentrate, but the effort seemed too much. The hammock swung away from him as he bent to sit on it, and with a thump he suddenly found himself lying sideways on the floor.

The two men laughed harder and helped him up. They spoke fast Italian and Brandon couldn't understand them.

Eyes closing, but determined, he tried again to climb onto the hammock and fell once more.

He swore at their chuckling, pushing them away as they helped him up again.

In the end, he stayed where he was, on the floor under the hammock. A blanket was thrown over him. Brandon drank straight from the bottle, not caring.

'No more women!' he yelled, raising a toast, but the two men were walking away, leaving the veranda and going home.

Saddened, Brandon wished for home, not necessarily England, or his parents' house, but a home of his own. He'd never had a home of his own before. He'd never had a place that was solely his or lived alone. He'd gone from his parents' house to boarding school, from school to university and from university to war. Then he toured countries with Vince.

Perhaps it was time to purchase his own home.

Maybe he'd buy a villa and stay in Italy…

Chapter Twenty

Prue took a deep breath and started climbing another steep set of stairs. Her legs protested at the constant walking up and down of stairs. She felt as though she had searched every shop and street in Positano. Alice and Vince were doing the same. However, Vince was doing it reluctantly, irritated that Brandon had been missing for three days. He wasn't worried but Prue and Alice were concerned. Vince believed Brandon had gone off in a sulk and would come back when he was ready.

She turned at the top of the steps and angrily stomped down another tight narrow cobbled alleyway between white painted houses. There was nothing here. She turned and climbed up another set of stairs. At the top she walked along another street, which on one side had a sheer cliff going upwards while the other side held a mixture of shops and houses, as always clinging to the mountainside.

There was no sign of Brandon's motor car, or him as she continued along. Church bells rang, echoing around the bay. The sun was high and hot. The pale pink cotton dress she wore stuck to her from the heat. It was too hot to be climbing stairs today. Sweat dripped down Prue's back as she groaned and faced another set of stairs leading up to the next street level.

Fed up and annoyed with Brandon, she turned and began the long walk back to the villa, which was on the other side of town and reached by two more stairways cut into a cliff face. Searching the town was fruitless. She refused to do it for another minute.

The sound of cowbells filled the air and Prue stepped to one side of the road as a farmer herded several cows along the cobbles. She gave him a small smile as she passed and rounded a bend. A little way along, she paused under an overhanging bougainvillea vine, it's purple flowers bright in the sunlight. The shade offered her a respite from the heat. She was dreadfully thirsty. The scent of lavender filled the air, and someone was cooking close by as the smell of garlic was strong.

A motor car's horn tooted, no doubt at the cows. Ignoring it, Prue continued, keeping tight to the side. For the last few days, since her argument with Brandon she'd tossed around the idea of going to France, to Millie's chateau for the rest of the summer. She'd even mentioned it to Alice, inviting her and Vince along, too. Alice had been up for it, but not so Vince. He was keen to do more mountain climbing, but promised he'd catch up with her once the winter arrived.

A motor car slowed down beside Prue and she turned enquiringly only to stop and stare at Brandon seated behind the driver's wheel.

Instantly angry, she glared at him. 'You are alive then, I see!'

'Apparently.' Under the brim of his hat, his gaze narrowed.

'Unfortunately, more like!' She strode off, torn between relief he was all right and an irrational urge to throttle him.

He drove at a snail's pace beside her. 'Can we talk?'

'Oh, *you* want to talk now, do you?' She waved him away. 'Sorry, you had your chance, but instead you stormed off like a child having a tantrum.'

'I'm sorry for doing that.'

'I don't care.'

'Prue!'

'What?' She spun towards the motor car and banged her fist on the bonnet. 'What do you want, Brandon?'

'I want us to talk, for you to explain to me why—'

'Explain to you?' She was incredulous. 'Why should I explain to you about anything? You're not my husband, father or brother. You are *nothing* to me! I *can* and *will* do as I like *when* I like.' She marched away, madder than she ever remembered being in her life.

'For God's sake!' Brandon exploded.

The motor car's door slammed, but she kept walking, ignoring him.

'Prue. Stop!'

'Go away.'

'I am sorry!' he yelled.

She turned to find him striding towards her, anger fought with a searing sadness. She blinked rapidly to fight the tears. She would not cry. 'Saying sorry, isn't good enough. Sorry doesn't fix everything. It doesn't stop me remembering the disappointment I saw in your eyes or from hearing the displeasure in the tone of your voice.'

'I reacted badly, I admit that, and I'm sorry. It was insensitive of me. Yes, I was disappointed, terribly. I hated to think that a man had touched you. I wanted it to be me. I wanted to be your first. I was jealous!'

'It can be you for many other firsts from this day forward until the day I die,' she said unhappily. She shook her head. 'But I'm not going to justify my actions to you for the rest of my life. I did what I did because I wanted to. Me. My decision. I was curious and defiant. So what? Why shouldn't women enjoy the experience of sex? I slept with a man once, Brandon, once. I wasn't the town whore. I'm twenty-four years old, not sixteen.'

Brandon took his hat off and ran his fingers through his hair. 'I overreacted. I'm sorry. Until you told me that I hadn't realised how much I loved you. But I felt betrayed. Ridiculous, I accept. I didn't even know you when you were in India.' He shrugged helplessly. 'What can I say? I'm an idiot.'

Emotion built hot behind her eyes. 'The damage is done. You see me differently now. I'm soiled in your eyes.'

He grabbed her arms. 'No! That isn't true!'

Her smile was watery as she fought the tears. 'I'm leaving Positano. Goodbye, Brandon.'

'Prue listen to me. I love you. I want us to get married.'

Such wonderful words. He loved her. He wanted to marry her. Yet, instinct told her it wouldn't work between them. She had to find someone else and never tell them her secret. Whoever she ended up marrying would believe she was a virgin on their wedding night. As much as she didn't want to lie, it was the only way to avoid disappointment, the accusations.

'Prue talk to me. What are you thinking? Do you want me?'

'Yes, I do, but it'll not work.'

'It will. I don't care if you've slept with someone else before.'

'But you do, Brandon. I suppose any man would. They don't want a wife who has known another man.'

'I want you! It's taken a three day drinking fest to make me come to my senses and a telling off from an Italian nona who made it clear I was a fool.' His voice became desperate, his face etched with pain.

'But what will you be thinking when we make love for the first time?' She raised her eyebrows, bracing for the hurt of leaving him. 'Will you always be wondering about that other man?'

He stepped back, pain in his eyes. 'I can't say. How can I know until that time arrives?'

'It's a risk I'm not willing to take.'

'I thought you were adventurous?' he half joked.

'Not with my heart.' She slowly walked away, silent tears dripping off her lashes.

~ ~ ~ ~

Brandon strained on the rope, his bad shoulder twinged with the effort. 'Vince, keep an eye on those clouds.'

'Yes, I see them. The wind has grown stronger.' Vince called back down to him from where he climbed the cliff face ten yards above.

The morning had been hot and clear, perfect for climbing, but now, steel grey clouds whipped by an ever-increasing wind, sped across the sky.

Thankfully, they were near the top of the mountain.

Brandon regretted the climb for many reasons, one being he should have gone to the villa this morning to talk to Prue again, but Vince persuaded him not to. Vince said Alice would talk Prue around, but Brandon wasn't too sure. He'd learned that Prue was stubborn, and really, was he entitled to her changing her mind? He'd treated her shamelessly.

Unwillingly, he'd agreed with Vince to go on this climb and give Prue some space to think.

This morning, he'd stopped at the villa on the way to the climb and finding Maria in the garden feeding the chickens, he'd given her a note to pass on to Prue saying that he loved her. He hoped it would be the start of Prue forgiving him.

Now, as the wind slapped him in the face, he gave his attention to finishing the climb. He looked up, curling his fingers into niches in the rock face. The cries of birds drifted on the wind as they swooped and dived near them. A drop in the temperature cooled the sweat on his skin.

Taking the weight on his good arm, he pulled himself up further, the toes of his spiked boots searching for grip. He fed the rope through the link, giving more slack, then glanced up to check on Vince climbing above him.

'Nearly there,' Vince shouted down, his words almost carried away by the wind that buffeted them.

Gritting his teeth, Brandon reached up probing for a hold. A trickle of apprehension shot through him as he grabbed at a fissure in the rock and missed. He fingers slipped on loose gravel and a barb of fear gripped his stomach. He had to get up to the top. Fast.

Concentrating on finding a foothold, he was shocked when the first hailstones pelted him. He swore and heard Vince shouting something to him.

Putting in extra effort, he climbed up a few yards with little regard to safety. Level ground was slightly above Vince's head and through the blur of hail, he watched his friend heave himself over the edge to lie on the ground. Safe.

Brandon swore again in relief, releasing a pent-up breath. The hail pitted against his face, stinging his skin and tapping him on the head like sharp knuckles.

Why were they putting themselves through this? Hadn't they climbed enough mountains now? Wasn't there more to life than trying to kill themselves? They'd survived the war, why push the limits with this?

The vision of Prue's face came to mind, and the cheeky way she smiled when wanting to get her way about something. He remembered again the way her lips melded to his. She was worth living for. He'd win her back, he had to. It was funny that for all these years he thought no one would ever match up to Claudia, yet within moments of meeting Prue, Claudia ceased to exist in his mind, and he was free of her, finally. He just wished the damage she'd done to him hadn't lingered, unknowingly. Prue wasn't Claudia.

And all he wanted was Prue. He had to convince her of that. The past was gone. The future was all he cared about.

His foot slipped. Scaring him. He must focus. He concentrated on the job at hand, which was not to fall to his death from this cliff. Later, he would call in at the villa and beg for Prue's forgiveness and do whatever it took for her to change her mind. Vince had called him all kinds of a fool when he had finally turned up at their hotel, and his best friend was right.

He'd been so stupid. Prue was his future. He had to get off this mountain and tell her so.

With care, he inched his way up, the hail had turned to biting rain and it dripped down his face. Blinking, he fixated on each placement of his feet and hands. Icy wind battered him, threatening to tear him off the cliff side. His bad shoulder ached severely, but safety and Vince weren't too far away now.

'There now, mate, nearly there,' Vince yelled against the bitter wind, hanging over the edge, his hand reaching down.

Brandon nodded, straining to keep a grip on the footholds. Pain stabbed his shoulder. Rain blinded him. He groaned and reached up and with his fingertips and touched the rocky ledge of the ground above, but the edge crumbled beneath his hand. Suddenly, the rope jerked. He lost his grip and jolted down a yard or two. He swung helplessly in mid-air.

'Vince!'

'Hold on! The anchor is slipping.' Vince disappeared back over the top.

Terror froze Brandon. No, not the anchor! He tried to pull himself up again, but pain shot through his shoulder. He moaned at the stabbing throb that filled his mind.

'Have you got a good grip? Can you haul yourself up?' Vince shouted, his voice reflecting his fear as he returned to lean over the edge on his knees.

'Yes, I think so,' Brandon called back, fighting the pain. 'This bloody shoulder has gone again.'

Inch by agonising inch, he heaved himself up the side of the mountain, praying to unknown gods that the anchor would hold should he fall again.

Close to the top, he held up his hand.

'I've got you.' Vince grabbed him to haul hard.

Whatever Vince was about to say ended in a yelp as a blast of wind knocked Vince off balance and he fell sideways and nearly over the side.

Instinctively, Brandon seized him with both hands, the motion upsetting his own balance and sending another ripping pain through his shoulder and down his arm, but he held on with a strength he didn't know he possessed.

'Get back!' He pushed Vince backwards, his good arm gripping a large rock.

Panting, Vince gained traction and scrambled away from the edge, dragging Brandon with him as the ropes tightened securing them from plummeting to the ground hundreds of yards below.

Adrenalin and fear pulsed through Brandon as he lay gasping alongside Vince.

Agony. His body was on fire and he knew he'd done much more damage to his shoulder this time. He swore violently, trying to steady his breathing.

Blinding rain and howling wind erased visibility. They were both soaked through and cold. The dark grey clouds seemed close enough to reach out and touch.

Brandon fought the need to vomit, the torture of his damaged shoulder filled his brain and he groaned.

'I don't want to think how close that was.' Vince shook his head, breathing hard. 'Are you all right? Christ, Brandon, you're white as a sheet.'

'Get me off this damn mountain, Vince,' he moaned.

'I'm not certain we can walk down, mate.' Vince glanced around, the storm wiping out landmarks as far as the bay in the distance. 'We need to climb back down, that's the fastest way.'

'I don't think I can.'

'We can't walk down. We don't know the way. We always climb up and then climb back down. That's how we do it,' panic crept into Vince's voice.

Brandon cradled his arm against his chest to try to ease the intense agony. 'Vince. We have to walk down. I can't hold the rope to descend.'

'Right, of course.' Nodding, Vince knelt beside him and unlatched the straps and ropes from Brandon's harness. With each movement Brandon fought not to faint. He had to stay on his feet for Vince's sake.

Vince packed up their gear and with an arm around Brandon, they tenderly made their way away from the cliff face and over the rise of the mountain's peak. Positano disappeared behind them and in front was only more mountains.

'How do we know which way will get us back to a village,' Vince spoke against the wind and rain.

'Once we are lower down, we'll find some sort of sign, a road or something,' Brandon encouraged, doing his best to ignore the pain.

'It's going to take us hours to get back to the motor in this weather and with your arm,' Vince muttered. 'It'll be dark by the time we reach the bottom.'

'Just keep going.' Brandon winced, tripping over a rock.

'It's like being back in the bloody trenches,' Vince scoffed.

'At least we aren't getting shot at,' Brandon tried to joke to take his mind off the throbbing ache.

Their wet clothes made them uncomfortable and the cold wind battered them. Within minutes, Brandon was gasping with every step. They were high above the tree line and had nowhere to take shelter. With reduced visibility, they had to watch where each foot was placed. The endless deluge turned the mountain into a grey slippery death-trap.

With a sudden yelp, Vince fell forward, the rocky outcrop he'd stood on was fast crumbling away beneath him.

In horror, Brandon watched him roll down a steep slope and drop over the side of the mountain.

'Vince!' Brandon ran to where Vince had disappeared.

In what seemed an eternity, Vince stopped rolling and lay still at the bottom of a gorge that separated one mountain from another.

'I'm coming!' Brandon stumbled and slipped down the slope, jarring his shoulder so badly he gagged, needing he'd be sick. With a thud, he landed on his knees at Vince's side. The pain in his shoulder had become unbearable, and he swayed fighting another faint.

'Vince!' He shook his friend's shoulder.

'I'm all right, I hope,' Vince murmured, dazed and bleeding from a cut on his forehead.

'Can you walk?'

Vince sat up and rubbed his forehead, his fingers came away with blood on them. 'I'm sure hope so.'

'Bloody hell. What a day.' Brandon wiped the rain from his eyes. 'I'm done with all this.'

'Me, too.' Vince reached for Brandon to help him up forgetting about Brandon's shoulder, and as he pulled on Brandon's arm, pain spasmed through Brandon's whole body. He yelled in agony and felt himself falling. Everything dimmed to black.

Chapter Twenty-One

Prue folded a skirt and placed it in the second half-filled suitcase. This morning she had gone down into the town and bought another suitcase to cope with all her extra clothes she bought when in Naples.

Yesterday, after finishing it with Brandon, she'd returned to the villa and started packing her trunk, much to Alice's dismay. Prue had then arranged for her trunk to be sent to England, leaving only clothes to take with her. Even so, she'd needed another suitcase.

Going into town to purchase it gave her an excuse to get away from Alice. She knew Alice meant well, but she didn't want to talk about Brandon, or her decision to end something that really hadn't even begun. It was best to do it now, before she became too deeply attached to him.

Grabbing another skirt, she flinched as the wind assaulted the wooden shutters on the windows. Rain fell heavily and despite it only being mid-afternoon, the light had gone as though it was mid-winter.

Prue closed the shutters and switched on the lamp beside her bed.

'I'm a little concerned,' Alice announced, coming into the bedroom and sitting down amongst Prue's clothes.

'Why?' Prue asked, adding a pair of sandals to the suitcase.

'Vince said he and Brandon were climbing today. The weather has turned dreadful'.

Prue's stomach tightened. 'They are likely to be back by now.'

'Yes, quite likely. I'll venture down to their hotel and see if they have returned.'

'In this weather? You're brave.'

'Well, on second thoughts, I'll ask Maria if her brother, Marco, will go instead.' Alice laughed. 'I don't want to ruin my new shoes.' She wiggled her feet showing off the expensive brand of red-heeled sandals she wore.

'Marco has a bicycle and has been happy in the past to run errands for us,' Prue agreed. 'Tip him well and I'm sure he'll do it, storm or no storm.'

'I will. Since it's your last night, perhaps we can all go out for dinner?'

'No, thank you. I have letters to write that I can post in Naples. A friend of mine, Laurence Richardson, has invited me to stay with him in Port Said, I'm seriously considering it, if only for a few days. Grandmama and I were going to stop and stay with the Richardsons on the way back from India, but I was still recovering from malaria and we didn't want to burden them.'

'Please don't go, Prue. I feel terrible about Brandon's behaviour, but it shouldn't stop us from having a good time here.'

'I told you, I can't stay here with Brandon so close.'

'We'll go elsewhere then.'

Prue shook her head and kept packing.

'Get Bridget to pack for you.'

'No, I can do it myself.'

'You're too independent!' Alice huffed and left the bedroom and Prue could hear her talking to Maria in the kitchen.

After another hour of packing, Prue tucked in a last pair of sandals and decided she was nearly done. At times her gaze would stray to the note Maria gave her that morning from Brandon. It simply said, I love you.

Part of her wanted to cave and go see him, but another, stubborn part of her rejected the words.

They weren't enough to change her mind. Brandon had judged her and found her wanting. Well, stuff him and his uptight morals! She didn't need his good opinion, or his love, which no doubt would lessen every time he thought of her and Ajay.

Ajay.

Why had she slept with him? If she'd known back then it would jeopardise her chance of having a future with Brandon she would never had done it. Her impulsiveness had led to the pain she suffered now. She had to learn from that.

She took a deep breath, annoyed with herself. No, she wasn't going to be ashamed any more. She'd done it and she had to live with it. Moreover, Ajay was dead, and she was alive because of him. She wouldn't sully their time together with regret. He deserved more than that and so did she.

Blast Brandon! Her thoughts whirled back and forth until she expected her head to burst.

She needed to leave Positano. Despite saying to Alice she'd stop and visit Laurence in Egypt, she knew she wouldn't. She needed to be with Millie in

France. There, she could put some distance between herself and Brandon and gain wise council from her older sister. She missed Millie enormously and with her heart broken about Brandon she needed Millie's hugs, and hopefully her mama's if she was there as well. Not that Mama would understand why she grieved so badly for a relationship that no one even knew about.

'Prue!' Alice's call drew her from the bedroom and into the sitting room.

'What is it?'

'Marco has returned, and Brandon and Vince have not arrived back from the climb.' Alice stood smoking by the closed French doors leading out to the balcony.

'Surely in this awful weather they would have abandoned the climb?'

'I should think so. They are sensible about that kind of thing.'

Prue glanced at the wild storm and then at the clock on the mantelpiece. Brandon and Vince had left at dawn and now it was close to four o'clock in the afternoon. 'Did Marco leave a note at the hotel?'

'Yes. I told him to.'

'Good. I might go and run a bath.' Prue gave an encouraging smile. 'Then we'll have some dinner.'

'Yes.' Alice drew deeply on a cigarette. 'Maria has cooked a fabulous lasagne.'

'I won't be long.' Prue didn't really want to have a bath but needed to do something to keep herself occupied.

~ ~ ~ ~

'Stop worrying, Prue. Heavens, you'll make me start soon, and I never worry. It's a waste of time and energy.' Alice sipped her morning tea at the table, her toast uneaten.

'Sorry.' Prue couldn't eat the breakfast Maria had made. A cup of tea was all she could manage as she stood by the balcony doors and watched the sun rise higher in a clear blue sky.

'They'll be in some little village getting fussed over by some old nona whose force-feeding them breakfast,' Alice said with false gaiety while flipping through a French women's magazine. 'Come and give me your opinion of this layout.' She held up the magazine.

Sighing, Prue sat beside her and tried not to worry over Brandon. 'I really don't have time, Alice. I've got to leave soon.'

'You're going to go without saying goodbye to Brandon and Vince?'

'I'll visit Vince when I'm back in London. I have his address in Sussex, too.'

'And have you considered more about what I offered last night?' Alice asked.

Last night, during the long hours they stayed awake unable to sleep, Alice had informed Prue about her idea of starting a new business venture, which was to create a women's fashion magazine in London. She'd been in Paris to meet with clothes designers and now thought to do the same while in Italy. After seeing how stylish Prue was, and her keen eye for wearing the latest fashion and even starting her own trends, Alice had offered Prue a job with the magazine as an editor.

The idea intrigued Prue, and if she was honest, excited her to be doing something interesting and worthwhile with her time. She'd pondered over the job offer and Brandon until nodding off just before dawn broke.

Prue sipped her tea. 'I'd like to be a part of your magazine, yes. I accept your offer.'

'Excellent! I'm so happy! Thank you.' Eagerly, Alice turned another page. 'See, here? The way the model is standing with no real interesting background? I don't like that. In my magazine I want themes for each page, or set of pages, depending on what they are wearing.'

'Yes, I believe that's a fine idea. You should also consider about adding accessories, too. Show women how to wear the right colours, jewels, shoes, that kind of thing,' Prue added, straining to hear a motor car pull up outside, and at the same time hoping one didn't. She didn't think she could face Brandon again.

'Absolutely. That's where you'll come in.' Alice took another magazine off the pile on the table. 'We should go to Rome tomorrow for a week or two and then to Venice afterwards.'

'I'm going to France. I'm not changing my mind.' Prue sighed. All night she had argued with Alice about her need to go to France. Although she was interested in helping with the magazine, she first wanted to see Millie and Mama. She needed to be with her family.

'Can you not go afterwards? Between us we could cover quite a lot of meetings.'

'Alice, please, try to understand. I want to be with Millie until the baby is safely born.'

'Very well. How about Paris next month? The chateau is not far by train from Paris you said. We could meet up there for a couple of days.' Pausing, Alice frowned. 'Sorry. I'm taking over, aren't I? I cannot tell you what to do, I apologise. I'm a terrible friend. Of course, you must be with your family. I'm afraid that once I get an idea in my head, I steam-roll right over everyone else to get it done.'

Prue smiled and grasped Alice's hand. 'I do want to help you and be a part of the magazine, please believe me, but I've not seen my family for over a year, and I miss them. Once I've spent some time with them, and the baby has arrived, then I will be eager and ready to help you in any way you want. I promise.'

'Good. You have divine style and a brilliant talent for knowing what to wear. You'll be extremely useful to me and the success of the magazine. I can be based in London and you can journey all around the world finding designers.'

'That sounds perfect to me.' Prue poured more tea into her cup. 'If you are serious about this magazine, then so am I.'

'I am. It's something I've thought about for some time. After my husband died, I had no interest in anything, but I can't live the rest of my life like that, I'll go mad.' Alice put out her cigarette. 'I have the money to start this business, but I need help with the running of it.'

Prue added a little milk to the cup. 'I'm honoured that you think I am worthy.'

'You are, but as I said, it'll be hard work.'

'I doubt meeting fashion designers is actually working. To me, it sounds like fun. And we could find a few adventures while we're at it.' Prue smiled and realised up to that moment she hadn't really known what she wanted to do with her life. Without Brandon, she might as well do something to keep busy. 'Actually, my first trip should be to New York. What do you think?'

'Agreed. And Brandon?' Alice raised her eyebrows in question. 'What about you and him?'

'There isn't an us.'

'I know my brother, and he's been trying to keep himself occupied since the war ended. But now, I feel he's fallen so deeply for you and he's ready to turn his mind to other things. To settle. It's time. My parents and I want him back in England. They've done enough worrying over him.' Alice flipped through the magazine again. 'I have a plan anyway for him. You see, Brandon has a good head for business. He's smart that way, and I intend to use him to help me with the magazine. You and I will do the fashion part, as we both have good taste in that area, but Brandon would be brilliant with all the other boring paperwork stuff such as tax, I really don't want to be concerned about. I'm going to ask Vince to help, too, he knows even more people than I do and will be fabulous at the marketing aspect of it.'

'Brandon will agree to be a part of the business?' Prue's heart pounded. That wasn't what she was expecting. She didn't want to be thrown into Brandon's company all the time.

'Yes, he will, for me, and for you.'

'Alice…'

'Listen to me, Prue,' Alice said seriously. 'I understand your reservations, but please give him another chance. He loves you, and my brother doesn't love lightly, I assure you.'

Prue looked at the clock again. They'd had no word in over twenty-four hours. Where was he? Had something happened? Why hadn't they returned to the hotel and sent a note?

'Stop watching the clock!' Alice sighed. 'Now you're making me worry.'

'I'm sorry, but I have the feeling that something isn't right.' Prue left the table and stood by the French doors. 'And I need to get down to the jetty. Stefano is taking me to Sorrento to catch the ferry.'

Alice rose. 'I'll go and ask Marco to go down to their hotel again. I will kill them both when I see them!'

Five minutes later, Alice returned. 'Marco has gone. What a good chap.'

Prue nodded. 'I'll bring my suitcases through from the bedroom. When Marco gets back, I'll ask him to help me take them down to the jetty.'

'Surely you want to know if Brandon and Vince are safe and sound, don't you?'

'Absolutely, and once they are, I can leave,' she said flippantly.

'You do love Brandon, don't you?'

'Is it love? I do care about him, a lot, but as we've discussed repeatedly, it'll not work between us. I don't match up to his expectations.'

'Nonsense. It would work if you gave it a chance, dear Prue. And I'm so happy that my brother has fallen in love with you. You'll be a fine addition to our family.'

'Alice!' No matter how many times she argued with Alice about the situation with Brandon the woman refused to give up hope.

'It seems a natural decision to me, why fight it? Grab life, Prue, it can be gone before you know it, believe me.'

Prue closed her eyes, her heart and mind torn. Grab life. That same saying was always being said to her. What would her grandmama do?

The flinging open of the door and Marco rushing in made them jump in alarm.

'Marco? What is it?' Alice snapped.

'*Sorrento!*' He panted.

'Sorrento? What are you talking about?' Prue frowned at him.

'*Signore ospedale!*' He spoke in fluent Italian losing both Prue and Alice completely.

'What is he saying?' Alice demanded.

'Maria!' Prue shouted, only to turn and realise Maria was standing right behind her.

Maria was wiping her hands on her apron. '*Signore* Brandon and *Signore* Vince in *ospedale* at Sorrento.' She paused to listen to her brother as he continued speaking. 'A note… sent to the hotel this morning …'

'What is an *ospedale*?' Prue looked from Marco to Maria.

'Hospital,' Maria supplied.

'Oh, my God!' Alice grabbed Prue's arm. 'Now, we mustn't be alarmed, it might not be serious.'

'Brandon.' Prue's hand flew to her throat as her heart dipped. 'I must go to him!'

Within a short space of time, Maria organised for them to be taken by a neighbour's horse and cart through the winding streets and down to the jetty.

In relief they saw Stefano was working on his boat, cleaning up after the storm the night before. He agreed to take them to Sorrento as he'd planned to take Prue anyway.

'Why are they in Sorrento?' Prue asked for the hundredth time as Stefano motored the *Rosa* around the headland, leaving Positano behind. She was thankful the storm had gone, and the sea was calm once more.

Alice gazed out over the water. 'As long as they are both all right, that is all I care about.'

Forty minutes later, they were docking in Sorrento's beautiful harbour. Stefano spoke with some men standing outside a café and one of them offered to take Prue and Alice in his taxi to the hospital.

Prue and Alice remained silent as the fat little man drove them through the cobbled streets of the town to the hospital.

In broken Italian and with lots of hand gestures Prue and Alice managed to make the nurse at reception understand who they wanted to see.

Along a corridor of an old red-bricked building they finally found Vince, who had scratches on his face and a bandage on his forehead.

Alice hugged him tightly. 'Are you both all right? Where's Brandon?'

'He's not great,' Vince replied, embracing Prue. 'He's going to be taken to Naples.'

'Naples?' Prue gasped. 'Why?'

'To have surgery on his shoulder. They're organising for an ambulance to take him now.' He told them before leading them into a room where Brandon lay. Speaking in Italian to the nurse, who was checking Brandon's condition, Vince ushered them closer to Brandon's bed. 'He's been sedated for the journey.'

Prue fought the tears, not willing to let them escape. She had to be strong. Brandon wasn't dead, not like Ajay. He was simply sedated. That said, he looked dreadful. His face was white as the sheet he was lying on. His arm was in a sling and she could see how much his shoulder was padded and bandaged.

'When do they take him,' Alice whispered.

'Soon, within the hour I was told.' Vince looked down on his friend. 'They need to try to save his arm.

299

The doctor has warned that the nerve damage in his shoulder could be too severe to save.'

Alice straightened her shoulders. 'Poppycock! I'll not have that! Where's the doctor, I'll speak to him.' She stormed out of the room.

Vince gave Prue a small smile. 'I feel sorry for that doctor.'

Prue swallowed back emotion. 'To lose his arm, Vince…'

~ ~ ~ ~

As Brandon's sibling, Alice could travel in the ambulance with Brandon, not that the hospital authorities had much choice for Alice was in a demanding mood and should anyone wish to argue with her they would receive a tongue-lashing. Alice's requirements for Brandon to have the best of everything, no expense spared, made her a force to be reckoned with, and Prue and Vince let her get on with it.

Vince hired a motor car from a garage whose owner happened to be a friend of Stefano's and he and Prue followed the ambulance to Naples.

'What happened?' Prue asked him as they drove the coast road.

'Everything was going so well,' Vince told her, staring straight ahead as he drove. 'We were near the end of the climb and out of nowhere the weather turned dreadful. Hail and winds, the lot. The storm came and made everything hazardous.'

'Yes, it was bad even at the villa.'

'In his rush to reach the top, Brandon must have strained his shoulder too much. There was no way he could manage climbing back down, which is usually what we do as it's the quickest way. We had to walk off the mountain instead. Only, with the storm raging we could barely see a few feet in front of us.' Vince rubbed one hand over his face tiredly. 'We hadn't gone far when I slipped and fell down a steep slope into a gorge. I remember rolling and banging into rocks and bushes and thinking I'm going to roll to my death, or at least break every bone in my body.'

'You must have been terrified.'

'I was, then I slammed against a rock and stopped. Brandon ran down to help me, he was in enormous pain. He could only use one arm to help me, but I was dazed, not thinking correctly and pulled myself up on his bad arm ... Brandon screamed and passed out.' Vince shook his head. 'God, what a bloody fool I am! My actions have probably made him lose his arm.'

'You don't know that.' Prue placed her hand on his arm in comfort. 'You can't blame yourself, you were dazed and in shock. It's not your fault. Brandon would never blame you. Besides, the damage might have already been done as he was climbing.'

Vince was quiet, a tortured look in his eyes. Taking a deep breath, he changed gear as they slowed to drive around a sharp bend.

'How did you get down the mountain?'

'I had to wait for Brandon to regain consciousness. Then, holding him up by his good arm, we slowly trekked down, stopping every few minutes to rest. We had no idea where we were, and it took us hours to reach level ground. There was a track, which led to a farmer's hut. Luckily for us, he was there and he took us on the back of his cart to the nearest village. Brandon passed out again from the pain of being jostled on the cart, but it couldn't be helped. We reached the village, I don't even know its name, and from there some people took us to Sorrento. They were extremely kind. I shall go back and thank them.'

'Yes, that would be a lovely thing to do.' Prue stared out at the stretch of water they passed by, but her thoughts weren't on the boats or the prettiness of the Gulf of Naples, but on Brandon.

Ever since finding out he was in hospital, she'd been on edge. The thought of him dying had overridden every other argument she had with herself about whether he was the man for her.

She couldn't lose him. It was as simple as that, and if Brandon was willing to try and see if they could be a couple, then she would as well.

She loved him. Life was too short.

'But first, we need to see what the outcome is for Brandon,' Vince said, breaking into her thoughts. He gave her a sidelong glance. 'I know you had called it off with Brandon, and I understand why, but he does care for you. He's not one to share his feelings with anyone, but I understand him better than he realises, and what he feels for you is true and real.'

She nodded. 'Thank you for telling me that.'

'Will you change your mind about him?'

'I already have.'

'Even if he has lost his arm?'

'It's only an arm, Vince. He has another one with which to hold me.'

Vince's cheeky smile returned. 'You're a corker, Prue Marsh!'

While Brandon underwent a lengthy surgery, Prue booked them into a small hotel, which was shabby but clean and the closest she could find to the hospital. She bought fresh clothes and toiletries for them all, as they'd not brought luggage with them.

It was past midnight before Brandon was brought out of recovery and into a ward. They weren't allowed to see him and only been told the surgery was successful, whatever that meant. No one seemed to speak English and Vince's understanding of Italian wasn't ideal. With lots of hand signals and shakes of the head, a strict and bossy matron declared the three of them would not be seeing Brandon tonight and were to go to the hotel and return in the morning.

Being so tired, they agreed, even Alice, who'd not eaten all day and survived on cups of coffee.

The following morning, washed and changed, Prue and Alice collected Vince from his room, and they headed back to the hospital. A nurse told them Brandon was awake and they could see him for a short time.

The three of them entered the room and stood quietly. Brandon had his eyes closed, his face pale, and his shoulder and arm bandaged and held rigid in a contraption attached to the bed and ceiling.

Prue sagged, seeing that he still had his arm. They'd not amputated it. With tear-filled eyes, she gripped Alice's hand.

Slowly, as if sensing their arrival, Brandon opened his eyes.

'Well.' Alice strode over to the bed and kissed her brother's forehead. 'That's enough of that then. No more climbing and scaring us witless. Understand? And before you say another word, I've got plans for you and Prue, and Vince if he wants it, concerning my new magazine. We'll talk later. Right now, you need to kiss Prue and apologise for alarming her so badly!' She turned to Vince, took his arm, and led him out of the room.

Alone together, Brandon and Prue smiled at each other.

Brandon cleared his throat. 'My sister is a law unto herself. What if I have plans of my own?' He shifted in the bed and a flash of pain etched his features. 'And I'm very sorry for causing you concern.'

'Are you hurting terribly?' She stepped closer. He held himself stiffly. The contraption made it difficult for him to move.

'They've given me something for the pain. I'll be fine, eventually.' He stretched out his good hand to her, and she grabbed it like a lifeline.

'I was so worried,' Prue gabbled. 'I knew something had happened, I just knew it, but I dared not say anything or I'd upset Alice.'

He brought her hand to his lips and kissed it. 'I'm sorry I worried you.'

'Promise you won't ever do such a thing again!'

'I promise. I'm done with climbing.'

'Good.'

'Marry me, Prue. It's crazy, too soon, only been months, but you're all I think about day and night. We can have a long engagement or whatever you wish, please say yes, and let me love you. I don't deserve a second chance, but I'll make it up to you.'

Her heart hammered, but she needed reassurance. 'Can you get past the fact that I've slept with someone else?'

'I can. In the last week I've done nothing but torment myself and I've decided that if he was the man for you, you'd never have left India.'

'Brandon, Ajay is dead. He died saving my life, but he wasn't the man for me. I didn't love him.'

'He saved you?'

'Yes. In a riot in Bombay. Rebels were shooting at us. A gun was aimed at me. Ajay threw himself over me and the bullet hit him instead.'

'Prue…' He shook his head. 'Why didn't you tell me?'

'You never really gave me a chance.'

'No, I didn't, and I'm a fool.' He winced as he moved. 'Is that why you were so upset when the Blackshirts came? Did you think it was another riot?'

'Yes.' She shuddered, remembering. 'I felt like it was happening all over again.'

'I wish you had told me.'

'I should have.' She glanced down at their joint hands. 'You must understand that Ajay is my past, and you are my future.'

He stared at her in surprise. 'Are you sure? Do you want time? I behaved badly. I said awful things.'

'I'm sure, and no, I don't need to think about it. I know what I feel.'

'Which is?'

'You first,' she challenged.

He chuckled. 'I fell in love with you the minute I looked at you that first night we met in Rome. I helped your grandmama into her seat and when I looked up you were there, and I couldn't breathe from that moment on. Since then, you've filled my head and heart.'

Her chest swelled with love for this handsome brave man. 'That's rather amazing, because that's exactly what happened to me.'

'You hid it well.' He gave her an ironic smile. 'I had no idea how you felt. I was consumed with jealousy when Antonio showed you attention and then I lost my mind when you confessed about sleeping with someone else. I wanted to be your first.'

'You'll be my forever, isn't that a better option?'

'Undeniably.' His smile was warm and loving. 'On that mountain all I could think about was you. I didn't want to risk it all and die, not before asking you for forgiveness.'

'You have it.'

'Will you marry me?'

'I will, my love.' She reached over and kissed him gently, not wanting to cause him any pain.

He rubbed his thumb over her knuckles. 'We'll do whatever you want, travel, see the world, or at least America.' He grinned. 'Or we can go home to England and raise a dozen children.'

Happiness filled her and she grinned. 'Can we go to New York?'

'I'll take you wherever you want to go, my darling.'

'All of that will have to be put on hold for a bit as your sister has plans for us to become involved in her magazine business. She's willing to offer us shares in it, in return for working with her.' Prue shrugged, not really caring about anything but the fact Brandon loved her and wanted to marry her.

'My damn sister,' he muttered with a smile. 'Do you want to do that?'

'Yes, I think I do.' A glow spread through her of being not only Brandon's wife but useful in creating a magazine. 'I want to be active. I'm not one for sitting around the house. I'll not be the typical wife, if that's what you're wanting,' she warned.

'Darling, there is no way I can ever expect you to be a typical wife. However, I'll have fun discovering just what sort of wife I'll be living with.' He tugged her close for another kiss, wincing at the effort.

'That works both ways, Mr Forster!' She laughed gently, then another thought entered her head.

'Brandon, about Claudia… Alice says she was the love of your life.'

'No, not really. I loved her yes, or at least what I imagined was love as a young man, but I soon learned she wasn't the right one for me. She didn't have the same feelings for me as I did for her. When she rejected me, I was hurt, my pride and ego dented.' He smiled self-consciously. 'I'm looking at the love of my life right now.'

A small nag of doubt still lingered. 'Truly? You're terribly sure I am the one you want forever. It's such a long time, you know, and I'm not the easiest person to get along with, simply ask Cece. I'm impulsive and reckless and—'

'Prue Marsh, you are all I want, I promise you, now and always.' He gazed at her with tenderness and desire. 'So, kiss me again before the others come back.'

She laughed and for once did exactly as she was told.

Author Note

Hello Readers,

I hope you enjoyed, *Prue,* book two of the Marsh Saga series.

Millie, book one, was a new era for me to write. I'd never written a story set in the 1920s before and had to research a lot about how women were stretching the boundaries of their independence and freedom. The end of WWI brought many changes, but at the bottom of it all, women were still expected to marry well and raise children. I wanted that for Millie because she is the oldest and would naturally lead the way for her sisters. Yet, I also wanted to show each sister as being unique.

Prue was a joy to write as she is very different to her sisters. They all have courage when needed and spirit, but unlike the others, Prue has a little of a devil-may-care attitude and is more reckless. I hope you liked her story.

I've added a short excerpt of the next book, which is about *Cece*, Millie and Prue's younger sister.

In order the books are: *Millie, Christmas at the Chateau*, a novella that fits between *Millie* and *Prue* that explores the family a little more, then *Cece* and finally *Alice.*

I hope you enjoy the series, which you can find on Amazon, or order from bookshops and libraries.

AnneMarie Brear
2020.

Acknowledgements

Thank you to my wonderful friends and fellow authors, Maggi Andersen and Lynda Stacey – you both listened to me going on about this series and giving advice where needed!

To my editor, Jane Eastgate, thank you for finding my mistakes.

Thank you to my family and friends. Your support means the world to me, especially my husband, who continually wonders when will there be a movie deal...

Finally, the biggest thank you goes to my readers, especially to the members of the Facebook group run by Deborah Smith who are so supportive of me and my books.

Over the years I have received the most wonderful messages from readers who have told me how much they've enjoyed my stories. Each and every message and review encourages me to write the next book.

Most authors go through times when they think the story they are writing is no good and I am no exception. The times when we struggle with the plot, when the characters don't behave as we wish them to, when 'normal' life interferes with the writing process and we feel we haven't got enough time in the day to do all we have to do those messages make us smile!

A few words from a stranger saying they loved my story dispels my doubts over my ability to be an author, at least for a little while! I can't express enough how much those lovely messages mean to me. So, thank you!

If you'd like to follow me on my author page on Facebook. www.facebook.com/annemariebrear

To receive my email newsletter, or find out more about me and my books, please go to my website where you can find all my book titles and also join the mailing list for updates.
http://www.annemariebrear.com

AnneMarie Brear

Chapter One

Chapter One

London. February 1923.

In the pouring rain, Cece Marsh hurried out of the taxi and nodding to the doorman, entered the Savoy Hotel in Westminster. She headed into the restaurant where her grandmama said to meet her at one o'clock. It was now one fifteen.

Mr Thomas, the well-known maitre'd took her coat and gloves with a warm smile. 'Miss Marsh, your grandmother awaits you.'

'Yes, I know I'm late.' She pulled a face. 'Traffic.'

He raised his hand, and another black-suited waiter was instantly by her side and directing her to where Adeline Fordham, her grandmama, sat nestled between a blazing fireplace and a large window. It was the table Grandmama reserved once a week when in London and had done for the last forty years.

'Oh, you remembered our appointment then?'
Grandmama gave her a piercing stare.

'I'm so sorry. The traffic was horrendous all the
way from the library.'

Grandmama's gaze rose to Cece's hair. 'Traffic? I
thought you had *walked* the entire way.'

Touching her wayward auburn curls and trying to
tuck them back under her hat, Cece knew she didn't
look her best and sighed. 'No. I didn't walk.'

'Shall you take yourself off to the ladies' room?'
The pointed remark was barely out of Grandmama's
mouth before Cece quickly left the table and hurried
to the ladies' room, where she half-heartedly
managed to repair the damage to her hair.

She unpinned her dark blue cloche hat and stared
into the mirror at the rain-frizzed red hair she'd hated
all her life. In her bag, she carried a small hair brush
and tortoise-shell combs, but nothing could be done
with it especially when it was raining. She wished she
had her sisters' hair. Millie's black curls were neat
and fell around her face in a delightful way, and
Prue's straight blonde hair was cut in a sleek short
bob and always stylish. However, Cece had inherited
her late father's fair colouring, which was pale skin
prone to freckles in the summer and wayward hair
that she couldn't control.

As other women, all elegant and sophisticated came
and went from the room, Cece became increasingly
frustrated. In the end, she squished her hair under her
cloche hat and with a last look at her plain brown
skirt and dark green cardigan, she returned to the
table.

Grandmama raised her eyebrows but said nothing.

'Have you ordered?' Cece asked, giving a small
smile to the hovering waiter.

'Just now. Lobster soup and sandwiches. Do you wish for anything else?'

'No, thank you, that's lovely,' Cece answered, including the waiter in her response.

'Since you're finally here. We can discuss what I want to talk to you about.'

'Grandmama, I only saw you at breakfast.' Cece unfolded her napkin. 'Why couldn't we do this at home?'

'Well, I simply assumed it would be nice for us to some time alone for a change. With Lesley at the house, it's difficult to get a word in.'

'Lesley is fine.'

'She's a loud American who outstays her welcome.'

'She was going to go home last week, and you prevented her.' Cece shook her head. Lesley Larkin, Grandmama's friend from America, was a nice woman, but Grandmama wasn't keen on Americans even though she adored Lesley, and so she'd pretend to all and sundry that she was only putting up with Lesley because she was a guest and guests are always treated with kindness and consideration.

'Yes, I prevented her from leaving because she hasn't visited to enough places. I don't want her returning to America and telling everyone that we British can't entertain our visitors. I'm not having that.'

'Lesley has been here for five weeks. She's seen and done more things in London than I have my whole life! And I've been coming here twice a year to stay with you since I was a child.'

'That's different. You are family not an outsider.' Grandmama paused while the waiter wheeled a trolley to their table and set out the tea service between them.

'Thank you, Robert,' Grandmama said as he left.

Cece poured out the tea into the thin porcelain teacups. 'Where is Lesley while we are here? You've not barred her from joining us, have you?'

'No, I have not! What cheek.'

'I didn't see her at breakfast this morning. Did she sleep late?'

'No, she left early to go on a tour of Cambridge that I organised for her through a friend. She'll be back tonight.'

'Did she enjoy the theatre last night?'

'She did, howled with laughter.' Grandmama's tone was disapproving. 'Most embarrassing it was. I ordered her to stop, but she didn't of course. She does it to spite me.'

Cece rolled her eyes.

'Anyway, enough of Lesley. I wanted to talk about you.'

'Me?' Cece was surprised at that.

'I know you objected me to taking Prue to India and Italy.' Grandmama sipped her tea.

'I felt left out, yes.' Cece didn't deny it. What would be the point? She was hurt that Grandmama had taken her sister Prue to India and Italy and not included her.

'You weren't ready to go on such a trip. We both know that.' Grandmama paused again as the lobster soup was brought out and the three-tiered cake stand full of sandwiches, little French pastries and miniature cakes.

'That is your opinion,' Cece muttered, eyeing the cakes.

'And the correct opinion.'

'Is this you apologising for not taking me?'

'Good heavens, no. Why would I do that? I am not sorry in the slightest. Prue needed that adventure and look how well it has turned out for her. She's married and is now part of a new magazine business with Lady Mayton-Walsh.'

Cece fumed inwardly. Yes, Prue had the perfect life, as usual. She thought of Millie her eldest sister, and admitted that Millie's life was also perfect, living in a chateau in Northern France with her husband and two children.

'You're thinking what about you, aren't you?' Grandmama sipped her soup. 'It's natural to do that. Millie and Prue are settled and happy, and then there's you.'

'Always last,' she tried to keep the anger out of her voice.

'Don't be self-absorbed. It's unbecoming,' Grandmama snapped.

Cece stared at her, a formidable woman she'd loved and admired all her life. Adeline Fordham was a force to be reckoned with and had spent her years as a young woman travelling the world and she ruled her family with a rod of iron, or once did.

'I have bought you a cottage.'

'A cottage?' Cece was so astonished her soup spoon was suspended half way to her mouth.

'In Scotland.'

'Scotland?' Cece lowered the spoon and sat back in her chair. 'Why?'

'Because I reason that you need it. You'll own something that is uniquely yours.'

'Why in Scotland? I don't wish to live in Scotland.'

'You don't have to live there permanently. It's simply a place that is yours alone for you to escape to when you need to.'

'Escape? What am I escaping from?'

'The world, family, yourself.' Grandmama continued to sip her soup.

Cece did the same, yet she didn't taste any of it. Her mind whirled. A cottage in Scotland? It sounded like banishment. Why couldn't she have a cottage in the Cotswolds, or Cornwall, or the south of France, or anywhere warmer than Scotland?

Cece will be released May 2020 in Kindle and paperback.

Prue

Made in the USA
Columbia, SC
15 March 2022

57719040R00193